# Around the Way Girls 4

# Around the Way Girls 4

Dwayne S. Joseph
LaJill Hunt
Roy Glenn

Urban Books
10 Brennan Place
Deer Park, NY 11729

ISBN 13: 978-0-7394-8622-1

Printed in the United States of America

*This is a work of fiction. Any references or similarities to actual events, real people, living, or dead, or to real locales are intended to give the novel a sense of reality. Any similarity in other names, characters, places, and incidents is entirely coincidental.*

# Acknowledgements

God: Thank you for being there.

Wendy: Thank *you* so much for helping me brainstorm! This story would not have existed without you. I love you! Tati and Nati—my drama queens. Daddy loves you!

My family and friends—you all are the best. Welcome to the family Nicole and Danielle.

La Jill and Roy: Always a pleasure to collaborate with you two!

To all of the readers and book clubs: Enjoy the stories! And thank you for all of your support and e-mails. Keep 'em coming! And watch out for my new book, *In Too Deep,* coming September '07.

Of course to my G-Men: Representing till I die! My wife's diehard now too! Keep doing it. Tiki, you will be missed. But Brandon Jacobs is a *BEAST!*

Dwayne S. Joseph
www.DwayneSJoseph.com (one day I'll get it updated, lol)
www.myspace.com/DwayneSJoseph

# All For Love

*Dwayne S. Joseph*

# Chapter 1

"**O**h my God! This can't be right."
I closed my eyes and prayed that when I opened them, the EPT results would be different. *One line, not two,* I thought.

"No," I whispered after opening my eyes again and staring down at two pink lines. There was no waking up from this nightmare. I was pregnant. "Love is gonna kill me."

I sat down on the toilet bowl and dropped my chin to my chest. "Shit," I said as my eyes watered. I knew better than to have sex without a condom, but like so many other females, I'd gotten caught up in the heat of the moment and made the stupid decision to do it anyway. "Love is gonna kill me," I said again.

I wiped my tears away and thought about the first time I met Love two years ago. It was my eighteenth birthday and to celebrate my first official day as an adult, I decided to get a tattoo. I didn't know what I wanted; I just knew that I wanted one.

Love was working behind the counter at Hood Tattoo when I walked in. " 'Sup shorty," Love said, nodding at me.

I nodded back. "Chillin'," I said.

Love smiled. "Right, right. So you here to get a tat or just browse?"

"I'm here to get one," I said looking up at the different samples posted on the walls.

"Aight, cool. Portfolio's on the counter at the end. Know what you want?"

"No," I said going over to the portfolio and skimming through it.

"Well, you kind of cute, so you definitely don't want anything hardcore," Love said.

"Thanks," I replied feeling a little uncomfortable about the compliment.

"Slim frame. Nice curves. You definitely want you a tat that reflects that."

I smiled, unsure as to how to respond.

"You Puerto Rican?" Love asked.

"Half," I said. "My mom is. Dad is black."

"You speak Spanish?"

I shook my head. "No."

"Your moms never taught you?"

"No," I said offering no more info. She didn't need to know that my mother had been too strung out to teach me anything.

Love nodded and then came from behind the counter. "You got nice eyes, shorty," Love said, stepping closer to me.

I took a small step back. "Thanks."

"No doubt." Love nodded again. "How old are you?"

"Eighteen today."

Love smiled. "Happy birthday."

"Thanks."

"You legal now."

"Yeah, I guess."

"So this a birthday present to yourself?"

I shrugged my shoulders. "Yeah, I guess. I don't see anything I like," I said closing the worn folder.

"That's because there ain't nothing in there that fits you."

"What do you mean?"

"I mean ain't nothing in there pretty or sexy enough."

"Oh," I said, blushing a little, but still very uncomfortable.

"I know the perfect tat for you though."

"You do?" I said giving a skeptical look.

"Yeah."

"What is it?"

"A word."

"A word?"

"Yeah."

"And what word is that?"

"Love."

"Love?"

"With a heart around it."

"What kind of tattoo is that?"

"Best one you can get," Love said. "Anyone asks what it means, you say you got Love for God. Love for your fam. Love for your boy or girl. Most importantly, love for self. You eighteen now, and you get this for yourself. Love. Feel me?"

I thought about it but didn't reply.

"What's your name, shorty?"

"Rayne."

Love smiled. "I like that."

"What's your name?" I asked.

Love smiled again. "I'll tell you after you get your tat. Deal?"

I gave Love another look of skepticism and then said, "Okay."

"So you got love for self, Rayne?"

"I do," I said with more meaning than she realized. The hand of life I'd been dealt so far had been a cruel one. My mother had been a junkie, and I hadn't seen her in six years. My father—and I use the term loosely—I hadn't seen since I'd run away from home two years ago. I got tired of him slapping the shit out of me. My mother's sister let me stay with her and her husband after that. My auntie always hated my father, and she felt guilty about my mother's addiction and abandonment. I stayed with them for two months, but when my uncle tried to fuck me after my auntie left for work one morning, I ran to the safety of the streets, where I occasionally robbed people, but primarily sold my body just to survive.

I did that for a year until one of my regulars ended up becoming my sugar daddy. He was fifty-two, I was seventeen. No longer wanting my lips around anyone else's dick, he rented an apartment for me, furnished it, and made sure I didn't want for anything. All I had to do was lay it on him good whenever and however he wanted. He wasn't good-looking, and he was overweight, but sucking and fucking him good kept me from having to sleep on the streets, or someone's unlocked car, or in a public bathroom. It wasn't love, but I was well-kept, and I would have kept him satisfied till forever, until one day I told him I didn't want to have sex because I was on my period and had terrible cramps. Like I said, I know my relationship with him wasn't based on love, but I had thought he cared about me. After he beat me up and then raped me, I realized I was foolishly mistaken. I had a job to do and it wouldn't have mattered if I had been on my deathbed; when he wanted to fuck, I was supposed to keep my mouth shut and open my legs. Two months passed before I left the apartment and all the comforts in it, with just the clothes on my back and escaped back onto the safety of the streets.

Love.

I thought about the word and the significance it never seemed to have in my life.

Love.

My mom had more love for the pipe. My father, who I'd

found out had divorced my mother, had more love for the stepkids I heard he was now raising as his own flesh and blood. All the guys I'd ever messed with had more love for my pussy than they ever did for me as a person.

Love.

It was true. There was no other tattoo more appropriate. In a lifetime of lovelessness, love for myself was the one thing I always had.

An hour and a half later, Love became my constant companion in more ways than one.

"So you got a man?" Love was cleaning off the equipment and throwing away the needles their tattoo technician, Amir, had used to brand me.

"No," I said, looking at the fresh tattoo on my shoulder in the mirror.

"Why not?"

"Men are a waste of time, and want only one thing."

"All men?" Love asked with a raised eyebrow.

"All men," I said.

"What about females?"

"What about them?"

"Ever messed with one?"

"Never. I don't roll like that."

"Never been curious?"

"Like I said . . . I don't swing that way."

Love nodded, but didn't say anything.

"So what's your name? You said you would tell me after the tattoo."

"Love," Love replied.

"Yeah. That's my tattoo."

"That's also my name."

"Your name?"

"Yeah."

"Love?"

"Love."

I opened my mouth to say something, but paused as it dawned on me that I didn't really know what to say. On one hand, I felt as though I'd been tricked into getting the tattoo, but on the other hand, I couldn't deny that the tattoo was as true a representation of me as I could get. So instead of replying, I closed my mouth, folded the directions on how to take care of my tattoo, and turned to leave the shop.

"You wanna get a bite to eat?"

I had one foot out the door when Love asked me that. "Huh?"

"Food. You wanna get something? I'm done here. Figured we could celebrate your birthday, unless you got other plans."

I shook my head. "No."

" 'No', you don't wanna get some food? Or 'no', you don't have other plans?"

I looked at Love for a long second. I was still a little uncomfortable with all of the questions and with the way the tattoo had been suggested, but at the same time, I was also a bit intrigued. There was just something about Love's confident approach. Something genuine. Something that made me wonder . . . could there have been something there that I'd never really had before?

"No," I said, stepping back into the shop. "I don't have plans."

"You like chicken?"

"Yeah."

"Cool. Chinese takeout on the corner has the best chicken in Brooklyn."

I laughed. "Okay."

I wiped another tear away as the memory of that day faded away, and touched the tattoo on my arm. I started seeing Love after that day. At first it was just a platonic thing. Love made me smile and made me feel like the world wasn't such a bad place. I was really never more secure or happier than when we hung out together. Love really helped me get my life together, by giving me a place to stay without obligations. With a secure and safe roof over my head, I was able to really focus on me and all the things I wanted to do with my life.

I owed Love a lot for that. Because of Love and the money Love gave, I was able to take classes at Baxter Community College. Love and I formed a good and tight bond. We were two very different people, yet we connected on so many levels. Under no circumstance did Love ever allow me to hurt physically or emotionally. Gradually as my walls of skepticism broke down, and my comfort level rose, we went from being just friends to being lovers.

"Love is gonna kill me."

# Chapter 2

"**Q** . . . I'm pregnant."

Q or Quincy as he didn't like to be called let go of me and stepped back. "Pregnant? What you mean pregnant? That shit ain't even possible because I pulled out."

"You ever heard of pre-cum?"

"Pre-cum," Q said in a what-the-fuck-are-you-talking-about tone. "Pre-cum my ass. I pulled out and spilled my shit all over your stomach. You ain't pregnant."

"Yes I am, Q. I have the EPT test with me."

Q shook his head. "You give the other nigga you fuckin' the same story?"

"What?" I said, slitting my eyes. "Don't even try that shit, Q. There ain't no other nigga and you know that."

Q gave me a serious, deadpan glare and clenched his jaws. It was easy to let it fly from his mouth, but he knew I wasn't talking to anyone else. Besides, even if I wanted to, he knew that between school, he and Love, I didn't have time to be messing with anyone else. He shook his head again and flared his nostrils.

I first met Q a year ago in economics class at the college. He was a junior and I was a freshman. We were both working to get our degrees in business. Q was always attracted to me, and tried his best to get me to go out with him, but I never did. It wasn't that I wasn't attracted to him or anything, because at 6'3", lean with Boris Kodjoe good looks, Q was fine. It was just that I had Love, and although Love wasn't perfect, the one thing Love didn't do, that no other guy had ever done, was make me feel alone or unwanted—at least not until later in our relationship.

Even though I never hooked up with him, over the course of the year, Q became a friend whose shoulder I could always lean on when things with Love started to get rough. Of course Love didn't know about him.

One night, after Love and I argued about how I felt like I was being cheated on—which was something I'd been feeling for a while—I went to Q's house to cry on that shoulder that he'd always made available. In the midst of my crying and venting, one thing led to another and we ended up becoming secret lovers.

More pretty boy than thug, Q was the complete opposite of Love. Q liked to hear me talk, whereas Love seemed to like to talk for me. Sexually, Love could be tender at times, but for the most part, liked to dominate. Q preferred to let me run the show. Love was great to me, but I didn't realize until I started messing around with Q, that I never really had a voice in the relationship. I was just kind of there, and although I wasn't being raped or beaten, just as it had been with my sugar daddy, I was kind of doing what I was supposed to do, and not necessarily what I wanted to do—at least not completely.

Being with Q really helped me realize that little by little, I was really becoming unhappy with Love. Q tried to get me to leave Love on numerous occasions, promising to give me the things Love couldn't, but I just couldn't bring myself to walk away, because I felt like I owed Love so much. At the same time, even though I felt guilty about it, I couldn't bring myself to stop seeing Q either, because he was making me happy. Surprisingly, Q accepted that and continued to see me. We'd only ever had sex without a condom one time. Now I was pregnant.

"That bitch Love know yet?"

"No. I just found out about an hour ago. Love wasn't home."

"You sure you're pregnant?"

I reached into my purse and pulled out the EPT test. "See for yourself," I said, handing it to him.

Q looked at it and then flared his nostrils again. "I ain't ready to be a father yet. I got plans. Shit I'm trying to accomplish."

"I do too," I said, my eyes watering slowly.

"How much?" Q asked with a sigh.

"How much for what?"

"An abortion."

"What?" I said, my mouth dropping open. I didn't really know what I was going to do yet, but an abortion had never really crossed my mind.

"That's what you're gonna do right?"

"I don't know, Q," I said, tears falling slowly from the corners of my eyes. "I haven't really had time to think about it."

"What do you need time for? We both have plans. We both ain't ready."

"I know but—"

"But nothing!" Q slammed his hand against the wall. "I'm not trying to be a father right now, and I ain't trying to have no kid out there that I ain't taking care of."

"So just like that you want me to have an abortion?"

"Yes."

"I need time to think," I said, my head throbbing from the frustration of the situation. "I think we both do."

"Time to think? Rayne, we're in college trying to get our

degrees and make something of ourselves. A kid would fuck all of that up."

"Not necessarily," I insisted.

"Not necessarily? Rayne . . . I got friends and cousins with kids that fucked up their plans. Don't give me that 'not necessarily' bullshit." Q passed his hands over his bald head. "Shit!" He squeezed his temples.

"People have succeeded despite having kids," I said.

"And people's lives have been fucked up," Q countered.

"That's a really selfish thing to say, Q. It's not the baby's fault."

"Selfish? Rayne, I know you're not talking about being selfish. You're in a fucking lesbian relationship, but still seeing me. Talk about having your cake and eating it too."

"Do you have to go there again? I told you, I'm not gay. Not really."

"So then what are you, Rayne?"

I shook my head. "I'm just . . . just confused."

"Confused?" Q said, spreading his arms wide. "Either you're a dyke or you're not."

"Shut the fuck up, Q! I've told you what my life has been like. You know what Love has done for me. You know she's the only one who's ever been there for me."

"And where the fuck have I been for the past year and a half?"

I gave him an incensed look and said, "I thought you were there for me too, until now." My tears were flowing heavily now. I had no idea what his reaction was going to be, but I never expected him to be like this.

Q shook his head. "I've been there, Rayne. Despite the fucked up circumstances, I've been there. Believe me, no other nigga would have put up with the shit I've put up with, and you know it"

"That was your choice, Q."

"Yeah it was. Dating a girl that's involved with another female that's more dude than most guys I know. Shit, I don't know what the fuck was wrong with me sticking around so long."

"Fuck you, Quincy!" I shouted grabbing my purse. "Fuck your tired ass!" His words had really hurt me. Heartbroken, confused, and scared, I stormed out of his apartment, regretting the day I'd ever met him.

# Chapter 3

It was rough holding myself together after my argument with Q. On the train I struggled to keep my tears from falling. On Frederick Douglass Boulevard, concealed by the darkness, I let the floodgates open. Q had truly shattered my heart. I knew the news was shocking, but why did he just instantly assume that having an abortion was what I was going to do? I know I still had the issue of trying to figure out which direction I had to take with Love, but why didn't the possibility of he and I raising the baby together ever come out of his mouth? Why didn't that ever cross his mind?

Abortion.

The word had come out of his mouth so easily, whereas I hadn't even really had time to think about it. Shit, I hadn't really gotten past the fact that I was actually pregnant and that Love would kill me if she knew.

What Q had said was the truth. Love was more dude than most dudes I knew. The way she moved, the way she talked. At first glance, you'd never know Love was a female. Hell, maybe even at second glance. Faded, near bald haircut. Eyebrows slit with parts. Battle scars on her right cheek and under her left eye. Oversized clothing to hide her god-given attributes. Pants hanging desperately onto her thighs. Calling

Love a female almost didn't even seem right because there was practically nothing feminine about her.

As hardcore and thugged out as Love was though, there was one thing that she couldn't keep concealed—her compassion. Men may have their broad shoulders or their strong arms to you in when you needed to break down or be protected, but the one thing they couldn't give a female was that soothing, almost motherly compassion. As hard as she was, Love was still a woman, and no matter how much she tried to pretend she didn't have any nurturing ways about her, she still experienced both pleasure and pain in only the way a woman could.

Like me, Love's life story had been one filled with pain and disappointment. Her mother died before she'd gotten to know her. Her father tried to raise her, but couldn't deal with her knowing and declaring that she was a lesbian since the age of twelve. The majority of her God-fearing family turned their backs on her.

Love knew pain like I knew pain, and it was that common bond between us that drew me to her. I wasn't a lesbian before Love, and I can't say that I was one even as we dated, but I can say for sure that I loved her, because with her, I felt safe, secure, and most importantly, cherished. She loved me and gave me her love like no one had before. She'd often tell me that she'd kill to protect me, or give her life if it meant saving mine. I believed her with all my heart, because she was my heart; my life raft to grab hold of whenever the river of life tried to take me under. I couldn't imagine trying to swim without her.

Love.

Like my tattoo, she was always with me. In a lot of ways, I felt as though I owed her my life, because it was only after she'd come into it that the once permanent clouds above my head, started to dissipate.

Q had fooled me, and made me second-guess my relation-

ship with Love. I mean why was I dating a female when I'd finally met a guy who was ready, willing, and actually able to
love me and do all the things Love could do? I was really stupid for thinking that he actually cared about me. I was stupid
for falling for the roses and romantic dates. Stupid for buying
into the whole "Never met a woman that makes me feel the
way you do" line. His reaction showed me that he was no different than any other guy who'd ever hurt me with their self-
ishness.

Walking down the dark street, I realized that an abortion
really was the only thing for me to do, because leaving Love
or the comfort she provided, was just impossible for me to
do. Some might say that by deciding to stay with her, I was
settling, but I saw it differently. In my mind, I was just doing
what I had to do to survive. After going through life the way I
had, being with Love and enduring all of the things she may
or may not have been doing, was still better than being alone
again. That was just something I wasn't willing to go through.
Not anymore. I'd make sure Q paid for it, and after that, I'd
make him a memory.

I took a deep breath and let it out slowly to calm my
nerves as I put my key in and opened the door to the apartment Love and I shared. Love was on the phone when I
walked in.

"Oh yeah," I heard her say, the tone in her voice softer
than normal. "Yo, you are a crazy bitch," she said laughing.

"Hey, baby," I said, walking up to her to give her a kiss. Before I could do that, she put up her hand to keep me at bay
and gave me a nod and continued on with her conversation.

"Yeah, yeah, I can do that. Oh word? You got skills like
that? Damn!"

I watched her as she carried on with whoever the fuck she
was talking to as if I weren't standing there waiting for her attention.

"Tonight? Oh yeah. Bet. It's on. I'll bring the 'dro."

Tonight?

"Love, who are you talking to?" I asked loud enough for the person on the other end to hear me.

"My warden?" Love said into the phone, ignoring me. "Bitch, I ain't got no warden."

As she laughed, I asked again, "Who's on the phone, Love?"

With her eyes alone, Love told me to back the fuck off and continued talking.

"Love," I called again, louder than before. Any other day, I would have backed off, but today was not like any other day. Today I needed her.

Love locked her eyes on me and said, "What the fuck is your problem? Can't you see I'm in the middle of a fucking conversation?"

I snapped my head back and felt a thud in my chest. "All I did was say hello, Love. Would it have killed you to do the same?"

Love gave me another you-better-watch-yourself glare and then said into the phone, "Yo, let me holla at you later. Oh aight. I'll be there. Aight. Peace." She ended the call and then threw the cordless phone to the couch. "What the fuck's up with disrespecting me like that, Rayne. I know you know better than that."

"Disrespect?" I said, taking my jacket off. "First of all, I'm not your child. Second of all, you shouldn't be talking about disrespect after the way you just disrespected me to whoever the fuck you were just talking to."

"Who I was talking to ain't important," Love said.

"Whoever the bitch was, she was important enough to keep you from giving me a kiss hello!"

"You know what, Rayne . . . grow the fuck up. So I didn't kiss you hello. So the fuck what? It ain't like you wasn't gonna get a kiss at all. Damn. We don't have to be all over each other all the time."

"I'm not trying to be all over you, Love," I said, trying my best to mask how much her callous behavior towards me was hurting. "I've just had a pretty fucked-up day, and it would have just been nice to get a kiss and hug when I walked through the door. I really needed one."

"Shit, I've had a rough day too," Love said, moving past me to the closet and grabbing her bomber jacket. "But I deal with it. You need to learn to start doing that. A hug and a kiss ain't always gonna be the remedy."

I looked at her and shook my head and fought back tears at the same time as I watched her put on her coat. "Where are you going? Who were you making plans with?"

"I'm going out to chill. And don't worry who I'm making plans with," Love snapped.

"How come you didn't ask me to go out with you?"

"You don't be drinking or smoking no weed, Rayne. What am I gonna ask you to go for?"

"Maybe I want to smoke and drink tonight."

"Whatever, ma. You just stay here and hit your books like a good girl."

A good girl.

I put my hand on my stomach. If she only knew, I thought. "Do you have to go out?" I asked as Love slid her cell phone into her pocket.

"What?" she asked.

"Stay home with me tonight. I really don't want to be alone."

Love sucked her teeth. "Chill with the needy shit, Rayne. For real."

"So you won't stay home? For me?"

"I'll catch you later, ma."

"Don't you love me anymore?" I asked, my eyes watering.

"You know I got love for you, Rayne."

"But do you love me?"

"I told you—"

As tears of hurt and frustration spilled from my eyes, I said, "What happened to you, Love? What did I ever do to you to make you treat me so cold like you do now? What did I do wrong? And when did I do it?" I pleaded with my eyes for an answer.

Love rolled her eyes and frowned. "I don't have time for this shit. I'm out." And just like that, without an answer and without another word, Love left.

Alone with only the memories from my argument with Q, and the stinging from Love's cold attitude, I sat on the couch and cried myself to sleep.

# Chapter 4

"So you gonna do it today?"

I kept my lips pressed tightly together, kept my eyes focused on a milk-white Escalade with a license plate reading *#1 Stunr*, and shrugged my shoulders.

"What do you mean by that?" Q asked. We were standing in front of his apartment building. I was there to get the money to abort the baby we'd created. "I'm not trying to give you three hundred and fifty dollars if you're not gonna do this today."

I shivered as a bitter November breeze whipped around us. I was wearing a bomber jacket that Love had bought for me the winter before, but it did little to help keep me warm. Of course as I stood there in front of Q, I couldn't help but wonder it was the wind or the idea of actually going through with the abortion that gave me the chills.

A week had passed since I'd found out about being pregnant. Without a doubt, it had been one of the worst weeks I'd ever had. I couldn't sleep at night because the minute my eyes closed and my body relaxed, my brain went into overdrive and gave me nightmares. I couldn't focus on my schoolwork during the day, which really sucked because finals for the end of the semester were coming up in a few weeks. If I wasn't tossing and turning at night, or failing miserably at concentrating on my studies, then I was fighting depression from being around Love and dealing with her getting-colder-by-the-minute demeanor and my guilty conscience for stepping out on her.

"'Sup, Rayne?" Q asked. "You gonna do this or what?"

I stared at the Escalade and its rims that spun endlessly. Two young black wannabe thugs stood outside, leaning against the hood, talking to two young females who were all too impressed by what they saw.

Could the project mentality of being nothing but hustlers, pimps or hood rat chicks be any more obvious, I thought. An Escalade in the projects. Bitches with their eyes glazed over niggas whose last stop would be a casket before they reached twenty-five. I wanted to get away from all of this. I wanted more. I needed more. More than the bad memories. More than the one-bedroom apartment Love and I shared.

I needed a future. I needed to know that there was a reason I'd gone through all of the heartache I'd gone through so far in my twenty years. That's what made saying a quick yes to Q's question so hard.

I didn't want to have a baby yet because I didn't want to lose Love and be alone. I wasn't ready to be a mother, and I didn't want to end up like too many females from around the way—a mother on welfare. But at the same time, I couldn't help but wonder if I'd gone through the twenty years of crap just to be a mother and give my baby the life and love I'd never gotten.

"Rayne, you gonna answer me or what?"

"Huh?" I said, looking away from the Escalade finally and looking up at Q.

"The abortion. You gonna do it or what?"

I took a breath and thought one more time about possibly keeping the baby. But even as I did, the fact that keeping it was probably going to mean that I'd be alone again and that was just too much for me. "Yeah," I finally said, feeling my heart sink. "I'm gonna do it."

"Good."

I gave him a you're-a-pathetic-piece-of-shit look and said, "Yeah."

I paused at the entrance to the women's clinic at Lincoln Memorial Hospital. Abortion; once I stepped inside, there was no turning back. In a lot of ways, my life wouldn't change, but it would also never be the same again.

I turned around and stared at Q as he sat in his car. He'd insisted on driving me to the clinic because he wanted to make sure I went through with it. Typical nigga. God, I thought he was different. But yet, just like so many other guys, he could fuck on a dime and then drop a dime to get out of handling his responsibilities. It was that easy for him and all of the other jerks in the world. They didn't have to deal with the physical and emotional baggage. In a lot of ways, I envied him.

"What's wrong?" he asked, getting out of his car and approaching me. "You're not changing your mind are you?"

I closed my eyes slowly and let out a heavy, stress-filled breath. "No. I'm not changing my mind."

"You sure?"

"Just get in your car and leave, Q."

"Shit. No way am I leaving. I wanna make sure you go in and don't come out for a long while. Besides, you're gonna need a ride home afterwards anyway."

"What the fuck do you care about me needing a ride?" I spat, getting angrier by the second.

Q gave me a serious and almost apologetic look and then opened his mouth to say something, but before he could, his cell phone started singing Lupe Fiasco's song, "Kick, Push." He answered it. "Hey Mom."

I rolled my eyes and turned to go into the clinic to get away from him when I heard him yell.

"What! Oh no! No! No! No!"

I turned back around to see him running to his car, jumping in it, starting the engine, and racing off, leaving me alone.

My heart skipped a beat and wondered what had happened to put the distress in his voice and make him run off like that. I stood still for a few minutes, seeing if he would come back, but after five minutes, I came to the conclusion that he wasn't coming back any time soon.

Alone.

I was alone in front of the women's clinic with a baby in my stomach. A baby I didn't have to abort. Not anymore. Not with Q being gone. I could have taken the money he'd given me and bought a bus ticket to somewhere and lived my life.

No Love.

No Q.

No one was around.

I could have left.

But I didn't.

I turned and stepped inside.

# Chapter 5

Light pink, nearly white-colored walls. Dark gray carpeting. Framed pictures of flowers that were somehow supposed to help calm your nerves. Four females sitting a few chairs apart from one another, flipping through magazines.

This was the scene that greeted me when I stepped into the clinic. I stood just inside of the door and took it all in, thinking to myself that I didn't have to stay. Q had left and I could have turned around, opened the door and escaped. I thought that with each step I took to the receptionist. But I also thought again about having to be alone if I did.

"Can I help you?" a heavyset black woman said barely looking up at me.

"Ummm . . ." I paused and cleared my throat. The words wanted to come out, but my mind was putting up a fight. "I have an . . ." I paused again as a shiver came over me.

"Yes?" the woman asked, looking up and giving me a you're-really-wasting-my-time look.

"I . . . uh . . . have a two-thirty appointment."

"Your name?"

"Rayne Morgan."

The woman looked through a scheduling book, put a check mark beside what must have been my name, and then pointed to a clipboard off to the right. "Sign in there," she said dismissively.

I moved to the clipboard.

"Are you over eighteen?"

"Yes," I said removing my ID from my pocket and showing it to her.

She looked it over and gave a nod. "Is there someone here with you? You can't drive after the procedure."

I nodded. "Yes. He's waiting outside."

"Okay. Just sign and have a seat. We'll call you when it's your turn."

I grabbed a pen to sign my name, and I suddenly felt a nagging, weighing feeling. Something hovering over me, bearing down on my back. I tried to ignore the feeling and just go ahead and sign my name, but I couldn't. The feeling was too strong; the pressure just too heavy.

I turned to the right slightly and looked back over my shoulder, and found the source of the discomfort I felt, sitting in a chair with a magazine laying facedown on her lap, glaring at me. Shonda Ellis. Love's ex.

Shit.

I hadn't noticed her when I stepped into the clinic. How long had she been there?

Shit.

We stared at each other but neither one of us said a word. I'd only seen her one time before. Love and I were out at the movies to see the *Fantastic Four*. We'd only been a couple officially for three months then. We were in line to get some Twizzlers and popcorn when I felt the exact same feeling. Just like I did now, I took a look to see where the feeling had been coming from.

Shonda was in another line, standing next to another female that sort of resembled Love, staring at me. You know the saying: If looks could kill. . . . Shit, if they could, I would have been a dead bitch.

"What the hell is her problem?" I asked Love.

"Who?" Love asked.

"That girl, looking over here," I said, pointing as discreetly as I could.

Love looked in the direction of my pointing finger, and then gave a dismissive wave. "Don't sweat her."

"You know her?"

"Yeah."

"Who is she?"

"She's just a blast from the past."

"A blast . . . who is she?" I asked again.

Love sucked her teeth. "She my ex, Shonda."

"Your ex?"

"Yeah. Me and her used to kick it for a while."

"A while? How long ago was that?" I asked looking back at Shonda, who'd suddenly looked off in another direction.

"What's with all the questions? You jealous?"

I rolled my eyes. "No, I'm not jealous. I just wanna know what the deal is since she was grilling so hard. When did you break up with her?"

"Couple of months ago," Love said. "I dropped her to be with you."

"What? I thought you weren't seeing anyone?"

"In my mind I wasn't. She was too fucking clingy. Always wanting to be under me and shit. Always wanting to be holding hands and be all affectionate. I couldn't stand that shit. I was already leaving her ass alone, but I really stopped fucking with her a few weeks before you and me became official. She was still trying to keep shit going though. Blowing up my cell, sending me text messages and flowers and shit. Clingy-ass bitch. Finally I had to really get in her shit and make sure she knew what was up. Like I said, don't sweat her. She just looking at you like that 'cuz she jealous because I moved on to better things. She ain't nothing to worry about."

I turned my body back around and put the pen down as

my heart did tribal war dances in my chest. I looked down at the sign-in sheet and thought about Love's words again.

Nothing to worry about.

I looked back over my shoulder. Shonda was still staring my way, giving me the same evil eye she'd given me at the movies. My hands were shaking. My nerves were shot.

Without giving it another thought, I walked out of the clinic praying that Love had been right. Deep inside though, I knew that she wasn't and that things were going to get ugly.

# Chapter 6

One week had passed since I'd seen Shonda, and so far nothing had changed between Love and me. Maybe Shonda hadn't recognized me like I thought she had. At least that's what I dared to allow my mind to think. Maybe Shonda had just confused me with someone else. I mean let's face it, if she was as jealous a bitch as Love said she was, she would have gone running to Love the minute she saw me. But like I said—a week had passed. I still had the whole issue of the pregnancy to deal with, but with seven days down the drain, I allowed myself to breathe a little easier, thinking that Shonda hadn't recognized me at all.

"You tryin' to play my ass?"

Those were Love's first words as I opened the door.

"What?" I asked.

By the sheer venom in her eyes and her tense, ready-to-pounce stance, I just knew Shonda had made her move. Fucking bitch, I thought.

I stepped inside but stayed close to the door. Dormant most of the time, when provoked or threatened, Love had a temper and a wicked streak no girl or guy wanted to fuck with. I'd never experienced her full, all-out explosion, but she had choked, kicked, and slammed me into a wall before. The reasons why, I don't really remember. Whatever they were, they couldn't compare to being pregnant.

"Play you? What do you mean?" I was doing the best acting job that I could do. Hopefully she wouldn't read my eyes, because if she did, she'd know that I knew what she was talking about.

"You know what the fuck I mean. Don't play that ignorant shit."

My back still inches away from the door, I shook my head. "I don't know what you're talking about, Love. Why would you ask if I was trying to play you?"

"Who the fuck is Q?" Love suddenly asked.

"Q?"

"Yeah, Q."

On the outside I'd been doing my best to sound and remain calm, but on the inside I was shocked and scared out of my mind. Sure, after Shonda's call, she could put two and two together about me being at the clinic, but how the hell did she get Q's name? I mean, had my seeing Shonda been a coincidence, or had she been following me?

Shit.

I watched Love as she watched me, waiting for an answer.

Q. She wanted to know who Q was.

I swallowed the little bit of saliva I had left in my throat and took an anxiety-filled breath. "Q's a . . . a friend from school. Why?"

Love's eyes closed a bit. "A friend?"

"A friend," I said getting hot with nervous sweat. "Why?" I asked again.

"You fuckin' him?"

My heart skipped a beat as I took a half breath.

She knew.

I shook my head. "N—no. Why would you ask me something like that? I told you he's just a friend."

"You ain't never mentioned him before," Love said stepping towards me.

"There was never a need to mention him before," I said, my heart galloping.

"And he's just a friend?"

"Yes. Why do you keep asking me about him?"

"He came by here."

"Who came by here?" I asked as my legs slowly turned to rubber.

"Your friend," Love said, stressing the word with a lot of attitude.

I almost felt like an asthmatic, as I could only manage to take a series of short, quick breaths. Q had been there, which could only mean that he knew I didn't have the abortion. I scratched my forearm nervously. "W—when?" I managed to say, despite feeling like I had cotton stuffed in my mouth.

"An hour ago."

"What did he want?"

Eyeing me fiercely, Love said, "He said you had some notes for him from your class."

I scratched my forearm nervously again. "Oh yeah . . . I forgot all about them."

"What class you got with him?"

"Economics. Is he . . . coming back?"

"He didn't say. You sure you ain't fuckin' him? Because I swear, if I find out—"

"No!" I yelled, wiping beads of sweat away from my forehead. "I told you, he's just a guy from my class."

"So now he's just a guy? I thought he was your friend?"

"He is."

"What? A guy, or your friend?"

"Both! Shit, Love, why are you all down my throat and shit? Have I ever messed around on you before?"

Love stepped just a few feet away from me. "I don't know," she said her voice low, her tone serious. "You tell me."

"Come on, Love!"

Love shrugged her shoulders. "Shit, all I know is, I'm here chillin', and some nigga I ain't ever seen or heard of before, shows up at the door looking for my fucking girl."

"His notes, Love. He came for his notes."

"Right. That's what you say."

"Love . . ."

"How he know where you live?"

"What?"

Love raised her eyebrow. "You heard me. How the fuck does he know where you live? He been here before?"

"No!"

"So then how he know—"

"I gave the address."

"You gave him our address? For what?"

"So he could come and get his notes," I said flustered and on the verge of tears.

"If that's the case, why were you so fucking surprised when I told you he came by?"

"I . . . I just forgot he was coming. I forgot about the notes." I wiped a tear of anxiety that had escaped from the corner of my eye away.

Love flared her nostrils. "What's wrong, Rayne?"

"Nothing," I said, trying unsuccessfully to keep more tears from spilling out.

"So then why the fuck are you crying?"

"Because . . ."

"Because what?"

"Because you're acting like I did shit behind your back, when you know I would never do you wrong like that!" I was crying hard tears of guilt now.

"I was just askin' you some questions, Rayne. You don't have to get all dramatic and shit."

"Well, you don't need to be asking me questions like that. I love you. You know." I watched Love intensely as my tears cascaded down my cheeks, and prayed that she would believe me and give up with her interrogation, because if she kept pressing, my guilt was going to get the better of me and I was going to crack.

Tense seconds passed with Love staring at me hard before the look in her eyes softened.

"Aight, ma," she said, wrapping her arms around me. "My bad. Stop crying aight. I didn't mean to trip like that. I just got all fucked up inside when that nigga showed up at the door."

"He's just a friend," I insisted again as Love caressed my cheek. "That's all."

"I know, ma." Love kissed me on my mouth. "The thought of you fucking around on me, especially with a guy, just really fucked with me."

"I'm all yours, Love," I said softly as she slid her hand beneath my shirt and under my bra to play with my nipples.

"Damn right you are," Love said, squeezing and pulling on it.

It hurt, but I didn't say anything about it. Instead, I let out a breathy sigh and said, "All yours, baby." I wasn't turned on in the least bit, but if giving Love some pussy was what it was going to take for her to believe everything I'd been saying, then that's what I was going to do.

Love kissed me aggressively, ramming her tongue into my mouth. I let out a moan, let my tongue dance with hers, and took my hands and grabbed her DD's—a body part she hated, but loved to have played with. She breathed out heavily and took her other hand and slid it down the front of my sweats, moved my thong to the side and worked her middle finger against my clit before sliding it inside of me.

"This is my pussy," Love said, guiding three fingers into me now. "My fucking pussy. Right?"

"Yes!" I moaned, no longer faking my arousal. One thing

Love knew how to do was finger-fuck me. I was dripping. "It's yours, Love. Shit. I swear!"

"Good," Love said. Suddenly, she pulled her fingers out of me, pulled her hand from my pants and grabbed me by my chin with her wet fingers and forced me to lock my eyes with hers. "Because, I swear to God, Rayne, if you ever give up my pussy to another bitch or nigga, as much as I love your ass, you're gonna live to regret it."

A chill rose from the base of my spine as Love gave me the most threatening scowl before pressing her lips against mine again.

Playing the aroused role again, I worked my lips and tongue with hers. Her hands were gripping the top of my sweats to pull them down, when her cell phone suddenly rang. "Shit."

"Ignore it," I said. I don't know why, but I just had an ill feeling in the pit of my stomach, and it wasn't the pregnancy.

Love frowned. "Nah, I can't. I'm expecting a call."

"Let them leave a message."

"Nah. I gotta answer it."

Love moved away from me and ran to the bedroom to get the call. The feeling in my stomach worsened as she said, "Shonda? What the fuck are you calling me for?"

Needing to hear nothing else, I grabbed my coat, my bag, and ran out of the apartment knowing that I wouldn't be able to go back.

# Chapter 7

"Why did you come to my apartment?"
Q had barely opened the door before I snapped the question at him.

He looked down at me. "Are you okay?"

I wiped a small stream of tears away from my eyes. I'd been crying since I left Love on the phone with Shonda. I walked the dark streets aimlessly, not knowing where the hell I was going to go, or what I was going to do. All I knew was that Shonda had made her move, and my life was never going to be the same again.

Shonda was a bitch for making the call, but I was a bitch for betraying Love. For betraying the love I'd never really had before her. Love had her ways, but she cared about, provided for, and protected me. That should have been enough. It was selfish of me to have ever been confused about my being with her. Selfish of me to think that Q and his words, affection, and attention were what I needed; what I was missing. I should have been happy.

I had ruined everything.

Tears of sadness, guilt, and anger poured from my eyes as I walked. Until I banged on Q's door, I'd really been oblivious to where I'd been going.

Was I okay?

Hell to the fucking no, I wasn't okay.

Wiping another stream of tears away from my strained eyes, I said, "I'm fine. Just answer the damn question. Why the hell did you come to my apartment?"

"Did Love do something to you?" Q asked, his face filled with concern, which threw me off a little.

"Just answer the fucking question!" I yelled.

Q closed his eyes a fraction and clenched his jaws. "I needed to see you."

"Why? To make sure I took care of your fucking problem?"

Q sighed. "No. I—"

"I didn't do it yet!" I snapped, cutting him off. "Something came up. But don't you fucking worry. I'll take care of it. So you don't need to come and fucking check up on me anymore."

"Rayne," Q said, his voice calm.

"I told you, I'll fucking do it!"

"Rayne," Q said again.

"Fuck you!" I screamed as the streams became floods.

"Rayne!" Q yelled, grabbing me by my arms. "I don't want you to do it!"

I looked up at him through blurred vision. "What?"

"I said I don't want you to do it."

"What?" I asked one more time.

And then I passed out.

When I opened my eyes, I was stretched out on Q's sofa, my head on a pillow, as he hovered above me, wiping my forehead with a cool washcloth.

"Rayne . . . you okay?" he asked, his voice filled with concern.

I tried to sit up, but he wasn't having it. "Just stay still."

I looked at him, trying to read him. Trying to understand

the words that had come out of his mouth before I'd blacked out. "You don't want me to do it?" I asked softly.

Q smiled that smile that I remembered before I'd given him the news about being pregnant. The smile that had lured me to him. "No," he said. "I don't."

"But at the clinic . . . you said . . . you were making sure . . ."

"I was an idiot, Rayne."

I shook my head slowly. "I don't understand."

"When I left you at the clinic, I went to go and see my sister at the hospital. My mom had called and told me that she had to be rushed to there because she was having complications with her pregnancy. When I got there, I was given the news that she lost the baby she was carrying."

I put my hand over my mouth. "I'm sorry," I said sincerely.

Q's eyes got misty. "She only had two more months to go."

"How?" I asked.

Q shrugged. "I don't know all of the details. All I know is that something went wrong inside of her, and she lost her son and the ability to ever have kids again."

"I'm really sorry, Q," I whispered.

Q fought and won a battle to keep from crying. "My mom couldn't wait to be a grandmother. She had the spare bedroom in her house all decked out in blue and yellow, with basketball, football, and baseball stickers all over the walls. She's devastated. Both for my sister and for herself." He paused and wiped away tears of his own, the battle having been lost. "About eight months ago, my mom found out she had cancer and that she only had about two years tops to live."

My mouth fell open. I stared at Q, unable to say a word. He'd never told me about his mom being sick. That hurt; I thought we were closer than that.

Q looked at me. "I know you're wondering why I never told you. It's not that I didn't care about you enough, or trust you enough . . . It's just . . ." He paused and clenched his jaws. "Accepting it is hard enough. Talking about it is just something I don't like to do. I hope you can understand."

I nodded. I'd lost my mother a long time ago and still didn't like to talk about it. "I do."

"I just wanted to finish school before my mom died. I wanted her to see me walk the stage and get my degree. I had finally turned my life around when I found out about her cancer. Before that, the only stage I was headed for was the one in the police lineup. I was a real knucklehead. I caused my mom a lot of stress when I was growing up. When she broke the news to me, I swore that day that I was going to turn my life around and make her proud.

"When you told me that you were pregnant, I flipped out on you because I felt like that was going to fuck everything up for me. All of the hard work and long hours of studying—I was just starting to get my shit together with school. Besides, I was ready to be an uncle, but I wasn't ready to be nobody's daddy. You understand?"

I nodded my head and reached out for Q's hand.

"Rayne, all the shit I said . . . the way I treated you . . . I didn't mean it."

"It's okay," I whispered as I gently caressed his hand with my thumb.

"I just have so much shit on my shoulders right now."

"I know."

"I just want my mom to see me succeed."

Tears were flowing freely from his eyes now, as they were from mine.

"My sister can't have any kids, Rayne. That shit's not fair. She didn't deserve to lose her son."

"Good or bad, all things happen for a reason," I said.

"I know, and before this shit happened with my sister, I just kept wondering why the hell you had to get pregnant. It's hard to accept, but now I know why."

I closed my eyes as bumps rose from my skin.

"I came by your place to apologize to you. I figured you'd had the abortion and I just wanted to tell you how sorry I was for forcing you to do it. Or at least for making you feel like you had no other choice. But you didn't do it."

"No, I didn't."

"Does Love know? Is that why you showed up in the condition you were in?"

I nodded my head.

"Did she touch you?"

"No."

"Rayne . . . I care about you. But I won't front and say I'm ready to get married, because I'm not. I mean I accept responsibility for this baby, but other than that . . ."

"I know, Q," I said, nodding my head. "I'm not sure what I want right now either. To be honest, I'm still trying to deal with actually being pregnant. I'm still trying to get my life together too. The thought of having a baby to raise and take care of scares me. In a way, it was easier when you did want me to have an abortion. Now . . . " I paused and looked up at the ceiling, focusing on a water stain. "Now," I said sighing, "I just have a lot to think about."

Q and I were silent for a few minutes, as we both thought about the tough decisions ahead of us. I know it shouldn't have, but even though I didn't know her, Q's mother's situation really made it hard for me. The consideration of others' feelings above my own has always been a flaw of mine.

"Rayne, why did you tell Love you were pregnant?"

"I didn't."

"So how'd she find out?"

For the next few minutes, I told him about Shonda and my seeing her first at the movies and then at the clinic.

"Damn," he said, when I'd finished. "She didn't hesitate to blow up your spot huh?"

"Nope."

"So what are you gonna do about Love?"

I frowned and looked up at the ceiling. "I don't know."

"You gonna go back home?"

I shrugged. "I don't know," I said again. "I don't know what I'm going to do." I wiped another wave of tears away as the stress of my predicament weighed down on me.

"You can stay here if you want," Q suggested.

I smiled. "Thanks, but it's probably better that I don't."

"I think you should stay. At least for a couple of days. I know you care about Love, but taking a few days will give you some time to really think about what you want. It'll also give Love some time to cool off."

I shrugged my shoulders again. "I don't want to cramp your style," I said with a half smile.

"Whatever," Q said with a laugh. "I'm so deep into the books, that I don't even know what style is right now."

I shook my head. "I'm not trying to put you out like that Q."

"You're not putting me out of anything," Q insisted.

"But—"

"But nothing, Rayne. You're gonna stay here and chill until you're ready. End of discussion."

"But—" I tried again, before Q put his hand over my mouth.

"Done deal," he said.

I looked up at Q as he smiled at me. With everything he was going through, and the goals he had and the reasons for those goals, I couldn't help but look at him with a great sense of respect. Without knowing his story, I would have never known just how much of a man he was.

"Q . . . would you hate me if I went through with the abortion?"

"No."

"But what about your mother, and her wanting a grandchild?"

"My mom doesn't know about you."

"But she was really looking forward to being a grand-mother before she passed."

"Yeah she was."

"And you wouldn't hate me for keeping her from being one?"

Q shook his head and then put his hand on my cheek. "Look . . . no matter what decision you make, you and I will be cool. Okay?"

I nodded and turned my frown upside down slightly. "I wish this decision wasn't so hard," I said, my bottom lip quivering as I started to cry hard tears again.

Q pulled me up to him and wrapped his arms around me. "Just give it a couple of days," he said.

I thought about the threat Love had made to me, and how serious the look in her eyes had been. Crying in Q's arms, I couldn't help but wonder if I'd make it a couple of days.

# Chapter 8

*Rayne, ma . . . please come home. I'm dying inside without you. I can't fucking breathe without you. I can't think. What did I do that was so bad that I deserved to be hurt like this? All I ever did was love you unconditionally. You're everything to me. My heart. Why are you treating me like this? I don't even feel like going on anymore.*

I hit the #7 button on my cell to delete Love's latest message, closed my cell, and then buried my face in my hands and broke down. I'd been staying with Q for two days now, and for two days, Love had been blowing up my cell phone, leaving me messages filled with rage and now heartache.

*Bitch, I was trying to give your ass the fucking benefit of the doubt. I didn't wanna believe Shonda's simple ass. But it's two in the fucking morning and your bitch-ass ain't here, so that means she was telling me the truth. There's only one reason you would have been at the fucking clinic. One! I warned you about giving up my pussy to somebody else, especially a dude, didn't I? Bitch I'ma find your ass. Believe that shit!*

That was the first message she'd left for me. After listening to it, I shook in fear for hours. I'd never heard so much anger in her voice before. So much hatred, so much rage.

Love's words to me before Shonda's call repeated themselves over and over again in my head, morning, noon, and night.

*. . . I swear to God, Rayne, if you ever give up my pussy to another bitch or nigga, as much as love your ass, you're gonna live to regret it.*

Live to regret it.

Live to regret it.

Live to regret it.

Initially, each one of the messages she'd left was worse than the one before it.

*What the fuck, ma? It's like that? You just gonna fucking disrespect me and shit? Bitch! Fucking, selfish, dick-sucking, ungrateful bitch! You keep hiding. You only making shit worse, bitch!*

They were so bad that I didn't even try to step foot outside of Q's door, for fear that Love was standing in a shadow somewhere, waiting to carry out with her promise.

But gradually, they began to change.

*Rayne, ma . . . look . . . I didn't mean to trip like I was before. I'm just hurt that's all. Give me a call so we can talk. I know it takes two for shit to happen, and if you went to the arms of some nigga, then that means I wasn't doing something right. Give me a call and let's talk.*

*Rayne, please . . . I didn't mean all of the other shit I said. You know how I am. You know I'm quick to blow a fuse. But trust me, ma . . . I wouldn't hurt you. No matter what. Come home, Rayne. Come home and let's talk. At the very least call me back so I can at least hear your voice and know you're ok. Just do that for me please, so I can sleep at night.*

"I'm sorry," I whispered, crying as I rocked back and forth. "I'm sorry, Love."

Hearing the pain and desperation in her voice was just more than I could bear. I never mean to hurt her like this. I never meant to do her wrong. Again I thought to myself that I should have never been selfish. I should have never been unsure.

"Goddamm it!" I yelled, slamming my palm down on the sofa. "Love, how could I have done this to you? You're not perfect, but you don't deserve to be treated like this. I need to make this right."

I wiped my eyes furiously, and then grabbed my cell phone and flipped it open. I still didn't know what I was really going to do, but I had to talk to Love. After all she had done for me I couldn't continue to hurt her this way.

My hands trembled as I found her number and hit the talk button. I didn't know what I was going to say exactly, but I just had to stop hiding.

"Rayne?" Love's voice was barely a whisper as she answered her phone.

I hesitated for a second before saying, "Hey, Love."

"Rayne . . . where are you?"

A new wave of tears cascaded from my eyes down my cheeks. "I'm sorry," I struggled to get out as the lump in my throat grew bigger.

"Ma . . ."

"I'm so sorry, Love."

"Rayne, where you at?"

I shook my head, clenched my jaws and cried heavily into

the phone, unable to respond. After a few seconds, I said again, "I'm sorry, Love."

"Where you at, Rayne," Love asked again. "You want me to come and get you?"

"No," I said slowly.

"No? You mean you not gonna come home?"

"No." I shook my head. "I mean no . . . I . . . I'm going to come home. I mean . . ." I paused, trying to think of the right thing to say. "We need to talk, Love."

Love was silent for a second and then said, "Okay. When are you coming?"

"Soon," I said.

"Soon? What's soon? I miss you."

"Give me an hour," I replied.

"You sure?"

"Yeah," I said. "I'm sure."

"Aight ma. One hour. I can't wait to see you. I love you."

I ended the call without responding and let out a long breath of air. I wasn't exactly sure what I was going to say when I got there, but after everything she'd done for me, I owed Love the respect of talking to her face-to-face.

During my stay at Q's place I really took the time to think about what I wanted, and what I realized was that I really needed some time alone, away from both of them. I needed to focus on myself without any outside pressure, intentional or not. Q and I had talked the night before and I'd told him about the decision I'd made. He was okay with it and had even agreed to go with me whenever I decided to tell Love, that way she would see that I was choosing me over both of them.

I called Q's cell to tell him what I was doing. He was probably gonna be pissed about me going without him, but after talking to Love, I decided that this was just something I needed to do alone. When his voice mail picked up I left him a message and then grabbed my purse, my coat and left.

# Chapter 9

I paused.

My key was in my hand, my hand was poised in front of my doorknob, and I paused. Love had been so angry, felt so betrayed. Even though her anger had seemed to have died down and been replaced by heartache, I couldn't help but wonder about how it was going to be when I opened the door. For a split second, fear and doubt crept up my spine, and I thought about just turning around and heading back to Q's place. But even as I thought about doing that, I put the key into the lock. Shit, I'd already betrayed Love once; I couldn't do it again.

I slid the key in and opened the door. I don't know why I expected the place to look any different, but, just as it should have been, everything inside was the same as before I'd left. I stepped inside and closed the door behind me. "Love?" I called out. I had expected her to be in the living room, waiting for me, but she wasn't. My heart did step routines inside my chest, my breathing quickened. That fear and doubt crept higher up my spine, almost reaching the back of my neck. "Love?" I called out again.

"In the bathroom," she finally answered.

I shrugged out of my coat and walked to the bathroom.

Expecting to see her sitting on the toilet, I was shocked to find the room lit with four candles sitting in each corner of the small bathtub, which was filled with bubbles. "What's this?" I asked surprised by the romance.

"This is for you, ma," Love said, blowing out a match she'd just used. She stepped to me and grabbed my hand. "I missed you, ma."

"I missed you too," I said, genuinely.

Love touched my cheek softly. "It's good to have you back home."

I gave a half smile. *Home*, I thought to myself. I still hadn't found that yet. But I would. "I'm sorry for hurting you, Love."

Love shook her head. "Shh . . . don't talk about that now." Then she brought her lips to mine and kissed me strongly.

I have to admit, I missed her full lips and her aggressive kissing style. There was just something about the way she did it; something so take-charge about it, that turned me on. My fear and doubt gone, I kissed her back just as strong, trying to match her hunger with my own, and let out a heavy breath as her hand found its way beneath my shirt to my nipple.

Love kissed and played with my hard nipple for a few more seconds before stopping to say, "Let's take a bath before the water gets cold."

I nodded. She gave me a smile and then helped me undress, before getting naked too.

"You look . . . good, ma," she said, looking me up and down from head to toe.

Nonchalantly, I draped my arm across my stomach, as I noticed Love's eyes remain focused there. "Thanks," I said, feeling extremely uncomfortable with the intensity with which she stared. "You do too."

She moved my arm away and held onto my hand. "Real good," she said, her focus unchanging.

"Love . . . I'm really . . . shit . . . really sorry—"

"Get in the tub," she said, cutting me off. In a not so subtle way, her tone had changed and become harder.

I looked at her. She was still looking down at my stomach. I knew right then and there that coming home had been the wrong damn thing to do.

"I'm a little hungry," I said, praying for a way out of the darkening situation I was in. "Why don't we go and get something to eat instead? We can take a bath later."

My heart was beating as though it were a heavy drum being pounded on. My legs felt like rubber. I started to shake. With or without my clothes, I knew that I had to get out of there. Unfortunately, I did too much thinking and not enough reacting.

"Get in the fucking tub, bitch!" Love screamed out suddenly.

"Love . . ."

Before I could get out another word, Love, who had finally looked away from my stomach, punched me hard in my mouth, sending me falling back against the sink. Blood erupted from my lip as tears poured from my eyes. In that instance, her threat came to my mind again.

"Shit Love," I whispered, touching my lip. I was physically and emotionally dazed from the punch. I know she had a temper, but I never ever thought she'd lash out at me.

"Get the fuck in the tub, Rayne. Now! Don't make me have to tell you again."

Swallowing my own blood, I moved on my rubbery legs and did what she'd ordered, and moved to the tub. "Please, Love," I whispered again.

"What the fuck did I tell you, bitch!" Love yelled out, pushing me violently.

Like a rag doll, I crashed against the porcelain side, and fell sideways into the tub, hitting my head along the tiled wall at the same time. The blow would have knocked me unconscious had it not been for the ice-cold water I'd fallen into. I cursed and screamed out and tried to stand up, but I lost my footing and slipped back down, landing hard on my hip. I swallowed water mixed with my blood and attempted to stand up again. But before I could get too far, Love stepped in front of me, put her hands on my shoulders, and pushed me back down.

"Stay the fuck in there, bitch," she ordered.

Crying, bleeding, and shaking uncontrollably from both fear and the cold, I sat down in the freezing water. Seconds later, Love stepped into the tub, and as though the temperature of the water were seventy degrees, sat down easily with her back to the faucet. "Come here," she said, opening her legs, her voice filled with venom. "Put your back to me."

Fearing another outburst, I turned my back to her and scooted back in between her legs.

"Fucking bitch," she said, splashing the cold water against my face. "Ungrateful, fucking bitch." She slapped me in the back of my head and then took a handful of water and let it rain down over my head.

On the verge of passing out from shock, I tried to plead with her again. "Please . . ." I stammered. "Please, L—Love—"

Love slapped the back of my head again. "Fucking ass bitch," she said. "Lying to my face and shit." She smacked me again.

"I . . . I . . . shit, I'm sor—sorry." I wanted to scream and fight my way out of there, but I was so paralyzed by the cold, that all I could do was beg and tremble.

"Sorry for what, bitch? Sorry for stepping out on me? Sorry for getting pregnant? Sorry for disrespecting me with your lies? Sorry for getting caught?"

I shook my head. "Yes," I said.

Love splashed water in my face again.

"I—I n—nev—never meant to . . . to . . . Love . . . please!"

Love grabbed a bar of soap from the soap dish attached to the wall, and began to rub it over my neck and breasts. "So tell me bitch . . . was it that nigga that came here looking for you?"

I tried to say no, but I couldn't get my mouth to work, and so I didn't say anything.

"Skinny ass nigga. What . . . you got tired of the dildos, and you wanted some real dick?" She grabbed hold of my breast and squeezed it roughly. "Is that what sent you to that motherfucker? His dick?"

I gritted from the pain, and shook my head. "N—no," I forced myself to say.

"So what . . . you ain't a lesbian no more? You like fucking guys, now?"

I shook my head again as tears fell from my chin into the water. "N—no. That's not it."

Love slammed the soap down into the water. "Bitch, I fucking loved your ass! Ain't nobody been there for you like I have!"

"I . . . I know," I said, my tears rivers now. "I'm sorry."

"You're sorry?" Love yelled, splashing my face and hitting the back of my head again. "Bitch, if Shonda would have never been at the clinic that day, your ass would have had the fucking abortion and I would have never known shit! Ain't that right?"

"No."

"Stop fucking lying, Rayne!"

"Love, please!"

"I could have dealt with you and another bitch. But a nigga? After all of the shit niggas have put your through, you went and let him cum inside of you! Inside of my pussy! Bitch, I should kill you for that shit."

That said, she slammed her hands down on my shoulders and began to push me down under the water. I screamed and tried to fight her, but I was weak and no match for her strength or rage. But I still tried.

Arms flailing, splashing water everywhere.

Legs kicking and pushing back on the tub.

Death.

Love hated me, wanted me dead. Despised me for betraying her, for hurting her after all she'd done for me. I hated myself too.

Death.

Water filled my mouth and went up my nose. I felt myself fading. The cold water didn't feel cold anymore. My head didn't hurt. My lip wasn't throbbing.

Death.

An ending to all of the shit I'd ever endured. An ending to the guilt. An ending to mental struggle of trying to decide whether or not to keep the baby.

And then it hit me: the baby.

For the first time, I didn't think of the child inside of me as just some mistake Q and I had made. There was a real, live growing person inside of me. A boy or girl that I could love like I'd never been loved. A boy or girl that deserved a chance.

My baby.

With that thought, I somehow found the strength to force Love's hands off of me and push myself up until I was sitting again, only I'd turned and was sitting, facing Love.

"Bitch!" she yelled again. She reached for me, her fingers bent and ready to grab me by my throat. I thought of my baby again and reacted. I grabbed her by her wrists, and pulled her towards me, only before she could fall into me, I moved to the side.

The blow I'd taken to my head when I'd been pushed into the bathtub had hurt like hell, but nowhere near as much as Love's face when she fell face-first against the back of the tub.

As she turned over, blood spilled from her nose and mouth and dripped into the water. Love moaned and tried to rise up, but with my newfound strength and determination to live, I hit her in her face twice. After the blows I'd taken, I'd barely managed to remain conscious, but Love wasn't so lucky. She fell forward, and hanging partially over the side of the tub, passed out.

I held back a scream as I climbed out of the tub and fell to the floor. I was shaking, but this time, it wasn't from the cold or my fear. I was just shaking from the anxiety of what had just happened. I looked up at Love. Blood dripped from her nose and mouth like a faucet with a leak. Part of me wanted to go to her and take care of her, the way she would have taken care of me. But then she moaned and I remembered that she had just tried to kill me.

I put my hand on my stomach. *My baby*, I thought. *My baby*.

"No one will ever hurt you," I whispered.

Love moaned again. I looked at her. "Bitch," I said.

No more thinking, I got up, got dressed, and got the hell out of there.

# Chapter 10

"What the fuck?"

That was Q's reaction when he opened the door after I'd banged on it.

"What the fuck, Rayne? What happened to you?"

I'd been holding them back the whole way back to Q's place, but as soon as he popped the question, I lost it. Collapsing into him, my tears erupted.

"Rayne? What the hell happened to you?" Q asked, holding me tight and walking me over to the couch. He helped me out of my coat and then looked at the cut in my head and then at my busted lip. "Who the fuck did this to you?"

I tried to answer him, but I was just too hurt, not physically, but emotionally to say anything. I still couldn't believe Love had flipped out on me the way she had. That wasn't the Love I knew. Like I said, I knew she had a temper, but the Love I knew wasn't an insane monster. I cried softly, as Q got up and went to the back. I was still crying when he came back with a warm, wet rag, and some Neosporin.

"Rayne," he said, wiping by my lip gently. "Talk to me. What the hell happened? Did Love do this shit?"

Again I tried to say something, but no words came out.

"Rayne . . . come on. Tell me something. Was it Love?"

I nodded my head slowly. "Yes."

"Fucking bitch!" Q yelled out, kicking his coffee table. "Fucking dyke bitch! I'ma fuck that dyke up. I don't give a shit if she's a fucking female!" He kicked his coffee table again. "How the fuck did this happen? Did she jump you?"

I shook my head and wiped my eyes, finally all cried out. At least for now. "No. I went to see her."

"You went to see her? But we talked about this yesterday. We agreed that I was gonna go with you when you went to see her."

"I know but—"

"But nothing! Why the fuck didn't you just do what we agreed? This shit could have been avoided!"

"I know, Q. I just . . ." I paused.

"You just what?"

"I just had to do it alone. I owed her that much."

"Owed her? Shit, Rayne. You didn't owe her shit."

"Yes I did. She was my fucking girlfriend, Q, and I stepped out on her. It's bad enough she found out I was cheating and had been at the fucking clinic, from her Shonda. Was I just supposed to go and throw more shit in her face by having you there too?"

"You shouldn't have fucking gone alone, Rayne."

"She didn't do shit to me, Q!" I yelled out. "She wasn't fucking perfect, but she never did anything to hurt me, and I know she never would have!"

"You don't know that, Rayne. Remember we've talked about how you thought she might have stepped out on you before."

"Yeah, but I never had any proof. Those were just feelings I had."

"A feeling is all you need."

"No Q, it's not. You need proof. I never had that. But she did!"

Q clenched his jaws and flared his nostrils. "So the fuck what, Rayne? Am I supposed to feel sorry for that bitch?"

"No."

"Then what the fuck are you defending her for?"

"I'm not defending her! I'm just saying, I couldn't roll up to her and shit with you there! I couldn't disrespect her like that!"

Q threw the rag across the room. "Fuck, Rayne! Have you seen yourself? Have you seen what she did to you?" His eyes suddenly got wide, and he lifted the front of my shirt. "Did she fucking hit you in the stomach?"

I shook my head. "No. She just punched me in the mouth."

"So how did you get the cut at the side of your head?"

Seeing what had happened all over again, I said, "She pushed me over in the bathtub."

"What?"

I sighed and told him all about the special bubble bath Love had prepared for me, and then about how she had tried to drown me and how I had fought back and escaped. When I was finished I was crying again.

Q sat forward on the couch with his elbows on his knees and his fingers locked together. His jaw was tight, his nostrils flared again, his eyes were black and cold. He looked just like Love had looked.

"Q," I said, sighing. "I'm sorry. There was so much pain and sadness in her voice. I felt bad and I was just . . . just trying to be . . . to be fair. I knew she was pissed, but honestly I didn't think she would have ever done some shit like this. I would have never gone alone if I had."

I looked at Q as he remained silent and staring forward. Two minutes passed before he asked, "Did you decide if you're keeping the baby or not?" He looked at me.

I went back to the tub and the moment Love had almost

drowned me in it. I'd never experienced a feeling so strong before. I'd heard mothers say it before: they'd sacrifice anything to keep their kids alive and safe. Before that moment, I never knew how strong those words were.

"I'm keeping it," I said.

Q flashed a half a smile and nodded. "We have to go to the hospital. We have to make sure the baby's okay."

My turn to nod.

Q got up and got his coat, and then came back and helped me up and into mine. We went to the hospital, explained that I was pregnant and had been jumped, and got seen right away. After getting four stitches in my lip, an ice pack for my head, and the word from the doctor that the baby was okay, which gave me great relief, Q and I went back to his place. We slept in bed together that night, but nothing sexual happened. We just talked about the baby.

Boy or girl—which did we want? Boy names. Girl names. Football, basketball, music star, or business exec—which did we want and hope he or she would be? Whose traits we wanted him or her to have?

We spent damn near half the night just talking about the baby and nothing else, before we finally drifted off to sleep.

The next day, before he left to go to his part-time job, Q made me swear on the baby's life to stay at his place and not go anywhere. I hadn't planned on leaving anyway, so swearing wasn't hard.

I was on pins and needles all day long, thinking about Love. I looked at my cell phone so many times throughout the day. I'd expected her to, and when she didn't call, I couldn't help but wonder why she hadn't blown up my cell. What exactly did her silence mean?

Was she out searching for me, determined to get her revenge and finish what she'd started?

Would she ever leave me alone?

Would she ever forgive me, or would she hate me forever?

I didn't really want her to, but I couldn't help but wonder why she hadn't called.

And then at just about eight o'clock at night, exactly four hours after Q had called to tell me he was going to be working late, she called.

# Chapter 11

Q's name flashed on my caller ID. I looked at the time; eight o'clock. I knew he was going to be late, but I figured he would have been back by now. I was just waking up from a two-hour nap. I was wired, my brain was on fire, but I just couldn't keep my eyes open. I flipped open my phone. Hopefully he was calling to tell me he was bringing something to eat, because I'd checked and he didn't really have shit in his refrigerator or cupboards. At least nothing that I'd considered dinner.

"Hey," I said, stretching out on the couch. "I hope you're on your way with some food, because I'm hungry. Plus I'm eating for two." I smiled. I struggled with being pregnant for practically two and a half weeks, stressing over whether to keep the baby or not, but the minute I accepted it, it was like I'd never struggled at all. I was scared, but ready to be a mom, and after the night Q and I had together, I was pretty confident that no matter what did or didn't happen between us, I wasn't going to be in this alone.

Silence was the only response from Q, and after a few long seconds, I called his name. "Q? You there?"

Silence again was all I got from him. That and slow, heavy breathing.

"Q? What's wrong?"

A few more seconds of silence passed before my heart practically stopped.

"Your boyfriend's a fucking idiot, bitch."

Love.

Calling from Q's phone.

Every hair on my body rose.

"Love? What the—Where's Q? How are you calling from his phone?" I asked, although it didn't really matter what her answer would be. The fact was she was calling from Q's phone; there was no good answer.

Love chuckled into the phone. "You should have warned him about who the fuck I am," Love said.

"Where the fuck is Q, Love?" I asked, my hands shaking a little. "How the fuck did you get his cell phone?"

"You got a couple of lucky hits in on me, bitch, but don't try to get some fucking balls now. That wouldn't be good for your baby-daddy."

"Love . . ." I paused to take a deep breath to try and calm my nerves down somehow. "What . . . what the fuck is going on?"

Love laughed into the phone. "Fucking skinny ass, soft nigga. Thought he could just come at me and dominate shit like he's the fucking man. Fucking stupid-ass faggot. He should have fired his piece when he had a fucking chance, instead of standing there running his mouth and shit. Dumb-ass nigga."

Fired his piece?

"Love . . . where the fuck is Q?" I asked again. My heart was beating triple time. "What the hell is going on?"

"You a stupid, bitch, you know that Rayne? You should have fucking killed my ass when you had the chance. Now this fucking nigga's gonna lose his life."

"Love . . ." I squeezed my eyes shut tightly. "Please . . . what the hell's going on? Let me speak to Q."

"Fuck you, bitch."

"Come on Love. Shit . . . please. Put Q on."

"I said fuck you!"

"Love . . . come on. Don't be like this," I begged. "I was the one who did you wrong. Not Q."

"Fuck you and this bitch-nigga!" Love snapped back.

Unable to hold myself together anymore, I snapped. "Put Q on the fucking phone!" I screamed out. "Put him on the phone or I swear to fucking God, I'm gonna—"

"You're gonna do what, bitch?" Love yelled, cutting me off. "Hurt me? Stupid trick . . . you can't hurt me any more than you already have."

"Love . . . shit. I told you I was fucking sorry. I'm human. I make fucking mistakes." I squeezed my temples and slammed my hand down on the cushion over and over again. What the hell had Q done? Where did he get a gun from? Why the hell did he go after Love? I slammed my hand down over and over again. "Love please! Let me talk to Q?"

Twisted laughter erupted in my ear. "How the fuck you gonna talk to a corpse, bitch?"

Corpse? No! No! She didn't. She wouldn't have.

"What did you do, Love? What the fuck did you do!" I'd been trying to hold them back, but tears of anger and fear were falling hard and fast now.

Love laughed again. "I ain't did shit yet, bitch. But I'm about to."

"Please, don't," I begged. I was shaking, I was so upset. "Don't hurt him."

"I fucking hate you, Rayne!" Love yelled out. "I gave you everything for two fucking years and instead of trying to make shit up to me, you're begging for this nigga's life, like he's the fucking world."

"Goddamn it Love! What the fuck do you want from me?"

"I want you to fucking die, bitch!"

I screamed out and banged my head against the back of

the couch. She was right; I should have never left her ass alive. I should have killed her just like she was trying to do to me. I screamed again, grabbed a cushion from the sofa and threw it across the room. When I put the phone back to my ear, Love was laughing.

"I'm gonna kill you, Love," I said, tears dripping from my chin. "I'm gonna fucking kill you!"

Love laughed some more. "You're welcome to try, bitch."

"Fuck you!" I spat.

"Tell you what, Rayne. You know where the fuck I'm at. You wanna run your fucking mouth. Come with it. I'll even wait to kill this nigga in front of you. But don't take too long or you'll miss it."

Click.

The call disconnected, I screamed out again, let the phone slip from my hand, and buried my face in my hands. I couldn't believe this was happening.

# Chapter 12

Love had to die.

That was the only option.

The wind whipped around me, as I ran the five blocks back to the place I used to call home, almost like it knew something was about to go down. My hands were buried in my coat pocket. My right hand opened and closed around a blade I'd had since my days on the streets, before all of the madness.

Love had a gun.

I had a knife.

Fucked-up odds, but still . . . Love had to die.

I prayed for Q as I hurried down the street. I prayed that he was still alive. Prayed that if he was, that somehow, some way, I'd be able to keep him that way. He was innocent in all of this. He was just a guy who fell for a girl, just like Love had. The girl was the only one who'd done anything wrong. Never in a million years did I ever think I would have been that girl.

When I got to Love's place, I was so tense I could barely breathe. My nerves were on fire. I'd gone over different scenarios in my head about what I thought would happen when I put the key in the lock and opened the door. Would Love shoot at me first and then talk shit later? Would she shoot Q the minute I walked in? Shit, was I going to have a chance at all to take her out?

My hand shook like crazy as I stood to the side of the door and reached over and put the key in.

"It's already unlocked, bitch," Love said from inside.

I took a slow, deep breath and thought about the scenarios I'd played out again. What the fuck was I walking into? I put my hand in my coat and wrapped my fingers around the switchblade. A trick named Rosa had given it to me a few years back. She was a Latina that didn't take shit from anybody. Not even the pimp she worked for.

For a few months, she'd been kind of like my surrogate mother, watching out for me, teaching me how to survive life on the streets, and teaching me how to deal with the people on them. In another life Rosa would have probably been some rich female executive. She was smart like that. But in this life, she was a coke-sniffing prostitute, who'd run her mouth one too many times to the man she called Papi.

Before she was killed, she'd given me her switchblade. A "family heirloom" she'd said, putting it in my hands. I never saw her again. And weeks later, I found out that Papi had decided to close her mouth for good.

She used to say this prayer sometimes. I didn't know it, but I pretended I did and recited it in my head. Then I opened the door, and making sure to keep most of my body hidden, took a look inside.

Love was sitting in a chair in the middle of the living room, facing me, with a gun in her hand. Q was slouched back on the couch beside her. I wanted to cry as I looked at him. Duct tape wrapped around his ankles, he was bleeding from his forehead, nose, cheek, and mouth. His right eye was swollen shut. The front of the white shirt he was wearing was soaked with blood, and I couldn't tell if it was from the damage done to his face or that he'd been shot in the chest. Q moaned, and I think that was his way of acknowledging me.

I looked from him to Love. She was sitting, her legs spread, her arms folded across her chest. She gave me a cocky smirk and then stood up.

"You're lucky I'm a patient bitch," she said. "I almost didn't wait for you to do this." Without warning, and as if it were nothing, she pointed the gun at Q and shot him in the chest.

"No!" I screamed. "Q!" I ducked back into the hallway. "You bitch!" I screamed. "You fucking bitch!" I screamed out again and squeezed my head in my hands. Just like that, she'd shot him. Until she had tried to drown me in the bathtub, I would have never thought Love would have been capable of doing something like this. I squeezed my eyes shut tightly, determined to keep tears from falling. I couldn't cry. Not now. I called out his name again and slammed my hand against the wall. Not Q. Not him. He was innocent, I thought to myself again. So innocent. And now he was . . . I slammed my hand against the wall again, screaming out on the inside.

"Come the fuck inside, bitch," Love said with a laugh.

I squeezed my eyes tight again. No tears, no tears. "Why Love?" I said barely keeping my composure. "So you can kill me too?"

Love laughed again. "Your baby-daddy ain't dead yet, but he will be right now if you don't get your ass in here."

I squeezed my eyes shut again, but tears escaped and fell this time. I covered my face with my hand and for a few seconds, gave in to the hard tears. But only for a few. Q wasn't dead. Not yet. At least that's what she said. Was she lying? Did she just want me to step out into the open so that she could shoot me just as easily as she had Q? I touched the blade in my pocket again. Unless I could make it fly through the air straight into Love's heart, the shit was useless.

I touched the blade in my pocket again and thought about Q in the room. Fear had a death grip over me, keeping me from moving, but for Q I had to shake it loose. I had to step into the room. I took a breath. A slow and deep one, and then slowly and cautiously, stepped into the apartment.

Love was sitting down again, arms crossed, legs wide. Who the fuck was she? She wasn't the same female I'd called my girlfriend for two years.

I looked over at Q. He was slumped over motionless on the couch. The couch was black, so I couldn't see the pool of blood that I'm sure had formed, which was a good thing. I willed for him to move. He didn't. I tried, but couldn't keep the tears from rolling down my cheeks.

"The cops are gonna be here soon," I said, looking at Love, who sat looking at me with a smirk on her face. "You won't get away with this shit, you fucking psycho bitch."

Love smiled. "This is the fucking Frederick Douglass Projects, bitch. Gunshots flow like water here. Ain't no fucking police coming to investigate shit, and you know it."

I stared at her, but didn't say anything. She was right. God himself could make a fucking 911 call from here and the cops still wouldn't come around.

"Love . . ." I said, shaking my head.

"What, Rayne?"

"This is . . . crazy. What you're doing . . . I mean, shit, all I did was step out on you. Is it worth all this?"

Love stood up and pointed the gun at me. "Disrespect," she said, her lips curled up into an Ice Cube sneer. "That's worth killing a motherfucker for! Someone disrespects my friends and the people I call family, they gotta die. They disrespect the person I love . . . they gotta die. They disrespect me . . ." Love walked towards me, her arm locked straight, her fingers opening and closing around the butt of the gun. "They disrespect me, and death ain't even enough."

I tried to fight it, but shook with fear. "Love—pl—please . . ." My bottom lip trembled as my tears fell. My chest tightened and I struggled to breath. "Please—d—don't."

"What's wrong, trick. You had a lot of fucking shit to say out your mouth before. 'Please don't'—that's the only shit you got to say now?" She pressed the muzzle against my forehead.

"Please," I whispered. I closed my eyes tight and braced myself for the split second of pain I was going to feel before my life ended.

"What the fuck did I do wrong, Rayne," Love asked suddenly. "What the fuck did I ever do to you?"

For the first time since this had all happened, the Love I knew had spoken. I opened my eyes and looked at her. The nigga-wit-an-attitude sneer was gone, replaced now by a frown. The intense hatred in her eyes was replaced by sadness and pain. Her arm that had been cocked and ready was shaking slightly.

Deep hurt.

That's what I saw looking at Love. I'd hurt her like no one else had ever. I could see it in her eyes and almost defeated body language. I could hear it in her voice. Up until now, she'd been hiding how bad she was hurting with rage. For the first time ever, I saw the female in her that she refused to accept.

A fresh wave of tears fell, but this time, they were more tears of regret than fear. I knew I'd hurt her, but I just didn't realize how badly until now.

"Love . . . I'm so sorry," I said softly. "Please believe me . . . you didn't do anything. You were . . . you are a beautiful, loving person."

"But I had to do something wrong," Love said, her eyes moistening. "I had to, or else you would have never stepped out on me."

I shook my head. "No, Love. You didn't do anything wrong. It was all me. I took you for granted."

"Why? I gave you everything you wanted. I gave you the love that no one else did."

"I know," I said, my heart shattering. "I know you did. I was just . . . I was just . . ." I sighed, but didn't say anything else.

"Were you gonna leave me?" Love asked. After you had your abortion . . . were you gonna leave me?"

I shook my head. "No, Love. I wasn't going to leave you. I made a mistake. Shit, a terrible mistake. And I realized that. I was just going to have the abortion and come home." It wasn't entirely true, but I knew that was what she wanted to hear.

"You were?" Love asked, her arm lowering ever so slightly.

"Yes," I said. My heart beat heavily as I prayed for her arm and guard to drop some more. She needed help, and I wanted to make sure she got it. But I had to get the gun out of her hand, and trying to force it out wasn't going to work. I had to win her trust again. "It was going to be all about you and me, Love. I was going to be with you forever."

"Forever?" she said, her lips curling ever so slightly into a half smile.

"Forever," I said, nodding. "Fuck anyone else." Her arm dropped some more. It was working. "Give me the gun, Love. Please. Give me the gun and let's just be together."

Love shook her head as tears fell from her eyes.

"Please," I said. "I love you. I need you. I was stupid to take a chance at losing you."

"You love me?" she asked.

I nodded. "With all my heart."

She smiled and dropped her arm to her side. I held my breath, but on the inside I let out a long sigh of relief. I was going to make it through this.

And then behind her back, I saw Q rise up from the couch and stand on shaky legs.

I shook my head. *No. No!*

He rushed forward.

"No!" I screamed.

And then everything slowed down.

Love spun around.

Q was too slow.

Love's arm rose with the gun again.

Q was too slow.

Love was about to squeeze the trigger.

Q was too slow.

Suddenly the switchblade was in my hand.

Q was too slow.

The blade sank deep into the back of Love's neck.

I screamed out as I lost control and drove the blade into her again and again and again and again. I screamed as Love dropped the gun, yelled out my name, and then fell to the ground. Blood covered my hands. Blood pooled on the floor where Love lay breathing her last breaths. I shook as Q dropped to his knees and collapsed forward, the top of his head barely touching the top of Love's. I shook as everything suddenly got quiet.

"Love," I whispered.

I dropped the knife, knelt down beside her, and took her in my arms, resting her head on my lap. "Love!" I said crying uncontrollably. "Love . . . I'm sorry. I'm sorry." I rocked back and forth cradling her. "I'm sorry." Tears fell from my chin to hers. "I'm sorry."

Love coughed and looked up at me, her eyes filled with pain and confusion. She opened her mouth to say something, but started coughing again. "R—Ra—yne," she struggled to whisper.

I caressed her cheek with my bloody hands. "Shhh," I said. "Don't speak. Don't speak."

I reached into my pocket, pulled out my cell phone, and with shaking hands dialed 911. When the operator answered, I could barely keep it together. "H—help please. I . . . need help. Love . . . she . . . I . . . Q . . . he's . . ."

"Ma'am, try to calm down and tell me what's wrong."

"They . . . they need help."

"Who needs help, ma'am?"

"Love and Q . . . they're . . . they're . . ." I paused and caressed Love's cheek again as she watched me and had another coughing fit.

"Ma'am, can you tell me where you are?"

"I'm . . . I'm . . ." I squeezed my eyes tightly. *Think. I had to think.* "I'm at eight fifty-four Nichols Street, Apartment five-C."

"In the Frederick Douglass Projects?"

"Yes. But please don't fuck around," I said, looking over at Q, who lay motionless. "They're dying."

"We have paramedics in that area already ma'am. We'll get them to you soon."

"Okay." I ended the call, dropped the phone.

Love coughed uncontrollably again. "I . . . I . . . love . . . love you."

"I love you too," I said. I looked over at Q again. I wanted to go to him, but I couldn't leave Love. I'd stabbed her. Again and again, I'd stabbed her. I looked back down at her, and knew right away that it didn't matter how soon the paramedics got there. They were going to be too late.

I leaned forward and kissed Love on her forehead. "I love you," I said again.

Love frowned. "I didn't . . . didn't want to be . . ." Love exploded with another fit of coughs, and then grimaced in pain before continuing. "I didn't want to . . . to be alone."

"I know," I said, kissing her again. "You won't be alone," I said. "I promise. I'm not going anywhere."

"You won't . . . won't leave me?"

I shook my head slowly. "No. Never."

Love smiled at me, and then her eyes widened with fear. "I'm get—getting cold."

I clenched my jaws and wiped tears away from my eyes,

although that was useless to do. "I'll keep you warm," I said, pulling her closer to me. "I'll keep you warm." I kissed her on her lips, and then her forehead again. Crying softly, I rocked her until she went to sleep forever.

Five minutes later, the paramedics arrived.

# Chapter 13

*Six months ago I became a killer. At least in my eyes I did. The police didn't see what I had done that way though. They said I was in a life-and-death situation and that I had to do what I had to do to make sure myself and my baby survived. That may have been the case, but Love died in my arms, so no matter what the cops or anyone else would say, I would always see myself as a killer.*

*Technically, I became a killer the moment I betrayed Love's trust. Everything had been sent into motion the moment my lips met Q's. Love's death was an inevitable and inescapable punishment. I realized that when I'd held her in my arms. There really was no other way for me to repent for what I'd done. At least not in my mind.*

*Speaking of mind . . .*

*Every time my eyes closed, I would see Love, see myself holding the knife as it went into her neck, and then I'd see her die.*

*Over and over again.*

*No matter how hard I tried, I couldn't get the images out of my head. I couldn't get away from all of the blood.*

*Over and over again.*

*I cried so hard night after night that I gave myself mini-*

migraines. Weeks passed before I was able to keep my eyes closed long enough to be able to get something that seemed like sleep. Really, that was all I could ask for.

Despite the stress and drama I'd gone through, Rachel was okay. That's the name I chose for the girl I was having. When the doctor told me I was having a girl, I cried for a long time. I named her Rachel Love to pay my respects to the only person who'd ever shown me unconditional love. I thought Q was going to have a problem with the name, but he never said a word about it.

Luckily, the paramedics had gotten there just in time to save him. He'd lost a lot of blood, and the doctors say that had the bullet been an inch over to the right, he would have never made it. I was in the hospital every day with him while he recovered. I actually got to meet his mom. If he wouldn't have said anything to me, I would have never known she was dying. Seeing her and the strength she had, helped me finally move on. She was dying, yet she was still living. I was living for two, and by spending time with her, I realized that I had to stop dying. I've been living ever since.

It hasn't been easy though. Some days I'd just keep reliving the nightmare, while other days, I was actually able to smile. Like I said, it wasn't always easy, but I was doing it.

Q was too.

Healed physically, he was back in school, focused and determined to walk across the stage to get his diploma with his mom watching from the crowd. If you didn't know him, you would have thought he was just fine. He'd survived a gunshot to the chest like it was nothing and kept stepping. That's the perception that pretty much everyone had when they saw him. But I knew better. Emotionally, I could see in his eyes that he was still trying to deal with everything.

*He had rolled up to Love like a true thug with a .38, ready to assert his manhood and defend my honor, but had to be rolled out on a stretcher. He'd probably never admit it, but I could tell that he was embarrassed by what happened. Even though she was more dude than anything, Love had still been a girl, and I don't care how secure a guy is, no guy wants to ever have to admit that he's had his assed kicked by a female.*

*After Q came out of the hospital, we barely talked about what had happened. Actually, we barely talked at all. Without really saying it out loud, I think we both just kind of silently and mutually agreed that although we were having a baby together, we weren't meant to be together. At least not yet. Q had things he wanted to accomplish, and I really needed to be alone to truly find myself.*

*And that's what I was doing.*

*I got a job working at the mall, eventually moved out of Q's place and got my own apartment, and took the time to just get to know myself. In my own space, keeping my own company, I realized that the relationships I had with Love and Q had really been one-sided relationships that I had used to keep from being alone. Did I care about Love? There was no question. But when I felt like she was pulling herself away, instead of giving her some space, I gravitated over to Q and the attention he'd been trying to give me. I was searching for love.*

*Love that my mother gave to her drug addiction.*

*Love that my father couldn't give me.*

*Everything I'd been through stemmed from those two missing links in my life.*

I closed the journal I'd been writing in and put my hand on my stomach as Rachel moved. I'd read about it happening in books and magazines, but the first time I actually experienced it for myself, it freaked me the hell out.

I smiled as I thought about that moment. Right after it had happened, I cried a little bit, and wished that drugs never existed so my mom could have been there.

I stood up and went to the kitchen to get some strawberries from the refrigerator. My stomach was a bottomless pit when it came to strawberries. Didn't matter how many I had, I never seemed to have enough. I shoved two of them into my mouth and looked at the clock. It was almost nine o'clock. Q had called me earlier in the day and told me he was going to stop by to check up on me after he got out of work. It had been my day off and I was bumming all day. I'd say I had about a half hour to wash my ass and make myself look half decent. I shoved three more strawberries into my mouth and then heard a knock at the door.

"Damn." I smelled my armpits and groaned. I went to the door. "You know," I said unlocking and opening the door. "You could at least call before—"

I paused as my heart dropped into my stomach. Love's ex, Shonda, was standing in the doorway holding a butcher's knife in her hand.

"Surprise, bitch," she said.

I looked down at the knife and then up at her. "What are you doing here?"

"What the fuck do you think?"

I moved as quickly as I could and tried to slam the door shut, but pregnancy and speed just don't mix, and before I could, Shonda put her foot to keep it open, and then pushed her shoulder into it. I stumbled back, but didn't fall.

"Get the fuck out of here, Shonda!" I yelled, backing up.

Shonda stepped inside. "I'm gonna kill you, bitch!" she screamed. "I'm gonna kill you the same way you killed Love! Except I'm gonna stab you right through your fucking stomach!"

"Help!" I screamed out as Shonda stepped forward and

swiped the knife at me. Luckily I'd moved out of the way in time. "Help!" I yelled out again.

Shonda lunged at me again. This time I wasn't so lucky, and she cut me on my arm. "Bitch!" she yelled. "I loved her! I loved her and you stole her away. Twice!" She swung out again, but missed as I moved to the side.

"Shonda . . . please!"

I screamed out again as Shonda swung out and this time just barely cut me in my side.

"I would have never stepped out on her!" Shonda yelled. "She was everything to me. You fucking bitch! You killed her!" Tears erupted from her eyes as she moved toward me.

"I'm sorry!" I said, stepping back, trying to keep distance. "Please Shonda . . . don't!" I shook with fear. "Please!" I begged again.

"Fuck you, you fucking trick! Why the fuck did you ever mess with Love if you knew you liked guys? You fucking bitch!" She let out a growl and lunged for me. I backpedaled and avoided the knife, but not the leg on my coffee table.

I tried my best to regain my balance and stay on my feet, but couldn't. I went down hard on my ass, my back banging against the front of the couch. "Please," I begged, looking up at Shonda, who was now staring down at me. "Please don't do this, Shonda. I didn't want to hurt Love."

"Liar!" Shonda screamed. "You meant to the minute you cheated on her!"

"No!" I said. I was crying hysterically. I was going to die. That was the thought running through my mind. I was going to die. Me and my baby. "Please, Shonda. I never meant to hurt her. I made a mistake!"

"Bitch!" Shonda said, kicking me in my thigh. "You didn't deserve to have her. She was too fucking good for you!" Shonda lifted her arm, holding the knife straight up into the air.

"Please Shonda . . . don't do this! I was just trying to protect my baby. I didn't want to hurt Love. You've got to believe me!"

"Liar!"

"Help!" I screamed, damn near bursting my vocal chords. "Hellllllllp!"

And then suddenly the knife was coming down toward me as Shonda attacked. Only when the knife fell beside my feet, and she fell over me and collapsed onto the couch, I realized she hadn't attacked me at all.

And then someone caught my eye.

He was standing where Shonda had been a second before, holding a thick biology book in his hands like a baseball bat.

"Q!" I screamed.

He helped me to my feet. "You're bleeding," he said, looking at the blood on my arm and on my side.

"I'm okay. She just grazed me."

"Fucking bitch!" Q yelled. He raised the book above his head to hit Shonda again, who lay unconscious.

I reached up and grabbed his arms. "No! Please don't."

Q gave me a look of confusion. "But she tried to kill you?"

"Please Q," I said, looking down at Shonda. "Just call the police."

"You've been cut, Rayne, by a fucking butcher knife. You can say it was self-defense."

I shook my head. I didn't want anyone else's blood on my hands. "Call the fucking police, Q."

"But Rayne . . ."

"Call them now!"

Q looked down at me and then frowned and pulled out his cell phone and called 911.

# Epilogue

Shonda had been stalking me since Love's death. She'd confessed everything to the police. She waited so long to do anything because she wanted Rachel to grow. Her plan was to stab me in my stomach and then watch me die a doubly painful death, knowing that I was going to die, but that my baby had died first. She hated me with all her heart and swore to the police that when she got out of prison, she was going to find me. Nothing was going to stop her.

I live in California now.

They'd given Shonda twenty years for attempted murder. She'd be eligible for parole in ten. Would she still hate me? Would she still want me dead? I ran all the way to the other side of the country to avoid finding out.

Even though she hasn't been released yet, not a day goes by that I don't feel her eyes on me, or feel like she's waiting in the shadows somewhere for the right moment to finish what she'd started.

Eight years behind us, and the fact that only his sister knows where we are, is the reason Q doesn't feel the eyes like I do. With everything we'd been through and the friendship we'd developed, we ended up falling in love and got married nine months after Shonda was locked up. That was five months before his mother died. She'd exceeded the doctor's expectations. Q was sad when she passed, but happy that she'd seen him graduate and become a husband and a father. His mother is buried here in Cali, so that he can visit her on a consistent basis. It cost an arm and a leg to make that happen, but just before he graduated, he was given a very nice job offer with a marketing firm.

After I told him that I wanted to move to Cali and why, he asked some questions at work and found out they had a branch on the West Coast. That's when we realized that we were meant to be.

Despite the apprehension I have, I'm happy. The love I'd always wanted, I get tenfold from Q and our smart-ass daughter, who is her father's spitting image. I give them all my love in return.

It was a long and crazy trip to get to this point, but I'm glad I went through everything I did, because I have a beautiful daughter, and a grown and sexy man to show for it. All the the drama made me the strong and the happy woman I am today.

I'm also licensed.

I have a .22 with me at all times. If Shonda does come looking for me, her ass is in trouble.

# Acknowledgements

To God, for once again, giving me the opportunity to utilize the talents you bestowed upon me.

To my family, for constant love and encouragement.

To my daughters, for inspiring and providing comic relief when Mommy needs it. I love you!

To Pastor Brown and the Mt. Lebanon Missionary Baptist Church family, thanks for your continual love and support.

To Carl and Martha Weber, for all you do.

To Roy Glenn, Dwayne S. Joseph and K. Elliott, my big brothers who are always there.

To Arvita Glenn for accepting my 50 million excuses!!

To Milly Avent, Omeida Cutler, Toye Farrar and Selena Johnson, thanks for always reading when I need you to!!!

To all the readers who support me and my dream—I appreciate you more than you'll ever know!!

Feel free to email me at MsLajaka@AOL.com

Be on the lookout: Coming November, 2007
*Old Habits Die Hard*

# Thug Passion

## La Jill Hunt

# Prologue

*Wake up! WAKE UP NOW!* Jovia's eyes opened and total darkness surrounded her. Something was wrong. She tried to inhale through her nose, but instead of taking in air, smoke filled her nostrils. She coughed and sputtered, gasping to breathe, her eyes scanned the blackness, desperately trying to find the source of her agony. She tried to call out to her mother, but she couldn't breathe. It felt as if someone was sitting on her chest. She found the strength to shift herself out of her bed, and shook her head repeatedly, as she moved about her small, cramped room. She could taste the stench of the smoke as she swallowed. Tears filled her eyes as her heart pounded. Once again, she tried to call out to her mother, but couldn't find her voice. Motivated by sheer panic, she crawled toward the doorway, praying that she would find her mother. As she made her way to the hallway, the smoke was even thicker and it was harder to breathe. *Help me*, she pleaded from within, unable to verbally call out. *Please help me*, she continued crawling. She remained close to the floor, remembering what her teacher had taught her during Fire Safety Week at school. Now, in addition to the smoke, she could feel intense heat. She opened her eyes and through her tears, she could see bright orange and yellow flames coming from her mother's bedroom. Her eyes darted through the flames to the sofa where she saw her mother lying, unmoving, an empty vodka bottle on the covers beside her.

"MAMA, WAKE UP!" She gasped and coughed. Her mother didn't move. Jovia tried to enter the room, ignoring the pain from the fire touching her back and shoulders, "MAMA, please! Mama!"

She fought her way through the flames, reaching for her mother. Just as she saw her mother moving, she could hear someone behind her, calling out. She continued to make her way through the extreme heat.

"Mama, please get up," she cried. Suddenly, she could feel someone pulling her away, "Let me go!"

"You gotta get outta here," the voice told her.

"MAMA, help me!" she yelled as she fought to get away from the arms that were now lifting her off the floor. She clawed and screamed, as she was carried out, "Let me go, let me go!"

She struggled to get away, but the arms held her tight. She opened her eyes once again, taking one last look at her mother, who continued to sleep peacefully through the blaze.

Jovia sat up in her bed. Her pajamas were soaked with sweat and she was panting. It had been so long since she had the nightmare of the deadly fire that not only left her homeless, but an orphan at the age of eight. She looked around, seeing that she was safe and sound in her room, filled with everything she could ever want. From the twenty-inch flat-screen television hanging on the wall, the computer and iPod on the mahogany desk, the walk-in closet filled with clothes and shoes, to the custom-built sleigh bed that she slept in, she was living every teenage girl's dream. Yet she was still haunted by the nightmare of her past.

# Chapter 1

"Wow, Jovia, that is amazing!"

Jovia barely glanced up from the painting she was finishing up. "Thanks, Mr. McKee."

"Class, this is what I was trying to explain. See the emotion that you can see in Jovia's piece. You can see the depth of what she is trying to portray. Remarkable."

Jovia could feel the stares of her classmates in her senior art class and fought the urge to run out of the room. She hated when Mr. McKee did this to her; made her the center of attention. She didn't want anyone to see the depth of the emotion she was trying to portray. She looked at the easel holding the painting of the little girl looking up at a hand that was reaching toward her. Jovia had become so consumed by painting the portrait that she forgot she was in the art room of her school, where everyone could see her work and not in the comfort of her room at home, where she waited to do her best work, alone. The bell rang, saving her from further embarrassment.

"Jovia, I need to see you before you leave," Mr. McKee told her.

"Uh, I have calculus with Mr. Durham, I can't be late," she

told him, removing her smock and gathering her book bag and purse.

"Don't worry, I'll give you a pass," Mr. McKee told her. "This is important."

Jovia stared at him. He was her favorite teacher even though he was corny as hell. He was a shorter white man with curly brown hair and a stocky body. He reminded her of a chubby John Travolta with his dimpled smile and bright eyes.

"Fine," she sighed.

Mr. McKee began gathering brushes and paints, saying good-bye to the other students as they filed out of the class-room. Once they were alone, he turned to Jovia and told her, "Jovia, you are one of the most talented artists I've had come through my classroom."

This wasn't the first time she'd heard that statement. All of her art teachers told her that through the years. This also wasn't the first time Mr. McKee told her that. She shrugged her shoulders and told him, "Thanks, Mr. McKee. You're a great teacher."

"I think it's time you start seriously working on your craft. What is it that you want to do with your talent, Jovia?"

Jovia blinked, not understanding what he was asking or where he was going with the conversation. She hoped this wasn't his attempt to get her to stay after school and possibly seduce her, because she was not the one. She had heard stories of male teachers who took advantage of their female students.

"What do you mean, Mr. McKee?" She gave him a look letting him know she wasn't down for any funny stuff.

"It's your senior year of high school, Jovia. Are you going to pursue a career in art? If so, are you going to go to art school on a collegiate level? Have you thought about working on your portfolio? Or is this just a hobby for you; something to do to get some easy credits?" He stared at her.

Jovia didn't know what to say. She hadn't really thought

about it. A career? In art? She was going to college, far away, of course. But as far as her art, she hadn't thought about it being a major part of her future, "I plan on going to college, Mr. McKee. But I was going to major in accounting."

"Okay, accounting is a great field, Jovia. I just thought that with your passion for art, you wanted to pursue it further," he told her.

"Not really," she said, shrugging.

Mr. McKee seemed a bit disappointed. "Well, we certainly don't want you to be any later for calculus, especially since you're gonna need it in your accounting field," he said with a half smile. He walked over to his desk and wrote out a pass for her.

"Thanks, Mr. McKee," she told him.

As she sat in her calculus class, she couldn't even pay attention to Mr. Durham droning about quantative analysis and equations. Instead, she thought about what Mr. McKee had asked her. Could she really pursue an art career and make money doing something that she loved? She took out her pencil and turned to the next blank page in her notebook. Before she knew it, the bell rang and class was over. She looked at the notebook and saw the vivid scene of caricatures she had drawn of her classmates, all staring at Mr. Durham as he taught class. She smiled at her handiwork and closed it.

"You want a ride home?"

Jovia looked up at her friend Kaitlyn Madison. Kaitlyn and her family lived down the street from Jovia. She was a nice girl and Jovia liked her. Like Jovia, Kaitlyn was quiet and unassuming.

"Sure, but can you wait a few minutes? I have to take care of something right quick," Jovia told her.

"No problem, I'll wait for you in the parking lot." Kaitlyn smiled. She had the most perfect teeth Jovia had ever seen. Until recently, Kaitlyn had also been overweight. But the past year, she had slimmed down considerably. Once the pimple-faced, fat girl who played the violin, Kaitlyn was now the one who turned heads as they walked down the hallway of St. Bart's Academy. And although her appearance on the outside had changed considerably, Jovia loved the fact that her demeanor had not changed not one bit. She was still the same Kaitlyn who she loved to watch movies with and made Jovia laugh with her goofiness.

"Thanks, Kaity." Jovia smiled and made a beeline down the hallway to the art room, hoping to catch Mr. McKee. She was disappointed to see that he was gone and the door was locked when she got there. She slowly turned to walk away.

"You leave something in the classroom?"

Jovia turned and smiled. "No, I was hoping to talk to you."

Mr. McKee walked toward her. "Really?"

"Yeah, I was thinking about what you said; about me having an art career."

"What about it?"

"Well, what kind of career? I mean, like having my paintings in a gallery?" she asked.

"Possibly, but there's a lot you can do with your talent, Jovia. There's graphic design, animation, fashion design, illustration, all sorts of careers. You just have to do a little research and like I said, work on your craft," he told her.

"How do I do that?" she asked.

"I'm glad you asked, my dear," he said, unlocking the door to the classroom and walking in. She hesitated and followed behind him.

"Man, what took you so long?" Kaitlyn asked when she finally arrived to the car thirty minutes later.

"I told you I had something to take care of," Jovia said, opening the door of the shiny black Acura and getting in. She was still thinking about Mr. McKee and all that had transpired. She knew that her life would never be the same again. She smiled as she thought about the things he said and the doors that he had just opened for her.

"What are you smiling so hard about?" Kaitlyn asked.

"Huh?" Jovia looked up. She hadn't even realized she was smiling.

"What's up with you?"

"Nothing, I'm just thinking about stuff," she answered.

"Must be damn good stuff," Kaitlyn laughed. "You wouldn't happen to be thinking about Jordan Capron would you?"

"Hell, no!" Jovia snapped. Jordan Capron was the farthest thing from her mind.

"Why not? Come on, Jovia, you know he's got it bad for you," she laughed. "He's fine as hell too!"

"I don't think so. Jordan Capron is not my type." Jovia shook her head. Kaitlyn was crazy to think she would be interested in Jordan. He was a pretty boy. The typical all-American who had all the girls at Saint Bart's after him, black, white, Hispanic, Puerto Rican, and Asian they all wanted Jordan. The school consisted of an equally mixed crowd of the crème de la crème, wealthy students whose parents could afford the 4,000-dollar per month tuition. He was senior class president, captain of the basketball team, and an all-around athlete. For some reason, he had set his sights on Jovia, and unlike all the other females at school, she was not impressed by him one bit. "I need someone a little more rugged than Jordan."

"Jordan is rugged," Kaitlyn replied.

Jovia looked over at Kaitlyn and said, "No, Jordan plays rugby, Kaitlyn, that's a far cry from being rugged."

"Rugged or not, he can get it."

"Get what?"

"It!"

Jovia looked over at her and couldn't help laughing, knowing full well that Kaitlyn was still a virgin and planned on staying that way until she was married. "You are so goofy, you know that?"

"Call it what you want," Kaitlyn said. "I heard he's going to ask you to go to the prom."

"No, he's not."

"If he asks, are you going to go?" Kaitlyn glanced over at her.

Jovia frowned and shook her head. "Hell no, I am not interested in Jordan Capron. Besides, he barely even talks to me. Why would he ask me to the prom?"

"Why not? You're smart, beautiful, and creative."

"We don't even talk to the same people," Jovia said.

"That's because you only talk to me, everyone knows that," Kaitlyn laughed. "That's probably why he had Carey Simmons ask me for your number."

"I hope you didn't give it to him, Kaitlyn!" Jovia's heart began racing.

"No, I would never do that without your permission. I gave him your e-mail address!"

"Kaitlyn, I can't believe you," Jovia screeched.

Kaitlyn laughed, reaching down and turning up her radio. They began bobbing to Fantasia's "Thug Boy."

"Now that's what I'm talking about," Jovia told her, snapping her fingers and singing along.

"Yeah, right. You want a thug boy, wife beater and jeans. But you and I both know that ain't happening. There's no way city councilman Marcus Grant would even allow that to happen," Kaitlyn told her as she turned into Wellington Estates, the neighborhood they lived in.

Jovia looked at the million-dollar homes with perfectly manicured lawns and sighed, "Well, guess what? City Councilman Marcus Grant may control a lot of things, but there are some things he has no control over."

Jovia knew there was some truth to what Kaitlyn was saying. Marcus Grant was definitely a control freak. He had just announced his candidacy for the city council when he received word of the fire that claimed the life of a young mother and scarred her young daughter in the Frederick Douglass housing project. Not one single apartment in the building had a smoke detector. Marcus Grant stepped up and made safer housing his platform. Not only vowing to improve the conditions of the housing development, but even adopting the orphaned little girl. On the day he won the election, he along with his wife, wheeled their new daughter out of the burn unit of Lincoln Memorial Hospital and took her to her new home. Marcus told her that she was now his responsibility and he would make sure he took care of everything. And he had. He took care of where she went, what she did, who her friends were, what she ate and everything in between. The rein he kept on Jovia was so tight, that she was beginning to feel smothered. If it wasn't for her adoptive mother, she didn't know what she would do. She tended to be a little more lenient with Jovia and reminded the councilman that she was a teenager and still had a life to live.

"Considering your high grades in mathematics, Jovia, I think you should consider majoring in accounting. I think that would make a great choice for you," he said the last time she got her report card.

"Accounting, that's so boring," his wife commented.

"Don't be discouraging." He frowned at her.

Jovia had already decided that she would go to college as far away from home that she could find, and if majoring in accounting would help her to get away, she had no problem with that. "I think that's a good choice too." Jovia said.

Now, all of that had changed. Mr. McKee had presented her with the opportunity of a lifetime; she just had to come up with a way to get Councilman Marcus Grant to loosen his grip on her.

# Chapter 2

"How was school?"

"It was fine, Me-Ma." Jovia walked over to the desk where her adoptive mother sat reading. She leaned over and gave her a kiss on the cheek.

"I went to the mall and picked up a couple of things for you. Nordstrom's was having a sale."

"Thanks." Jovia smiled. She loved this woman. From day one, Karen Grant had loved and nurtured her as if Jovia was her own child. She was a beautiful woman who people often compared to Phylicia Rashad, the woman who played Clair Huxtable on *The Cosby Show*. Her smooth café au lait skin, perfectly styled dark hair, and always pleasant demeanor played a major part in the comparison. It only recently occurred to Jovia to wonder why her adoptive parents didn't have any children of their own. She wondered if it was even possible. She didn't ask, nor was it discussed. They seemed content with Jovia.

"The councilman and I have a dinner engagement tonight, so we won't be home," she told her. "You want me to run you to get something to eat after you change out of your uniform?"

Jovia shook her head. "No, I'm good. I can make a sand-wich or something out the kitchen."

"What was the point of taking driver's ed if you weren't going to get your license, Jovia?"

"I did try to get my license, Me-Ma."

"You took the test one time. . . ."

"And I failed," Jovia sighed. She hated the fact that she failed her driving test two years ago and had yet to get up the nerve to retake it. She didn't want to chance failing it again. "Why do I need to drive? You take me wherever I need to go. Besides I can always catch the J."

"Jovia Grant, that is a cop-out and a sorry one at that. To think you'd rather ride that raggedy, dangerous piece of pub-lic transportation than get your license and have your own car. The J train, why would you even wanna ride that? As a matter of fact, I'd better not even catch you near the station!" Me-Ma shook her head in horror. "The councilman would have a heart attack if he heard you talking like that. You know what he always says: That train doesn't head anywhere but to trouble in the hood and only people looking for trouble ride it, hoodlums."

"Me-Ma, I'm kidding," Jovia quickly told her. Turning to depart to her room, she added, "I have homework."

"Don't forget to try the clothes on and let me know if you like them."

"I will," she said. She ran up the stairs and into her room. Tossing her book bag on the floor near her desk, she flopped onto her bed. *That train doesn't head anywhere but to trouble in the hood* . . . Me-Ma's words echoed in her head. The J train was the way she and her mother traveled when she was alive. They didn't have a car, and to even have a cab come to Frederick Douglass was damn near impossible, and even if it did, they didn't have money for cab fare. Everyone in Jovia's old neighborhood took the J train. It was how those who were lucky enough to have jobs uptown got to work. It was how they got to the mall, the store, even to church. *Hoodlums*. Were she and her mother and everyone they knew indeed hoodlums? If the councilman had his way, he would have the train shut down. He felt that it was a waste of tax money. She thought about the old neighborhood where she was from. For some reason, she had been thinking more often than not about Frederick Douglass and the life she and her mother had there. She realized that she missed it.

Jovia looked over at the two large shopping bags beside her. She reached over and dumped out the contents. Jeans, sweaters, shirts came tumbling out. They were all items that she had mentioned she liked when she and Me-Ma were out shopping last week and things that she knew Me-Ma thought she would like. Picking up a pink wrap shirt and holding it against her frame, she stood and stared into the full-length mirror on her closet door. Slipping out of her knee-length, red-and-gray plaid uniform skirt and white Polo shirt, she tried the shirt on along with a pair of jeans. The outfit was a perfect fit. The shirt accented her small waist and cocoa-brown complexion; the low rise jeans hugged the curves of her hips just right. She turned around and admired the way her behind looked in them. She heard the remarks of guys in the hall when she walked by. *Damn, look at that . . . that's what I'm talking 'bout . . . that's what's up . . . onion butt.* Although she pretended to disregard their comments and ignore them, she couldn't help being somewhat flattered by the attention. She was happy when she realized that her figure was just like the one her mother had. Men always turned to look when her mother walked by. Felicia Parker had a walk that turned men's heads for blocks and she knew it. Now, Jovia had the same walk. Felicia was also the best dancer in FDP. A party wasn't a party if Felicia wasn't there. Smiling, Jovia reached for the remote of her stereo and turned it on.

She began swaying and bouncing to the beat as Ciara's voice sang through the speakers. She closed her eyes and pretended her mother was in the room with her, laughing and encouraging her to *"go on girl"* like she used to when Jovia was little. Jovia danced harder and harder, and for a moment, she could feel her mother's presence. She smiled and suddenly stopped.

"I guess you like them?" Me-Ma was standing in the doorway grinning at her.

Embarrassed, Jovia grabbed the remote and turned the music off. "Yes, Me-Ma, they're a perfect fit. Thank you."

"You don't have to turn it down, Jovia. I didn't mean to embarrass you. You looked like you were in the zone." Me-Ma sat on the bed. Jovia walked into the closet and took out several hangers. She began hanging her uniform up along with the new clothes she had just gotten.

"I guess I was, huh?" Jovia smiled softly.

"I saw some gorgeous prom dresses at the store. Have you decided what color you wanted to wear?"

"I probably won't be going this year," Jovia told her.

"Why not? I thought you'd be excited about finally being able to go," Me-Ma told her.

"I'm not interested."

"But it's your senior prom, Jovia. You should go," her mother told her.

"I'm just not interested in going. You sound like Kaitlyn."

"And Kaitlyn's a smart girl. I like her."

"Like who?"

They both jumped at the sound of the councilman's voice. They looked up to see him standing in Jovia's doorway.

"Marcus, you scared us." Me-Ma rose to greet her husband.

"Hello, Councilman," Jovia said as he walked over and gave her a hug.

"You two shouldn't be gossiping and then you wouldn't be so jumpy," he said, smiling at them.

"You know we weren't gossiping, Marcus," Me-Ma scolded him. "We were talking about Jovia's *not* going to the prom and how I think she should attend."

"If she doesn't want to go to the prom, you shouldn't force her," he said.

Jovia looked over and gave Me-Ma a smug grin. "Thank you, Councilman."

"Jovia has more important things to think about," he added.

"Like what?" Jovia and Me-Ma said, simultaneously.

"Well, I was speaking with a colleague of mine at Coleman and Associates, they're a CPA firm, and it seems as if they are hiring students for the summer. I told him about Jovia and he doesn't have a problem with her working there."

"A job? You got me a summer job?" Jovia asked. She was happy that he was letting his tight leash up enough to allow her to out the house for the summer, but upset that he would get her a job without even consulting her first. She had considered getting a job in the mall this summer, but hadn't gotten the courage to ask, thinking that her parents wouldn't approve. Hearing the plans the councilman had for her now presented a problem with her entering the art program.

"Well, it's only part-time, but it'll give you great experience. And I've asked him to pull a few strings to see if he can get you a position," he said, nodding.

"You want her to spend her entire summer working, Marcus? I don't think that's fair," Me-Ma told him.

"Why not?" he asked.

"It's the summer before she leaves for college, Marcus. She should spend it enjoying herself, not slaving away in some stuffy office."

"It's okay, Me-Ma. I wanted to get a job anyway," Jovia responded.

"Jovia, believe me, you have the rest of your life to work.

You should take advantage of this freedom while you have it," Me-Ma told her.

"For God's sake, don't discourage the girl, Karen. If she wants to work, then we should let her. It's only a couple of hours a week," the councilman told her. In that brief moment, Jovia almost gathered the nerve to share with him the summer program Mr. McKee had told her about. It was an art program for high school students that exposed them to several areas. He had given her an application, a catalogue, and a brochure to share with her parents. She wanted to tell the councilman and Me-Ma that this was what she wanted to spend her summer doing. But somehow, she couldn't. She was scared.

"Come on, Karen. We have to be ready to leave in thirty minutes," the councilman said. "Those jeans are too tight, Jovia. You look like one of those hootchies from FDR."

"Yes sir," Jovia sighed.

Me-Ma walked over and kissed her forehead. "I love you. Enjoy your youth, sweetheart. Don't waste it away slaving for someone else. And those jeans are fine. You look like a beautiful eighteen-year-old girl."

"I love you too, Me-Ma," Jovia replied. Alone, she stared at herself in the mirror again for several moments, trying to see if it really was her staring back. The girl looking back at her was a far cry from the small girl who used to ride the J train and dance with her mother in the FDP. Gone were the chin-length ponytails and crooked teeth, replaced by picture-perfect teeth, thanks to four years of braces, and a shoulder-length bob. She stepped further toward the mirror, looking at her face. She didn't see herself as being pretty, although Kaitlyn and her mother often told her she was. To her, she was plain. Her nose was keen, her chin pointed, and her eyes dark and wistful. *I look like my mother*. The longer she stared, the sadder she became. She quickly turned away and removed the shirt. Glancing over her shoulder, she caught sight of herself in the mirror again. This time, her eyes fell on the reflection of her back and shoulders, darker than the rest of her body, and distorted. The scars from the fire still remained, although she had gone through several skin grafts and cosmetic surgeries. They weren't visible when she had her clothes on, but noticeable when she was nude. A constant reminder of where she had come from, what she had been through, and what she had endured.

She reached into her bag and removed the paperwork Mr. McKee had given her. She clicked on her computer to further research the program.

"You've got mail," her computer announced.

She clicked on the mailbox and scanned her in-box. She scanned the messages and was dumbstruck when she saw there was a message from JCAPE8 with the subject: *What's up wit u!* Thinking that this may be some kind of sick joke Kaitlyn was playing, she opened the e-mail.

Hey, what's up . . . got ur email from Kaitlyn . . . I'm tryin'to holla at u later . . . if so, hit me on my cell: 549-8808.
J-Capron

Jovia stared at the e-mail and read it continually for a few minutes. Jordan Capron was e-mailing her. She was shocked, but not impressed. She had no desire to call him. Jovia clicked out of the e-mail and put thoughts of Jordan out of her head. She had more important things to think about than his conceited ass. She went to the art programs Web site and began her research.

# Chapter 3

"Well, did you talk to him?" Kaitlyn asked the following day on the way to school.

"No, I didn't," Jovia told her.

"He didn't e-mail you?"

"Yeah, he did." Jovia shrugged.

"What did it say?"

"He wanted me to call him."

"Why didn't you?"

Jovia was becoming frustrated by Kaitlyn's inquisition. It was as if her friend couldn't believe that there was no possible way that Jovia couldn't like Jordan. "I keep telling you that I don't like him, Kaitlyn. What part of that don't you understand?"

"Jovia, what's there not to like? He's cute, smart, he's a great athlete and—"

"He's arrogant, conceited, and sarcastic as hell," Jovia interrupted her. "You along with the entire school have him thinking he's God's gift so he acts that way."

"That's not true, Jovia. He's just popular."

"Whatever." Jovia shook her head. They pulled into the student parking area of the school that looked more like a luxury car lot. Kaitlyn pulled her Acura between a Mercedes coupe and a Jaguar.

"Well, don't look now, but here comes God's gift now," Kaitlyn laughed as they got out of the car.

Jovia prayed she was joking, but sure enough, walking toward her was Jordan Capron, along with his trusty sidekick, Carey. Dressed in khaki pants and white oxford shirts, they looked more like brothers than best friends. Each stood 6'2" and had the same coffee-colored complexion along with the same close haircut. But where Jordan walked with an air of self-importance, Carey sauntered. She liked Carey; he was cool without trying to be, unlike Jordan.

"What's up, ladies?" Jordan said.

"Nothing, what's up with you?" Kaitlyn gushed. Jovia rolled her eyes at her friend's overt cheerfulness.

"Hey Carey," Jovia said as she walked past them. Kaitlyn paused then followed Jovia.

"Same old same." Jordan shrugged. "Carey the only one you see, Jovia?"

"Hey Jordan," she sighed. The boys began walking beside them.

"I e-mailed you yesterday so you could call me," he told her.

"I know," she told him. "Carey, you finish your questions for contemporary lit?"

Carey glanced over at Jordan and then said, "Yeah, I did. You?"

"Yeah, but I had the hardest time figuring the last one out. I didn't understand what she meant by figurative direction of the main character," Jovia said.

"Yo, I feel you. I didn't know if she meant the husband or the wife because to me, they were both main characters." Carey nodded. "But since I could understand things from a male perspective, you know which one I went with."

Jovia laughed. "And since I can understand things from a female perspective, you know which one I went with."

"Uh, I hate to break up this little homework hotline discussion but I believe Jovia and I were having a totally different conversation," Jordan announced.

"We were?" Jovia questioned.

"My bad," Carey said. "I'll see you in class, Jovia."

"We'll see which one of us gets it right," she laughed as he sauntered ahead of them.

"Damn, I left my history book in the car," Kaitlyn snapped. "I'll catch you in third bell, Jovia."

"Cool," Jovia told her.

"Damn, alone at last." Jordan smiled as they continued walking into the school.

"I hardly call this alone," Jovia told him, glancing at the multitude of students who were bypassing them as they walked into the building.

"You know what I mean," Jordan told her. "So, you got my e-mail and you didn't have the decency to call?"

"I had other stuff to do," Jovia said.

"Oh, yeah, contemporary lit, I forgot." Jordan glared.

"Yep," she told him, turning down the hallway that held her locker. "But, being that we're alone at last, you can go ahead and tell me why you wanted me to call."

"Because I'm trying to holla at you, that's why. I wanna take you out." He smiled, leaning against the locker next to hers. People continually spoke to him as they walked by and she knew that by lunchtime, everyone would be talking about how he was at her locker.

Jovia twisted the knob on her lock and popped it open. She didn't respond as she took books out of her bag and placed them inside, and removing the materials needed for her morning classes. Thinking long and hard before closing the locker door, she told him, "Look Jordan, you're a nice guy, but I'm not interested."

Jordan looked as if she had slapped him in the face. "What?"

"I'm not interested in going out with you," she told him, watching his reaction turn from shock to disappointment to anger. It was obvious he wasn't used to being turned down, and didn't know how to handle it. "I gotta get to class."

He didn't say anything as she turned away from him and walked to her class. As she took her seat, she hoped she hadn't hurt his feelings. She had been straight-up honest with him and felt that he deserved that much. Besides, he probably had another girl waiting for him by the time he made it to his class.

"What was I supposed to say?" Jovia asked Kaitlyn as they sat in the courtyard eating lunch.

"How about 'Cool, what time are you picking me up?'" Kaitlyn shrugged.

"But I don't like him, Kaitlyn," Jovia told him. "What's the big deal? I tell you what, since you like his ass so much, why don't you go out with him?"

"He doesn't like me, he likes you. Believe me, if he did like me, I would be on his ass," Kaitlyn told her. "I hope you know everyone is talking about how you dissed him."

"I don't give a damn what everyone is talking about, Kaitlyn." Jovia's voice became louder. She looked around and saw that people were looking at her as they had been doing all day. "And if the fact that I'm not interested in going out with Jordan Capron is all they have to talk about then they are even more pathetic than I thought."

She got up and grabbed her bags. She could hear people whispering as she walked past. She became even angrier. She had to get away. She ignored Kaitlyn's voice calling her name and decided to leave. She cut through the back of the building and crossed the street. The nearest main street was three blocks, and she quickly hailed a cab.

"Where to?" the driver asked, and stared at her shapely legs as she got in. She pulled her skirt down to try to cover her flesh.

Jovia had no idea where she was going. She couldn't go

home; Me-Ma didn't work and she didn't want to chance her being there. Jovia thought of the longing that had been pulling at her the past few months and said, "The train station."

Her cell phone rang for the fourth time. Knowing it was Kaitlyn, she cut it off completely. She quietly stared out of the window as the cab drove through the traffic-filled streets. The shiny glass buildings quickly turned to dark cement structures and the smooth black pavement became gravel-ridden concrete as the cab pulled in front of the station. She stared at the once familiar building, still shocked that she was here.

"Fourteen dollars," the driver told her. She reached into her Coach purse and gave him the money. She still didn't get out, and he asked, "You sure this is where you wanna go?"

"Yeah," she said softly and opened the door. She got out and he pulled off. She took a deep breath and walked inside. The busy station was filled with people coming and going. She waded her way through the crowd and bought a token. She walked over to the platform and waited for the J. She read the signs and billboards as she waited. She smiled at a little girl who looked to be about five, sucking on a lollipop and holding the hand of a woman. *This is crazy*, she thought. *Why? You don't even know where you're going. Yes*, I *do*, she told herself. *Home.*

The train pulled up and she got on. She tried to decide rather to sit or stand. She had never stood before, Felicia always told her she was too little. Now that she was big enough, Jovia decided to stand. Grabbing onto one of the hanging leather handles, she braced herself as the train jerked forward. Feeling someone's eyes on her, she turned. A man was staring at her, looking her up and down like he was sizing her up. She pulled her book bag and purse close to her, and quickly gave him a "what the hell you looking at" look back and rolled her eyes so that he knew that even though she may not look like she was from his neck of the woods, she was. He turned away. Before she knew it, she was walking down the streets of the FDP. It was as if nothing changed. The orange bricks of the building still held tags of rival gangs and lover's names. Graffiti; it was the first form of art that Jovia had fallen in love with. She walked over to the small park that was located in the center of the projects. Small children played on the ragged swings while men of all ages shot dice and drank beer. Jovia sat on a nearby bench and took out a small sketch pad. She began drawing the scene, capturing each detail so she wouldn't forget.

"Damn, you got skills," the deep voice startled her. She was so engrossed in what she was doing that she didn't notice him standing behind her. Taken off guard, she quickly closed her pad and grabbed her belongings. "Whoa, wait, my bad."

Jovia stood up without saying a word.

"Come on, don't be like that," he said and she felt his hand on her shoulder.

She quickly snatched away. "Don't put your hands on me."

"My bad, I wasn't trying to scare you or nothing like that," he said. "Don't leave on my account. Go ahead and finish."

Her intentions were to cuss him out, but when she turned to face him she was so stunned by how attractive he was, that she was speechless. The combination of his smooth mahogany complexion and his hazel eyes entranced her. He sported cornrows, parted in perfect zigzags. She knew he was barely six feet, but what he lacked in height, he made up for in the muscular cut of his body that she noticed through the long-sleeved T-shirt and jeans he wore. Jovia stared at him, from the top of his braided hair to the butter-colored Timberland boots he wore on his feet. She knew it was rude, but she didn't care. She couldn't help it, she wanted to take in every inch of him and etch it in her memory.

"What's wrong?" he asked, looking confused.

"I gotta go," she said and rushed away.

"Wait, hold on!"

For the second time that day, she was beckoned from behind, only this time, unlike the first, she wanted to turn around. But she kept going.

It was well after six o'clock by the time Jovia arrived at home. She prayed that Kaitlyn had sense enough not to come by her house looking for her. She was relieved when she saw that the councilman's Range Rover wasn't in the driveway. As she entered the house, she tried to think of a story in case she needed one.

"Me-Ma!" she called out. When there wasn't an answer, she hurried upstairs to her room.

"Jovia!" She heard Me-Ma calling her name.

"Yes," she answered.

Me-Ma entered her room, putting on a pair of diamond earrings. Dressed in a pair of black tuxedo trousers and a pearl-colored sweater, Jovia knew she must have another dinner engagement with the councilman. "Hey sweetie, I was beginning to worry. I called your phone and you didn't answer. Hurry and get changed."

"Changed for what?"

"The councilman called and we have to meet him for dinner."

"Do I have to go?" Jovia asked. She had a long day and she needed time to herself to reflect.

"Yes, you do. Now get dressed." Me-Ma kissed the top of her head. "Hurry, we have reservations at Cristobel's and we can't be late."

Well, at least it's at a decent restaurant, Jovia thought as she reluctantly walked into her closet and rummaged for something to wear. She settled on a simple green-and-white tunic dress and matching shoes. She dabbed on some of her favorite cologne, grabbed a sweater and by the time Me-Ma called her name again, she was ready to walk out the door.

Cristobel's was the latest craze for the city's elite. It always tickled Jovia the way the upper class catered to whomever they thought were to be the latest and greatest. The owner of Cristobel's claimed to have worked with the world's greatest chefs and in some of the finest restaurants. Having said that, anyone who thought they were anyone just had to dine at Cristobel's. To Jovia, the food was good, but not worth the prices on the menu.

"Mrs. Grant, how lovely to see you again," the maître d' greeted them. "And young lady, you're looking more and more beautiful each time and I see you."

"Thank you," Jovia said, politely.

"Claude, you are so kind." Me-Ma smiled.

"Come along," Claude told them, "The councilman is already waiting."

They followed Claude through the restaurant to a large round table. Jovia counted the number of chairs, totaling six. She began to regret not faking sick and staying home. This was probably going to be one of those long, drawn out, politically motivated dinners with a humdrum supporter and his wife. Jovia hated those dinners.

"I see my two lovely ladies have arrived," the councilman stood and welcomed both of them with a kiss on the cheek. "Thank you, Claude."

"Hello, Councilman," Jovia said, taking her seat.

"I'll bring the rest of your party back as soon as they arrive, sir," Claude said, nodding.

"Who else is coming?" Jovia asked.

"The associate I was telling you about at the CPA firm," the councilman answered.

Jovia became nervous. "Is this going to be like an interview?"

"No, sweetheart, nothing like that; relax," Me-Ma assured

her. "Marcus, you didn't tell me there would be other people eating with us. I thought this was a family dinner."

"I didn't know, Karen. He called while I was on the way and I mentioned I was coming here for dinner. Some kind of way he invited himself and his wife," the councilman replied.

"Just him and his wife? But there are three chairs here," Me-Ma said, picking up her menu.

"I don't know, he just told me there would be three of them. There they come now." The councilman stood and smiled.

Jovia turned to see. Her heart began pounding and she could feel beads of sweat forming on her forehead.

"Councilman Grant, this is my wife, Natalie, and my son, Jordan," the man said.

Jovia stared into the eyes of Jordan Capron, who was giving her the sickest smile she had ever seen in her life and she knew it was going to be a long night.

# Chapter 4

By the time they left the restaurant, Jovia was furious. Jordan had played her like a fiddle in front of her parents, paying her all types of compliments and telling everyone at the table about what a great student and artist she was. Before she knew it, he had asked the councilman if he could be her escort to the prom and the councilman agreed. Both mothers were ecstatic and you would think he had proposed by the way they were acting.

"Jovia, I don't understand where this attitude is coming from, and I don't like it," Me-Ma said on the way home.

"I told you I didn't even want to go to the prom, Me-Ma. You know that," Jovia told her.

"I know what you said, Jovia. But trust me, this is going to be one of the most exciting experiences of your life. I don't want you to miss out."

"I'm not going to miss out, Me-Ma, I can always go next year," Jovia tried explaining again. It was as if the world ignored her and what she wanted didn't matter.

"You'll have fun, Jovia. Jordan seems like such a nice boy and he'll be the perfect date for you. I keep telling you to learn to enjoy your life. You're too blessed to be acting this way. I'm beginning to think you're ungrateful."

It was the first time her mother had spoken to her like that, like she was some orphan girl from the projects that she had taken in. She turned to face Me-Ma and said, "I'm grateful for everything that you and the councilman have done for me, Me-Ma. If going to the prom is what you want me to do, then I'll go." Tears filled Jovia's eyes and she got out the car.

"Jovia, wait, that's not what I meant," Me-Ma said.

"No, you're right. I'm tired," she said and went inside. Now as she lay in her warm bed, she wanted nothing more than the cramped, damp apartment she shared with Felicia. There was a knock on her door and she knew it was Me-Ma. She thought if she ignored it, she would go away, thinking Jovia was asleep. No such luck. Jovia heard the turn of the knob and Me-Ma walked in and sat on the side of her bed.

"Jovia, I want to explain to you what I meant," she started.

"No, you don't have to explain. I told you I would go to the prom," Jovia said, looking away.

"It's not about the prom, Jovia. I need for you to look at me."

Jovia turned and stared at her. "Yes."

"When I said that you were acting ungrateful, I didn't mean to us and what we've done, I meant to yourself and all you've accomplished and have become. Jovia, you're a beautiful, talented young lady. You're gifted in so many ways. But sometimes, I don't think you see yourself in that way. You are so . . . what's the word I'm looking for. . . . introverted and you don't let people in. I just don't want you to miss out on anything because you're so busy being selfish with yourself," Me-Ma said. "I want nothing but the best for you. I promised you that a long time ago, remember?"

Jovia nodded, she did remember. It was the promise Me-Ma made to her the first night they brought her home.

"I meant that then, and I mean it now," Me-Ma told her, rising from the bed. "I love you."

"I love you too, Me-Ma," Jovia told her. "Can we start shopping for my prom dress this weekend?"

"If that's what your heart desires." Me-Ma smiled. She paused, looking down at Jovia's desk. "What's this?"

Jovia sat up, seeing the brochure and catalogue for the art program in her hand. "Oh, some information about a program this summer at the community college Mr. McKee gave me."

"Nice," she said, flipping though the information. "Are you going to apply?"

"I was thinking about it," Jovia said. "But the councilman wants me to work this summer."

"That's your decision, Jovia," Me-Ma said, closing the door. "Good night."

Unable to sleep, Jovia got out of bed and walked over to corner of her room that held her drawing table. She reached into her book bag, taking out her pad. She critiqued the drawing she had done earlier that day. *Damn, I do have skills*, she smiled to herself. She turned to the next blank sheet and closed her eyes. She envisioned the guy she saw in the park and picked up her pencil. With precise strokes, she guided her hands as she always did, until what she saw in her head was a vision on the paper. *His eyes, they captivated me. His voice, it drew me. His presence, it appealed to me.* For hours, she drew until she felt herself nodding from tiredness. She gave the portrait a final glance and then, kissed her fingertips and ran them along his lips.

"I'm sooo glad you changed your mind," Kaitlyn squealed when she told her she was going to the prom with Jordan. "It's gonna be the bomb, girlfriend, wait and see."

"Whatever," Jovia remarked as they walked through the racks of clothes. She felt bad about storming off the day before, so to make it up to Kaitlyn, she told her she would be attending the prom and suggested they start looking for dresses the following weekend.

"What about this one?" Kaitlyn held up a slinky silver dress that looked more like a costume for a Cher look-alike than a prom dress.

"I don't think so," Jovia told her.

"So, are you gonna tell me where you ran off to yesterday?" Kaitlyn asked, hanging the dress back on the rack and continuing her search.

"Just around," Jovia told her. She had contemplated going back but decided that skipping an afternoon of classes without getting caught one day was lucky enough and she wouldn't chance it again.

"Around where?"

Jovia knew Kaitlyn was going to keep asking until she told her. "You have to promise not to say anything to anyone. You know how you and your big mouth can be, Kaitlyn."

"Okay, I promise." Kaitlyn nodded quickly.

"I took the J train and went down to Frederick Douglass."

Kaitlyn stopped and stared wide-eyed at Jovia. "You went where?"

"I took the train to FDP," Jovia answered and held up a black dress, "This is cute."

"Jovia, you rode the train by yourself? My God, you coulda been killed." Kaitlyn shook her head in disbelief. "What if someone would have robbed you? People get mugged all the time down there."

"You sound crazy, Kaitlyn. People get killed and mugged everywhere all the time," Jovia replied. "You're beginning to sound prejudiced."

"How can I be prejudiced and I'm black," Kaitlyn snapped.

"Prejudice has nothing to do with race, it's about prejudging," Jovia told her. "I would hate to think you believe you're better than anybody because you live in the upper east."

"No, I just feel safer here." Kaitlyn smiled. "Jovia, I know that's where you're from and I don't blame you for wanting to go back from time to time. Next time you feel the need to venture down there though, let me go with you. You don't need to be going by yourself."

"You wanna roll with me to Frederick Douglass?" It was Jovia's turn to be shocked.

"You're my best friend, Jovia, why wouldn't I," Kaitlyn told her. "Besides, I heard it's some fine guys down there. Just let me know when so I can have my mace and whistle with me, just in case, of course."

"You are such a bigot," Jovia couldn't help laughing.

Before she knew it, it was the day of the prom. Jordan called her that morning to express his sheer delight and anticipation of the evening that lay ahead. "I can't wait until tonight, Jovia. I have great plans for us."

"The only plans you have for us is to go to dinner, the prom, and back home," Jovia told him. For some reason, she was still hesitant about going with Jordan. There was something about him that made her uncomfortable, but she had promised Me-Ma so she pushed her concern aside.

"Well, Carey and some of the guys are having an after party and I thought we'd swing through there after we left the prom."

"Look Jordan, I said I would go to the prom with you, not an after party. Now if you wanna roll to the party after you drop me off at home, by all means, feel free."

"Why do you have to act so anti, Jovia? It's an after party with your classmates, you need to lighten your ass up a bit and chill out. I'm beginning to think what everyone says about you is true," he huffed.

"And what the hell is that?" she asked.

"That you think you're better than anyone else. That's why you walk around with your nose in the air as if you're higher and mightier than everyone," he answered.

"You and everyone else have lost their fucking mind, Jordan. I don't walk around like anything. I keep to myself because I don't want y'all nosy asses in my business like you all are," she snapped.

"What business? Please," he scoffed at her, "you don't hang out, you don't participate in anything, you hardly talk to anyone except Kaitlyn—oh, and Carey of course."

"You sound a little jealous, Jordan. I talk to who the hell I wanna talk to. I talk to the people I feel are worth talking to. As far as you and all those other high-class, uppity people, I don't give a damn about them or you for that matter. The only reason I agreed to even go with you to the prom was because your ass put me on the spot at dinner. Now, if you still want me to be your date, I suggest you get off my phone and let me get dressed," she told him.

There was a long silence, until he finally said, "I'll be there at six," and hung up the phone.

"You look beautiful," the councilman said when she walked down the steps. Me-Ma had found the perfect dress for her. It was an ivory sequence gown with a Chinese collar and a long split. She wore gold high-heeled sandals that she had practiced walking in all week. Her hair was pulled on top of her head in an upsweep and Me-Ma even had a professional come to the house to do her makeup. Jovia felt like a princess.

"She's gorgeous," Jordan's mom gushed. He was waiting on her along with his parents. Jovia blinked from the flash of the cameras. Mr. Capron was taking pictures, the councilman had the video camera and Me-Ma was snapping shots with both her cell phone and her camera.

"Wow." Jordan smiled. Jovia hated to admit it, but he did look handsome in the ivory long-coat tuxedo he wore. He held his hand out to her and she hesitated then saw that he had a corsage for her. "This is for you."

"Thank you," she told him as he shakily slipped it on her arm.

"You two make a nice couple," Mr. Capron said. "Smile."

They posed for a few more pictures until Jordan announced that they had dinner reservations.

"I'm so proud of you," Me-Ma whispered, hugging her. "Please have a nice time. I love you."

They walked out of the house where an ivory Chrysler 300 was sitting in the driveway next to what she assumed was the Caprons' Mercedes SUV.

"Be careful with that rental car, son," Mr. Capron called out.

"He knows that, Kevin, don't embarrass him," she heard his mother say.

Jordan opened the door of the car for her and she got in, admiring the leather interior. "This is nice," she told him when he got in.

"Yeah, my parents went all out for tonight, not that you'd appreciate it," he said, checking the mirrors and pulling out the circular driveway.

"Look, let's not argue, okay? I do wanna have a nice time tonight," she told him. Her cell phone began ringing in her purse. She knew who it was, without even looking at it. "Yes, Kaitlyn."

"Where are you?"

"We're on our way to Cristobel's," Jovia told her.

"Are you going to Carey's party after the prom?"

"I don't think so," Jovia said, glancing over at Jordan who was now on his cell phone talking to someone. He was probably making alternative plans since she would be ending her evening with him early.

"All right, I'll see you all when you get here," Kaitlyn told her.

If anyone didn't know better, they would've thought the

prom was being held at Cristobel's. Limousines were lined up out front and ball gowns and tuxedos filled the entry-way. When she and Jordan walked inside, all eyes were on them and people actually looked stunned that she was with him.

"Why are they looking at us like that?" she whispered to him.

"Because no one thought you'd actually show up," he told her. "And because we look like Will and Jada walking into this piece."

She looked up at him and although she tried not to, she laughed.

"Oh my God, you guys are fly as hell!" Kaitlyn rushed over to them, pulling her date, Garland, by the hand. "Jovia, I hardly recognize you. You look like a model."

Garland looked Jovia up and down and said, "Damn sure do. Wow."

"Back off my date before I knock you out, Garland," Jordan teased.

Jovia began to loosen up and actually started to enjoy herself. Dinner was fun and the prom was even better than she thought it was going to be. She was having a great time.

"Okay, go ahead and say it. I'm waiting," Kaitlyn said while they were in the bathroom of the hotel where the prom was held.

"Say what?" Jovia asked, touching up her lipstick.

"You are having a ball."

"It's okay," Jovia said, shrugging.

"Come on, it's more than okay. You're even laughing and joking with Jordan. Come on, come to Carey's party. Be-sides, I thought you and Carey were cool."

"We are," Jovia said, contemplating whether she should agree to go or not. She had to admit, the evening was turning out to be enjoyable.

"Just for a little while," Kaitlyn pleaded.

"Fine, for a little while," Jovia agreed, hoping she was making the right decision. Jordan was ecstatic when Kaitlyn told him Jovia had changed her mind about the party.

"I guess we can be on our way then," he said.

"I guess so," she told him.

# Chapter 5

Carey's house was packed by the time they arrived. Some people had changed out of their prom attire and had on casual clothes. She followed Jordan around the house and into the backyard where music was blasting from speakers. The entire yard was lit up in what looked like white Christmas lights and long tables with all kinds of food. There was even a bar set up near the pool. Jovia looked at her classmates who were dancing and saw that they were drinking.

"Carey's parents must not be here," she said, motioning toward some of the basketball players who were standing near a beer keg.

"Naw, his older brother Simon is here somewhere, though. He's chaperoning."

"Didn't he just graduate last year?" Jovia remarked.

"Year before last," Jordan said, then added, "I'm going to grab a beer. You want something?"

"No, I'm good. I told you I'm only hanging out for a little while, Jordan; I mean it."

"Relax, girl, damn," he said, taking off his tuxedo jacket and tossing it over his shoulder. "I'll be back in a sec."

Jovia scanned the backyard and spotted an empty seat in the corner. Her feet were starting to ache. As soon as she sat down, she noticed Kaitlyn and Garland dancing near the pool. *They make a nice couple*, she thought. Kaitlyn gave her a quick wave and she waved back.

"Enjoying yourself?"

Jovia nodded to Carey who was now sitting beside her. "Yeah."

"Then why are you sitting over here all alone? Where's J-Cape?"

"He's somewhere getting a drink, I guess," she told him. He had changed out of the black tuxedo he wore earlier and now wore a pair of jeans and a black T-shirt. "You looked really nice in your tux. I didn't get a chance to tell you that earlier."

"Thanks, you know how I do," he laughed. "But you are the one looking like a supermodel. You are wearing that dress! You and Jordan look good together, I'm glad you worked things out."

"We ain't work out anything," she said.

"My bad, I thought you two were together," he told her.

"Yo, Carey, I need some more lighting. You got a lamp or something I can use?"

Chills ran along Jovia's spine and she looked up. It was him. The guy from the park. The voice, the eyes, it was no mistaking it.

"Yeah, where are you setting up anyway?" Carey stood.

"The garage," the guy answered. His attention turned to Jovia and their eyes locked. Once again, she felt the undeniable attraction to him.

"Hey Jovia, this is my cousin, Amir. Amir, this is my friend, Jovia."

"What's up?" he asked, reaching his hand out to her. She was afraid to touch it, fearing that there would be a jolt of electricity.

"Hi," she said, her voice barely audible.

He smiled and she nearly melted. If she thought he was

nice-looking before, after seeing his smile, she thought he was gorgeous as hell. His teeth were sparkling and he had deep dimples in his cheeks. She wondered if he remembered her as vividly as she remembered him. She looked down at his hand that still held hers. It was soft, yet rugged.

"You look really nice," he said.

"Thank you," she told him.

"Amir here is a tattoo artist. He's doing them tonight if you ain't a punk," Carey told her. "Jovia is an artist herself, A. She can draw her ass off."

"Is that so?" Amir nodded. "Cool."

"Go get the lamp, Carey. Your people are waiting and I ain't trying to be here all night," Amir told him.

"Oh, yeah, I'll get it. Be right back, Jovia," Carey excused himself.

"Tattoos?" she said, stretching her legs out.

"Yep, you game?"

"I don't think so," she told him, shaking her head.

"Why not?" He stared at her with such intensity, that she couldn't turn away if she wanted to.

"Well, because first of all, this isn't an appropriate place to get a tattoo," she said.

"Why not? You've never been to a tattoo party before?"

"Actually, no I haven't."

"Ever seen anyone get a tattoo before?"

"Nope," she tried to act as nonchalant as possible.

"I think you'd get off on it being that you're into art." His eyebrows raised and she could see he was teasing her. She was about to come back with a response as seductive as his when her thoughts were interrupted.

"A'ight, Amir, you straight." Carey walked up with Kaitlyn by his side. She had an empty cup in her hand and Jovia could see from the way she was smiling that her friend was tipsy.

"Cool," Amir said.

"You getting a tat, Jovia?"

"Hell naw," Kaitlyn laughed, "and anyone who does is crazy. Don't you know you can get all types of diseases from dirty needles? Can you say hepatitis?"

Carey frowned. "My cousin is a professional, so shut the hell up. He's been doing this for a minute and he's clean."

Kaitlyn gave Amir the once-over and said, "Whatever."

"Girl, you'd betta stop trippin' before . . ." Carey started.

"She's drunk, Carey. Don't pay her any attention." Jovia shook her head.

"It's all good, cuz. Don't worry about it. I can see the little rich girl can't handle liquor," Amir laughed. He looked at Jovia and said, "I'll check you later."

"Okay, how ghetto can you be?" Kaitlyn sighed. "A tattoo party after the prom."

"You are a trip. You know that?" Jovia stood up.

"Where's Jordan?" Kaitlyn asked, wobbling and grabbing onto Jovia to regain her balance.

She had completely forgotten about Jordan. She looked around and didn't see him. "I don't know. He said he was going to get something to drink and he didn't come back."

Kaitlyn shrugged. "He's probably in the game room upstairs. They're having an Xbox championship or something going on up there. Or he could still be getting a drink. You should try the punch, it's delightful," she said, smiling.

"If it makes you act like this, I'll pass," Jovia said.

"Well, there's Garland," Kaitlyn pointed. "I guess it's time for us to be going. What are you about to do? Look for Jordan?"

There was no way she was going to be on a scavenger hunt for Jordan Capron's rude ass. She couldn't believe he just left her alone and went off somewhere. Any chances of their getting together were now null and void. She was finished with him.

"Hell no," Jovia told her, grabbing her purse and walking off. "I'm going to watch!"

"Watch what?" Kaitlyn called out.

Jovia didn't bother to answer. She quickly found Carey's garage where a number of people were standing in line. As she walked toward the front, she could hear moans and complaints about how she was skipping the line.

They had actually set the garage up as if it were a real business. Simon was seated at a desk with a binder of pictures, helping those who were brave enough to partake of the venture, decide on a design. Amir was hard at work with what looked like a dental drill, focusing on Jordan's shoulder. Balls of sweat were pouring from her date's head and he was squinting and looking as if he was trying his hardest to hold back tears. Jovia couldn't help laughing.

"What's so funny?" He scowled at her.

"You are, you big punk," she replied.

"Hey, she can't just go to the front like that," a female whined.

"Gotta wait your turn, Jovia," Simon told her. "Large tats are fifty, small ones are thirty-five."

Amir looked up at her. "Changed your mind?"

"Yeah," she said and he looked surprised. "About watching."

"And you called him a punk?" Amir looked at Jordan. "Simon, grab a chair for her, will you?"

Simon quickly grabbed a chair from the corner and positioned it near Amir. He proceeded to finish the design he had started. Jovia became engrossed in watching him work. It was like watching herself. The focus, the strength, and the will to bring forth what was inside your head. It was power. She could feel the buildup as his hands quickly moved. Her heart beat faster and faster in anticipation of what it would become. Then, what started as black lines and curves soon

turned into a soaring eagle on his shoulder. When Amir finished, he sat back and admired his work, smiling. She knew
how he felt. It was climactic.

"Wow," she said.

"Damn, that shit is tight," Jordan said.

"You like it?" Amir asked.

"Hell yeah," Jordan answered, and then realized the question wasn't directed at him, but at Jovia.

"That is amazing," she told him.

"You ready to go?" Jordan snapped. Jovia looked up to
see him scowling at her. She didn't care.

"No, I think I'm gonna sit here and watch," she told him.

"I thought you only wanted to stay for a little while," he
said.

"I changed my mind." She shrugged.

"Hey, Jordan, let me check that out," someone called. Jordan paused and looked from Jovia to Amir before walking
away.

"Your boyfriend?" Amir asked when he was out of earshot.

"No, my prom date," Jovia told him. "I don't have a
boyfriend."

"Really?" he said and began preparing for the guy who
had come and sat down.

"Really," she told him. She liked him. She more than liked
him. She barely knew his name but she felt as if she needed
to be near him. She remained by his side, talking and laughing as he tattooed her classmates. It suddenly dawned on her
that he may be thirsty. "You want something to drink?"

"Yeah," he said, "I could use a drink. Yo, Simon, I'm taking
a break for a minute."

"No problem," Simon told him.

They walked back out into the yard and over to the bar.

"What you need?" a guy who looked no older than nineteen asked.

"Thug passion," Amir told him. "What you drinking?"

"I don't drink," she told him. "I'll have a ginger ale."

"Coming right up," the guy said and passed them their drinks.

"Should you be drinking and doing this at the same time?"

"Girl, I'm from the hood," he said as he took a long swallow of the green liquid. "This is nothing. I can handle a hell of a lot more than this."

"What's in that?" she asked.

"Wanna taste it?"

"No," she answered.

"Yeah, we wouldn't want you to get like your little girlfriend," he joked. "We know how you Northside girls are; can't handle your liquor."

"I'm not from Northside," she said, matter-of-factly. "I'm from Frederick Douglass, thank you."

"Yeah, right," he told her. "I lived out FDP for years and I ain't never seen your ass. And what the hell are you doing going to St. Bart's if you're from FDP, they damn sure ain't got no school bus that comes out there and pick you up every day."

"I don't live there anymore," she told him. "I used to, a few years ago."

"Guess you're like the Jeffersons and moved on up, huh?"

"Guess so," she told him.

"It's all good though. I ain't mad at you."

They stood in silence for a few moments when she looked up and spotted Jordan stumbling toward her. Obviously drunk, he yelled her name out. "Jovia! What the hell you got in your hand, girl? Come here!"

"Here comes your date," Amir told her.

"Amir, you still got a line of folks back here," Simon called from the garage.

"Guess we both gotta be going," she said.

"Guess so," he told her. "I'll see you around, homegirl. You should come back through so you can finish what you started."

She stared into his bewitching eyes. "And exactly what did I start?"

"Your picture, the one in the park," he replied before walking away.

He did remember her. She thought he didn't recognize her, but he did. She smiled to herself. Her self-satisfaction faded when she felt Jordan's hand on her shoulder.

"You done watching yet?" he said, his voice full of sarcasm.

"You're drunk, Jordan," she told him. "How the hell are we supposed to get home?"

"Drive," he said, his eyes half open.

"You must've been smoking too if you think I'm going to get in a car with you driving."

"No, Jovie-Hovie, I mean, you drive." He smiled and held the keys out to her.

"I don't have a license," she told him.

"It's three fucking streets over. What? You think the cops are doing a stakeout or something?"

"No, but . . ."

"Come on, Jovie-Wovie, take me home, pleeeeeeaaaaa-sssssseeee!"

Jovia looked down at her watch. It was after two in the morning, way too late to call her parents and she was tired. *He's right, it is only three streets over*, she thought. You can drive that far. She grabbed the keys from him, "Come on, let's go!"

*You can do this*, she told herself after they got into the car. She looked at Jordan who was slumped over on the passenger door. She tried to remember everything she had learned in driver's ed. Putting on her seat belt, she checked the mirrors, light and turned the key in the ignition. The engine purred and she pulled out of Carey's driveway and onto the street. It was a short ride to Jordan's house, which was completely dark.

"Jordan, Jordan, get up. We're at your house." She shook his arm. He barely moved. "Come on, Jordan, get out!"

Jordan's head turned to her and his eyes opened. "Huh?"

"Get out, you're home."

He closed his eyes again and she became frustrated. She opened her door, got out and walked over to the passenger side. She opened the door and his body almost fell out the car. She grabbed him just in time.

"Jordan!" she yelled, not caring if the neighbors heard. "Get your drunk ass up right now!"

As if jolted by her voice into temporary sobriety, Jordan halfway sat up and smiled at her. "Jovia-Wovia, you are so pretty."

"And you are such an asshole," she told him. Putting her arms around his waist, she helped him stand up and struggled to lead him to the front door. She rang the doorbell several times, hoping his parents would come and open the door. *I don't know how the hell he's gonna explain this to them, but that ain't my problem*, she thought. "Why aren't the answering?"

"Because they're not at home. They went to my aunt's condo at the beach," he giggled and then closed his eyes.

"Where the hell is your key?"

"On the key ring," he whispered.

She looked down at the keys in her hand and realized that there was a house key on it. She put it in the door, turned the knob and it opened. Suddenly, she could hear the beeps of the burglar alarm and saw the flashing red lights from the small console on the wall.

"Jordan, what's the security code?" she asked.

"Huh?"

"The code, asshole, the code?"

"Uh," he paused, "Eight, eight, four, three."

She quickly pressed the numbers on the panel and the aggravating noise stopped. She helped Jordan stand up and led him in. Once inside, she was tempted to drop him and let him fall to the floor, but decided to at least get him to the den. It was difficult to see in the dark, but she made her way down the hall and soon spotted the family room. She was relieved when they made it to the sofa. The weight of his body pulled her on top of him when he fell and his eyes opened. She struggled to get off of him and was shocked when she realized he was holding her tightly.

"Jordan, what the hell are you doing?"

"I just wanna kiss good night, Jovie-Wovie," he said, still not releasing his hold on her.

"Let me go, Jordan, I mean it," she said, straining to move.

"Not until I get a kiss," he said.

"You betta get the fuck off me, I mean it," she said, her anger rising.

Without warning, Jordan had shifted and she fell to the floor. Before she could get up, his body was on top of her and his lips were crushing hers. She felt his tongue in her mouth and could taste the alcohol on his breath. She tried turning her head away, but his hand grabbed her chin and he groaned as he kissed her. *This can't be happening*, she thought, and tried to get away. Her dress was rising above her thighs and she could feel his hardness. She tried to scream but couldn't. His hands were tearing at her underwear, ripping them off and he forced her legs open with the strength of his thighs. In one swift movement, his pants were gone and she felt his penis on her stomach. *Please, God, don't let him do this*. She tried to plead with her eyes, but when she looked at him, she saw the loathing. She thought of his fresh tattoo, grabbing his shoulder and squeezing it. He screamed in pain, but instead of loosening, his grip on her tightened.

"Shut the fuck up and open your legs, Jovia," he whispered.

"Jordan, no!" she screamed.

Again, he covered his mouth with hers and with a quick thrust, he entered her. She felt like fire was spreading through her body and shut her eyes. Fire . . . heat . . . burning . . . she was now living a nightmare of a different kind, and yet it was still the same. Tears streamed from her eyes and she silently prayed for God to let her die then and there. He continued pumping in and out of her until she could feel his stickiness on her stomach and inner thighs. His body collapsed onto hers and she rolled him off of her.

"Jovie-Wovie," he said, and wore a look of contentment on his face. His eyes closed and she stared at him. Within moments, she could hear him snoring. She sat next to him, not knowing what to do next. She thought about killing him, but couldn't gather up the nerve to do so. Tattered pieces of her corsage were all over the floor. Her underwear was lying on the floor nearby, nearly shredded. Ivory, to match her dress. She picked them up and silently walked out, closing the door behind her. The car door was still open. Jovia reached inside and got her purse out. She slowly walked home.

Confused, dazed, and still in state of shock, she walked directly up the stairs and into her bathroom. She took of her dress and balled it up. She sat on the toilet and contemplated whether or not what she thought had just happened really did happen. Maybe it was a dream, she said, it was a vivid nightmare. Looking down and seeing the dried fluid on her thigh, she knew it was reality. She wanted it off her. Fuck what you've seen *on Law & Order, CSI, Crossing Jordan* and all the other crime shows you've seen on television, take a shower. Get it off . . . wash. . . . cleanse . . . forget. She turned the water on in the tub as hot as she could take it. She reached under her sink and took out bottles and bottles of shower gel, bath oil, bath salts, and soaps. Bath & Body Works, Victoria's Secret, Clinique, Calvin Klein, Tommy Hilfiger, they all went into the tub together, along with alcohol, peroxide, and Epsom salt. Jovia didn't care. She pulled each and every bobby pin out, and shook her hair free and got inside the garden tub, rubbing herself with a loofah sponge until her skin was raw. She bathed and scrubbed for hours until she looked out the window and instead of the darkness of night, an array of pink hues was in the sky. She told herself it was a sign, that it was over and she was now clean. Once she had dressed for bed, she went back into the bathroom, retrieved the now hated dress of the previous evening and placed it far into her closet, under some old boxes. *Forget it ever happened . . . forget. Just like the fire, forget. Forget about it and move on*, she reminded herself. She willed herself to sleep, knowing that she would now have a new nightmare to replace the one that had been haunting her for years.

# Chapter 6

"What's going on with you?"

"Nothing," Jovia said, picking at the food on her plate.

"You've been in a fog for the past month. It's almost summer vacation and it's like you don't even care. Something's wrong," Me-Ma told her.

Life for Jovia had become a series of going through the motions. Go to school, come home, and fighting sleep. She hated to close her eyes, because when she did, she was either reliving the fire that cost her mother's life, or the rape that cost her innocence. She tried to figure out what she had done to deserve such madness and found no answers.

"Are you worried about working?" the councilman asked, looking concerned.

She had been waiting to break the news to him that she wouldn't be taking the job with the CPA firm this summer, knowing he wouldn't be pleased. She also knew that she had better have a damn good reason for not taking it. She looked up and said, "I've decided not to work this summer."

"What do you mean? I guess you're gonna hang out with your friends and waste your entire summer rather than do something worthwhile."

"Marcus, that's not fair," Me-Ma snapped.

"No, I am going to do something worthwhile," she replied.

"And what's that?" He waited for her answer.

"I'm taking art classes this summer at the community college," she said, looking over at Me-Ma for support. She was glad to see the faint smile on Me-Ma's face.

"Community college? Art classes? What the hell for? You already know how to draw," the councilman's voice became louder.

"I want to work on my talent. I am thinking about majoring in art," she told him.

"That's the dumbest thing I've ever heard in my life." He shook his head.

"Marcus! That's enough!" Me-Ma's voice matched his.

"Here I am trying to prepare her for the future and she's trying to be a damn starving artist. What? You wanna be broke as hell and go back to living in the damn projects? Fine, go ahead!"

Jovia tried to hold back the tears that were starting to form. The councilman was finally showing his true colors.

"Marcus! How dare you?" Me-Ma stood up, "I can't believe—"

"And how the hell are you gonna get over to the Southside everyday to get to these ART CLASSES?" he continued.

"I can take her," Me-Ma snapped.

"Not in your car? What, so it can get jacked?"

"I can catch the train," she said, determined not to be discouraged.

"The train? You really do have a death wish." He folded his arms.

"Shut up, Marcus. Just shut up! Of all the prejudiced, mean, hateful things to say. What Jovia does with her life is her decision!"

"And it's my job as her father to see that she makes the right decision!"

Unable to stand the yelling, Jovia ran upstairs to her room

and slammed the door. She wanted to get away. She went into her closet and grabbed a duffel bag and began tossing clothing and items in that she thought she'd need. Her sketch pad was the last thing she stuffed inside. Her life seemed to be getting worse and the only thing she could think to do was flee. She could here Me-Ma and the councilman still arguing when she came back down the steps and slipped out the door into the darkness.

Jovia had no clue where she was headed. She knew she had to get as far away from her neighborhood as quickly as possible before they came looking for her. She took long strides and walked as fast as she could. Tears were still streaming and she used the sleeve of her sweatshirt to wipe her face. She was almost out of the neighborhood when she heard the engine of a car. Her heart began to pound and she darted behind a nearby bush. She was relieved when she saw that it was just a pizza delivery car. Seeing that the street was empty again, Jovia continued her escape. She walked another thirty minutes until she reached the closest shopping center and called a cab. It didn't take her long to figure out where she was going and she didn't hesitate to direct the driver to the J train station.

Just as the cab dropped her off yards from the station, she could hear the sound of another loud engine. She turned to see a motorcycle slowing down as it approached her. She picked up her pace as the bike got closer and closer. She was about to walk away when the bike stopped in front of her, cutting her off. She turned to run in the opposite direction when she heard the driver call her name.

"Jovia?" a male voice called, causing her to stop and spin around. The helmet was removed and she squinted in the darkness to see who it was. He got off the bike and took a step closer to her. "Are you okay?"

She took a step back, still unsure of who it was. "I'm fine, leave me alone."

"You need a ride?" He took another step toward her.

"No, I'm fine." Her voice was shaking. As he got closer, she realized who it was. "Amir?"

"Yeah, it's me," he said.

Jovia relaxed a little and said, "Oh."

"You sure you're okay? Where are you headed? You need a ride?"

Seeing the headlights of another car approaching in the distance, she told him, "Yeah, I do."

"Where to?" he asked.

"Home," she said. "To FDP."

"You sure?"

"I'm positive," she told him.

"Well then, let's ride," he said and climbed back on the bike. Without hesitation, she got behind him, wrapping her arms around his body, flinging her bag across her back. Thinking that her life couldn't get any worse than it already was, she tightly held on as they pulled off.

The wind felt good against her face as they traveled. *What the hell are you doing? This is stupid and you're going to be in big trouble*, her intuition cautioned her. But the rebel inside her head quickly retorted, *what are you staying for? It's just as much misery here in the suburbs as it is in the projects.* The familiar sights of Frederick Douglass Parkway welcomed her and knowing that she was forty minutes away from Wellington Estates put her at ease.

"You hungry?" Amir asked, yelling over the engine of the bike, as they stopped at a traffic light.

"Not really," she told him.

"Well, I am. You mind if I get something to eat?"

"Nope," she replied. The light changed and he turned into the parking lot of a nearby shopping center. It was so run-down, that she wondered if any of the stores were still open. He parked the bike in front of what looked like a dimly lit bar.

They got off the bike and he strapped his helmet to the seat. He held the door open for her and she entered. It wasn't a bar, as she thought, but a sub shop. The smell of fresh bread filled her nose and her stomach began growling.

"What's up, Amir!" The old man behind the counter greeted him.

"Frankie, my man, what's up?" Amir walked over and slapped hands across the counter.

"Nothing much, where you been? I ain't seen you around lately."

"You know how I do, Frankie," Amir laughed. "I been working hard."

Jovia wondered what it was that Amir did. Did he draw tattoos for a living or did he do something else. It dawned on her that she knew nothing about him except that he was Carey's cousin and was from her old neighborhood.

"What can I get for you? The usual?" Frankie asked.

"You know it," Amir answered, then looked over at Jovia. "You sure you don't want anything?"

"A soda, please."

"That's it?"

"Yeah," Jovia nodded, removing the bag from her back. She walked over to a nearby table and sat down.

"And a soda for the lady, here, Frankie." Amir sat across from her.

Jovia looked around the small restaurant, which consisted of a counter, three small tables, and an empty candy machine. The faded menu hanging over the counter read *Frankie's Philly Style Subs* and she assumed Frankie was the owner. She looked into her purse and checked her cell phone, knowing she probably had several missed calls. Sure enough, Me-Ma had called six times and so had Kaitlyn. *They must know I'm gone*, she thought, closing the phone and putting it back in her bag.

"So, why are you running away?" Amir asked.

"What makes you think I'm running away?" she responded, staring at the concrete floor.

"I don't know, I guess because number one, you were running down the street with a duffel bag and ducking behind trees. That was my first clue," he told her. "So, you wanna talk about what's going on?"

*Should I start with the fire that killed my mother that I still haven't recovered from? Or how about my classmates who are conceited, self-absorbed people I go to school with? No, maybe I should tell him about the wonderful man who was gracious enough to take me in, only to want to take total control of my life and have me do what he wants me to do? Or how about how I was raped by my prom date?*

"There's nothing going on," she mumbled. "I just need to get away, that's all."

"And where are you getting away to?"

"Away from Wellington Estates, that's all I know."

"You don't have a plan? Then you ain't gonna get very far," Amir laughed. She looked up and gave him a look to let him know that she didn't think it was funny. "Don't get mad at me. I'm just trying to be the voice of reason."

"Well, I ain't in a reasonable mood, shit," she snapped. She was mad at him because he was right. She didn't have a plan. She had nowhere to go. No family, no friends, no one. She had about 200 dollars cash on her, and she had money in her bank account. But she knew using her check cards and credit cards were out of the question, they would lead her parents directly to her.

"I feel ya," Amir said.

"Okay, food's ready," Frankie called and Amir stood up.

As he walked over to the counter, Jovia couldn't help noticing the sexiness of his walk. His jeans were well-worn yet the black boots on his feet looked brand new. The red Phat Farm sweatshirt he had on was big on him yet she could still make out the frame of his muscular torso. *Damn he's fine!* He came back to the table carrying their tray of food.

"Hungry?" Jovia questioned, looking at the huge sandwich and mass of chips.

"A little." He grabbed a handful of chips and popped them in his mouth. "You sure you don't want any?"

Jovia's mouth watered as he picked up half the cheesesteak and bit into it. She was starving and regretted that she didn't order anything. She picked up her soda and took a sip. "No, I'm fine."

"You a damn liar," he teased. "You know you want some of this."

She blinked, and then realized he was talking about the sandwich. She looked into his handsome face and smiled. "You're damn right," as she reached over and grabbed the other half of the sandwich.

His hearty laughed echoed, "Oh hell naw!"

"You offered, I accepted," she said. God, this is wonderful, she thought as she took a large bite. It was the best thing she had ever tasted. She didn't know if it was because she hadn't had an appetite lately or whether it was actually that good.

"So, you thought of a plan, yet?" he asked as they ate.

"No, not yet." She shrugged. "I got money though, that's a start."

"Let me ask you a question, how old are you?"

"Eighteen," she answered. "How old are you?"

"Twenty."

She didn't think he was that old. She thought he was nineteen at the most. He was a grown-ass man. "Oh."

"You thought I was older," he stated.

"No, younger," she confessed.

"Hmmm, I don't know if I should take that as a compliment or not." He sat back.

"So, you're eighteen, still in high school and a runaway with no plan. You know they're gonna come looking for you, right?" He stared at her, and she was once again drawn into his eyes.

"They won't be able to find me," she told him.

"Are things that bad at home that you had to leave like that?" She could hear the concern in his voice. "It's hard as hell out here in the streets, believe that. Are your parents that bad?"

"They aren't my parents. My mother is dead and I never knew my father. I just live with them," Jovia told him.

"Oh, so they took you in after your moms passed? Are they family?"

"No, just some people that needed a token kid, I guess."

"That's deep. How long you been with them?"

"Eight, almost nine years." She picked at the chips on the plate that they now shared.

"Ain't nobody touching you or nothing are they? They putting their hands on you?" He sat up straight and frowned.

She frowned back at him, thinking of Jordan and his attack on her, then said, "No, my parents have never hit me. They're good people for the most part. But my adoptive father acts like he wants me to forget where I'm from at times, and I don't like that."

"I feel ya, but don't all caring parents want their kids to be better than they are? Is it that he wants to forget or be better?"

"I don't know, and I don't want to get to the point in my life that I think I'm better than anyone. That's not right." She thought of Kaitlyn and her other arrogant classmates. "I will never be like that. I embrace where I'm from, not reject it."

"But you also have to embrace where you're at now," he told her.

She thought of all she had been dealing with the past few weeks and responded, "One hell ain't better than another one. I've lived in both, I know."

"Damn, you're right about that," he said. They silently

stared at one another until he finally looked down at his watch and said, "Damn, you ready?"

Jovia hadn't thought about the fact that she was keeping him from doing something. *Shit, he probably has a girlfriend he has to get to or something.* She got up and walked over to the door as he cleared the table. In the parking lot, she saw a group of teenagers gathered, laughing, dancing, and talking. Unlike her peers at St. Bart's, they weren't decked out in 200-dollar jeans and there wasn't a 80,000-dollar car in sight, but they looked as if they were having more fun than she had seen any of her classmates having. She longed to go over and join them.

"You ready?" Amir asked from behind.

"Yeah," she told him, tearing her gaze away from the crowd.

"Yo, Amir," a guy called out. "You gonna be around this weekend? I wanna get my tat done."

"You got your money yet?" Amir asked.

"Of course, why you trying to carry me in front of everybody?" the guy asked, having to yell over the laughs of his friends.

"Because you always coming to me about a tattoo and don't ever have no loot, DeJuan, that's why!"

The crowd continued laughing and the guy retorted, "Whatever. I heard about your doing tats for the One and his crew and now you too good for a brother like me?"

"That ain't it at all, DeJuan, you think your money is too good for a brother like me. I don't see you going down to Hood Tattoo and asking Love for a free tattoo."

"That's because he know Love will kick his ass!" someone shouted.

"Get at me this weekend, DeJuan, you know I got you," Amir laughed. He put his helmet on his head and looked at Jovia. "You rolling or what?"

"I don't wanna keep you from anything or anyone," she told him. "You don't have to babysit me. I can handle myself."

"Girl, get your ass on the bike so we can go." He shook his head.

"Who the hell you talking to like that?" She stared at him like he was crazy.

"You! You're the one that swears you're a hood chick, so don't front like you ain't. Let's roll!"

She rolled her eyes at him and he grinned. She put her bag back on her back and took her place behind him on the bike. "Watch your mouth, son!"

# Chapter 7

Amir weaved the bike in and out of cars along the parkway until he turned into the housing complex. She looked at the familiar buildings and memories came flooding back. She recalled her and Felicia walking along the streets and visiting neighbors. The cookouts the families would gather together and have in the courts and the fun she would have playing. She turned her head and looked up at the structure that held the apartment she and her mother shared. It still looked the same. Her arms tightened around Amir's waist and she put her chin on his shoulder, inhaling the scent of Kenneth Cole Black.

They continued through the complex until he turned in the last court and parked in the lot. "Uh, my bad, did you have somewhere you needed to go?"

"No," she said as she got off, looking around.

"That's right, I forgot you don't have a plan," he laughed. "Come on."

There was something about Amir that made her feel safe, in spite of all she'd been through. Being with him brought her a comfort that she couldn't explain. She followed him inside the building and up the stairs. She could hear music coming from one apartment and a baby crying from another. The air was filled with the combination of incense, fried chicken, and burnt hair, just like it had in her old building. He used a key and opened the door. They walked inside the apartment and were greeted by an older woman and a girl who looked to be about Jovia's age.

" 'Bout time," the girl said, looking up from the television. "You know I was supposed to go braid Deidra's hair forty-five minutes ago."

"And you could been gone," the woman replied. "Don't let her fool you 'Mir, she was watching TV."

Amir walked over and gave the woman a kiss on the cheek. "I know she was, Granny. But she know she better not have left you here by yourself."

"I don't know why y'all insist on treating me like I'm some kind of invalid. I'm fine," the woman insisted.

"We know you are, Granny, and that's why I stayed here til he got home; to make sure you're fine." The girl stood up. "Hi, I'm Starr."

"Hi," Jovia said. She recognized the girl from somewhere. "I know you from somewhere. Do you go to Chamberlaine?"

"No, she doesn't. She goes to St. Bart's with Carey," Amir told her. "You swear you know everyone."

"Wow, St. Bart's," the girl commented, giving Jovia the once-over. "Impressive. Your parents must be loaded. What're you doing hanging with a lowlife like my brother?"

"How is my other favorite grandson, Carey?" the woman asked. She looked to be at least seventy with her head of gray hair and aged skin. Jovia could still see that she was very attractive.

"Other favorite?" Amir grinned. "You have three grandsons."

"And they're all my favorites," she said and then asked, "What's your name again, sweetie?"

"Jovia," she answered.

"I knew I knew you!" The girl snapped her fingers. "You're Jovia Parker!"

It had been years since Jovia had heard that name. Once she had been adopted, her name changed to Grant, like Me-Ma and the councilman's. "Yes, that's me."

"It's me, Starr. We were in Ms. Anderson's class together!" The girl walked over and Jovia immediately recognized her from elementary school.

"Oh my God, Starr Simmons!" Jovia and the girl hugged.

"Apologize to your sister, 'Mir. She did know your friend."

"Whatever," he said. "Did you eat, Granny?"

"Starr made some pork chops for me," his grandmother told him. "Have a seat, Jovia. I don't know where my grand-children's manners are."

"You don't remember her, Granny? She's the girl from the fire in two-oh-six some years back," Starr said. "I can't be-lieve it. After all these years. You look so good."

"Thanks." Jovia's voice was barely above a whisper. She sat on the sofa.

"I remember that. It was so sad. That man and his wife took you in after your mother passed, didn't they?"

"Yes ma'am, Councilman Grant and his wife." Jovia nod-ded. She looked back at Starr. She had grown into a lovely young woman, and looked just like her brother.

"Your dad is the city councilman? You know they're gonna have the SWAT out looking for you," Amir groaned where only she could hear.

Starr's cell phone began ringing and she reached into her pocket and answered it. "Hey girl, I'm on my way . . . I am right now. . . . Amir just got here, and guess who's with him? Jovia Parker! I'm serious. . . . I don't know . . . she goes to school with Carey . . . girl, please, Carey ain't thinking 'bout you . . . okay, I'll tell her . . . I will! Jovia, Deidra Franklin says hello and told me to tell you she's having a birthday party next month and wants you to come. It's gonna be at the community center. You should come. I know everyone would love to see you."

"Jovia ain't thinking about you and your hoodrat friends," Amir told her.

"Look, I gotta go, but Jovia, it was good seeing you. Remember when you drew that cartoon of Ms. Anderson? That was so funny. Are you still drawing?"

"Yeah, I am." Jovia smiled, recalling the picture she got in trouble about years ago. Everyone else thought it was hilarious, except Ms. Anderson.

"And you're still talking people to death, jeez!" Amir shook his head. Jovia couldn't help laughing. He was right, Starr was known for her nonstop talking.

"I'm outta here. Amir, give her my number. Call me, Jovia, I'm serious," Starr said as she walked out the door.

"That girl has always been a motor mouth," Granny said.

"I remember," Jovia giggled.

"You want something to drink?"

"No, I'm fine," she told him.

"Well, I'm gonna go on retire to my room. Jovia, it was nice meeting you. You tell my favorite grandson I send my love," she said, grunting as she rose from the recliner she was seated in.

"I will," Jovia assured her.

"Good night, Granny," Amir gave his grandmother a kiss.

"Good night, favorite grandson," Granny told him as she walked out the room.

When they were alone, she told him, "Your grandma is funny."

"Yeah, she is." He nodded. "So, you think of a plan yet?"

"I'm still thinking," she told him.

"Your folks are probably worried about you," he said.

"Probably," she agreed. "Can I use your restroom?"

"Sure, I'll show you where it is." He stood up.

"I know where it is," she told him. "It's probably in the same place ours was."

"Funny," he told her.

Jovia walked down the hallway and into the restroom, neatly decorated in mauves and pinks. She removed her back and sat on the toilet. She reached inside and checked her phone. There were several missed calls from her parents and Kaitlyn and several text messages. A twinge of guilt went through her and she wondered if she was making a mistake. When she was walking out, she noticed the room directly across the hall. There was a full-sized bed and a dresser that held a TV and a small stereo. Decorated in gray and black, she figured it had to be Amir's. She walked further inside to get a closer look. The walls were covered with sketches and drawings.

"You get lost finding the bathroom," his voice startled her.

"You are really good," she said, not turning around.

"You're better," he said.

She saw the tattoo equipment sitting in a corner. "Are tattoos difficult to do?"

"Not really," he told her. She could feel his presence directly behind her and could feel the hairs on her neck start to stand. "To me, it's just like drawing. People tell you what they want. You get the picture in your head and bring it to culmination."

"That's a big word," she laughed.

"Thugs use big words too. You ain't know that?"

A piece of drawing paper on the dresser caught her attention and she walked over to see it. She blinked several times as she picked it up and gasped as she realized what it was. She turned to face him, not knowing what to say.

"Oh," was his only response to her actions.

She reached into her bag and showed him the last picture she had been working on. It was his turn to be shocked. He reached his arms around her and pulled himself to her, kissing her fully on the lips. She opened her mouth slightly and welcomed his tongue, tasting what she had longed for from the moment she laid eyes on him. As they kissed, the portraits they had each done of each other lay on the floor beside them and Jovia knew that for the first time in her life, she was in love.

After several moments of enjoying and savoring one another, the two finally released.

"You really do tattoos for the One?" she said, impressed that he even knew the famous rapper.

"Yeah, I do," he said, shrugging.

"I want one," she told him.

"One what?"

"A tattoo."

Amir looked around his room. "This doesn't look like an appropriate place to have a tattoo done."

"That's not funny," she said, sitting on his bed. "Will you do it for me or what? I have money."

"I'll do it if you let me take you home afterwards," he told her.

"What?" He had to be kidding. There was no way she was going home.

"What? At least until you get a plan together. If you're gonna dip out on your folks, I don't have a problem with that. But be smart about it." He began gathering the equipment from the corner. "Be right back."

"Where are you going?"

"To get the lamp and some towels," he told her. "Oh, and a drink. You're gonna need it."

"A drink?" She started getting nervous. She didn't know what she feared more, the tattoo or the thought of going home.

"Thug passion, of course."

# Chapter 8

*WAKE UP! WAKE UP NOW! FIRE!* Jovia could feel the heat covering her body and she began screaming in pain. She opened her eyes and Jordan was standing over her, pouring gasoline all over her body. Her flesh was melting away and he was smiling as he tortured her.

"Jovie-Wovie!" he cackled.

"NOOOOOOOOOOOO!" she cried out.

"Jovia, wake up! Come on, baby, open your eyes," a calming voice said in the darkness. She felt someone touching her face, wiping the tears away. Her eyes opened and she realized she had once again been dreaming. She looked around, trying to figure out where she was. Amir . . . it was his voice she heard . . . his touch she felt. She sat up in the bed and he gently wiped the sweat from her forehead. "It's okay, you're safe, I'm here."

He pulled her to him and she fell into the security of his arms. She remembered now that she was in his room. She had spent the night. It had taken him nearly three hours to cover the scars on her shoulders with the tattoo. She wasn't really sure what she wanted and told him to just "be creative" and cover them. He was the first person she had ever let see them. She even felt comfortable enough to take her shirt off in front of him.

"Wow, a phoenix," she said when he finished.

"You like it?" he asked, stretching his arms. She could see the exhaustion in his eyes.

"I love it." She smiled and kissed him. He agreed that he was too tired to take her all the way back home and she should just stay the night. They talked until they were both drifting off to sleep. He kissed her good night and retreated to sleep on the sofa. Now, here he was by her side, comforting her.

"She okay?"

They looked up to see Granny and Starr standing in the doorway. Embarrassed, Jovia nodded. "I'm sorry."

"No need to be sorry. It's okay," Granny assured her. "Starr, go get her some cold water."

"Yes, ma'am," Starr said and hurried to the kitchen. Granny walked over and said a prayer over Jovia's head. The tears continued to flow from Jovia's eyes. Suddenly, she felt better. Granny slowly walked toward the door.

"Thanks, Granny," Amir told his grandmother.

"You're a survivor, don't ever forget that," Granny said as she departed.

"She's right," Starr said as she walked in with a tall glass of ice water.

Jovia took the glass from her and drank it. It was actually refreshing. "Thanks."

"Granny thinks ice water cures everything," Starr told her.

"She may be right because I feel a lot better," Jovia laughed.

"I'm gone back to bed," Starr said. "You need anything else?"

"Naw, we're good," Amir told his sister. When they were alone, he took her hand in his. "Damn, you scared the shit outta me."

"Not you, Mr. Thug Passion," she sighed, looking at him. He was wearing a pair of sweatpants and a wife beater. She touched his face.

"You are beautiful," he said, kissing her fingertips. "No wonder your parents are worried to death."

"How do you know?" she asked.

"I called Carey last night. He told me they've been calling everyone and everywhere looking for you. I think you should call."

"You called Carey? You told him where I was? He's gonna tell them and they're gonna come looking for me. Why did you do that?" Jovia hopped out of the bed and grabbed her clothes off the dresser. *I shoulda never went with his ass. I should've never gotten on the back of that damn bike.*

"Wait, calm down. Carey ain't gonna say nothing to nobody," he told her.

"He's gonna tell Kaitlyn and she's gonna tell my parents. They are gonna blow a fucking gasket! I should've never come here!" She went to storm out and he grabbed her arm.

"You're right, you shouldn't have and I never should've picked your ass up, either. But you did. Now get dressed so I can take your ass home."

She looked down at his hand on her arm and then back up to him. "Let me go. I don't need for you to do shit for me."

"Don't be ridiculous. Your dad is the fucking city councilman. He probably has all of the city's finest looking for your ass! I know you're pissed and you're hurt, but running away ain't helping your situation. No matter where you're at, that same nightmare is gonna be there. Go home and deal with whatever's going on. But know that when you go back, I'm right here for you. You're not by yourself this time." He pulled her close to him and she cried in his arms. "I'm right here for you."

* * *

The ride from Amir's home to Wellington Estates seemed to be the quickest ride of her life. Her heart beat fast in anticipation of what was going to happen once she arrived. She expected a brigade of police cars to be waiting when she arrived. Instead, there was just one unmarked car sitting in front of her house. Amir pulled into the circular driveway and parked behind Me-Ma's SUV.

"You want me to go in with you?" Amir asked as she climbed off his bike.

"No, I think I'd better go in alone," she lied. She really did want him to take her by the hand and go with her to face her parents, but she knew better.

"You sure?"

"Yeah, I am. I'll call you later," she promised. She reached over to hug him and at that moment, the door to the house opened and her parents walked out, followed by an officer.

"Jovia!" Me-Ma rushed over and hugged her. Jovia could see that she had been crying and instantly felt bad. She really didn't want to hurt Me-Ma, but it was inevitable.

"You are in deep trouble, young lady," the councilman said, then scowled at Amir. "And who the hell are you?"

Amir didn't seem intimidated at all. "Amir Simmons," he said nonchalantly.

"You have some ID on you sir?" The officer asked, walking over to Amir.

"Yes, sir." Amir reached into his back pocket and passed the officer his license. the officer took it and told the councilman he would be right back.

"Jovia, we've been worried sick," Me-Ma said, rubbing her hair.

"I'm fine, Me-Ma," Jovia told her. "I'm sorry. I just needed some time to myself."

"And how the hell did you end up with him?" The councilman nodded toward Amir. "Is there a reason you had my daughter all night without our permission?

"No, sir," Amir said, taking a deep breath. Jovia realized that she had gotten him involved in the middle of her mess and it wasn't even his fault.

"He just gave me a ride home, that's all," Jovia told her parents.

"Well, thank you, young man," Me-Ma told him.

The officer walked up and said, "He's clean," and held Amir's license out to him.

Without warning, the councilman snatched it and looked at it. As he read it, he became enraged. "You're twenty damn years old! Do you realize my daughter is a minor?"

"She's eighteen, Marcus, she's not a minor," Me-Ma sighed.

"He just gave me a ride, Councilman," Jovia yelled.

"I bet he did," the councilman hissed. "And she's still in high school so that makes her a minor to me."

"Marcus, you need to stop it. That's why we're in this mess now," Me-Ma told him. "Give the man his property, now!"

The councilman held the license out and when Amir reached for it, he grabbed his arm and pulled him toward him. "Stay the fuck away from my daughter. If I catch you anywhere within twenty feet of her, I'll have your ass arrested for statutory rape, and I mean it!"

"MARCUS GRANT!" Me-Ma yelled.

"Councilman, you're wrong," Jovia told him.

"I understand, sir, but get your hands off me." Amir's eyes filled with disgust. "Mrs. Grant, it was a pleasure. Officer, am I free to leave?"

"Uh, yeah," the officer stuttered.

"That was totally uncalled for. Why, Marcus?" Me-Ma asked.

He didn't answer her. Instead he turned to Jovia and told her, "I'd better not catch you anywhere near him again."

*  *  *

Jovia had been in her room for an hour, waiting. She figured they would come in at any moment. The tension was so
thick that she thought she could see it. Her bag was now un-
packed and she was laying across her bed, flipping through
the channels on her television. She wanted to call Amir, but
wasn't sure if he would even answer her call even if she had
his number, which she didn't.

"Jovia," she heard Me-Ma call her name softly.

"Yes," Jovia answered her, sitting up and wincing from the
pain of her tattoo.

Me-Ma walked in and sat beside her. "You ready to talk?"

"About what? I don't have anything to talk about, Me-Ma,"
she said, shrugging.

"Well, for one, your father said some hurtful things to you
and he needs to apologize," Me-Ma said.

"He's not going to apologize." She shook her head.

"Yes, he is and he will." Me-Ma gave her a knowing look.
"He had no right to say those things to you."

"He just said what he felt, that's all. He's entitled to his
opinion."

"He's not entitled to be rude and disrespectful. He's not entitled to make the demands of you and your life that he's trying to do."

"He can. He took me in when no one else wanted me and
saved me from the horrors of the projects. If it wasn't for him,
I would be a young, welfare, alcoholic like my mother."

"That's not true, Jovia. That's not what I meant by what I
said." The councilman stepped into her room. "I just want
you to be everything that I know you can be. You have so
much going for yourself and I don't want you to get distracted by anyone or anything."

"How am I going to be distracted?" Jovia asked him. "I
love art. I love to draw, to paint. It's my passion. Isn't that
why you went into politics, because it was your passion?"

Me-Ma looked from Jovia to the councilman, happy to see the spark in Jovia's eyes, something that she had never seen in her.

"And that's fine if you want to do that as a hobby. . . ."

"Why? You already said that I'm talented and destined to be great. Why can't I be a great artist? Don't you think you've raised me well enough to know that if art doesn't work for me, I have other talents I can use? Or are you limiting me, Councilman?" She stared at him, waiting for his answer. Being around Amir and his sister reminded her of the things she used to enjoy doing and the person she used to be. She had been denying that part of her and she refused to do that anymore.

"I would never do that." He sounded offended. "Why would you say such a thing? I always encourage you."

"You encourage me to do the things you want me to do," she told him.

"She's right, Marcus, you only have an interest in what you want her to do. You didn't even care if she went to the prom or not until you found out Capron's son had asked her. Then you were all gung-ho about it," Me-Ma told him.

"I'm so sorry if you two feel that way," he told them. "I apologize for making the comments I did last night. It was disrespectful and uncalled for."

"It's okay," Jovia sighed, knowing that the worst was over. She was about to apologize for running away when he continued.

"But I will not apologize for looking out for your best interest. That little stunt you pulled last night was immature and irresponsible and most of all, stupid. If you ever find it necessary to run away again, don't bother coming back home," he said and walked over to her. He pulled her up. "You had your mother worried all night and I won't have that happening. She does too much for you. It wasn't fair to either one of us. We love you."

"I love you too, Councilman." Jovia hugged him back.

"And I mean what I said earlier. If I catch you around that man again, it's gonna be ugly," he said and walked out of her room.

Jovia knew from the tone in his voice that he meant it. She turned to Me-Ma. "Now what?"

"Now you get ready to take your driver's test. You're the one that wants to take classes at the community college and I'm not taking you down there everyday," Me-Ma told her.

# Chapter 9

Jovia stared at the driver's license in her hand. She couldn't believe she had actually passed the test. Even her picture had come out nice. She was smiling so hard, that her face hurt.

"I told you it would be a piece of cake," Kaitlyn told her. She had brought her to the DMV after school to take the test. Jovia didn't even tell Me-Ma she was going to take the test. She hadn't even known she was going to take it until she talked to Amir on the phone during lunch.

"Stop being a punk and go get the damn license," he told her. She could hear the roar of machines behind him and knew he was working his regular job at the shipyard.

"I'm not a punk," she told him. "I just don't want to fail it again."

"You're not gonna fail, Jovia. You just need to stop being nervous. You know how to drive."

"I don't know . . ." she told him. She missed him so much. He worked at the shipyard Monday through Friday and had been doing tattoo parties on the weekends. The councilman had basically put her on lockdown, but she was able to sneak out twice in the past two weekends to meet him at Carey's house.

"You're the one who is talking about how bad you wanna take art classes this summer," he told her.

"I do want to take the classes."

"Then put up or shut up, boo. They done already told you they ain't driving you. Take the test," he said. "Look, I gotta get back to work. Do what you gotta do. Call me later."

Passing the test was just one of many things Amir had been right about.

"Wanna drive home?" Kaitlyn asked.

"I don't think so," Jovia told her. "Thanks a lot, Kaitlyn. I really appreciate this."

"You're my best friend, Jovia. You know there's nothing I wouldn't do for you."

Jovia knew that she had been distant with Kaitlyn the past few weeks. She still hadn't shared with her the rape nor the fact that she had fallen in love with Amir. The only person who was aware of that relationship was Carey and that was only because they met at his house.

"So, what kind of car are you thinking about getting?"

"It's not up to me," Jovia told her. "Believe me, if the councilman knows I'm gonna be driving it to the Southside everyday, it will probably be a hooptie."

"No, it'll probably come with an alarm system, a Club, a watchdog, and a security guard."

"You're probably right about that," Jovia laughed. It seemed as if her life had gotten better since meeting Amir. She could laugh and enjoy it.

"Oh, I have a stop to make before I take you home. Is that okay?"

"Sure," Jovia said. She continued to stare at the license once again. She had picked up her phone and was about to text Starr when she saw that they were pulling into the driveway of Jordan's house. "What the hell are we doing here?"

"Oh, I have some CDs I borrowed from Jordan that I

needed to drop off. It'll only take a second," Kaitlyn said reaching into the backseat.

"I'll walk the rest of the way home," Jovia said reaching for her purse.

"Jovia, don't be crazy. I just need to drop them off, I'm not staying or anything. What's the big deal with you and Jordan anyway? You've been acting weird toward each other ever since prom night. You'd think the two of you slept together or something," she snickered as she grabbed the handful of CDs and got out of the car.

Jovia didn't find the joke funny and replied, "Just hurry up."

Kaitlyn skipped toward the front door and Jovia watched as Jordan opened it. The two chatted for a few minutes and then Kaitlyn walked back to the car, "See, I told you it wouldn't take but a second."

"Thanks," Jovia told her. "Can we go now?"

They were about to pull off when Jordan called Kaitlyn's name and came running out to the car. Kaitlyn stopped. Instead of going to the driver's side of the car, he walked over to Jovia and tapped on the window. She turned away and told Kaitlyn, "pull off."

"Stop being silly," Kaitlyn said and rolled down the window.

"What's up, Jovia." He grinned at her.

"Leave me the fuck alone, Jordan," she told him and looked away.

"Don't be like that," he said. "Kaitlyn told me you got your license, congrats."

She didn't respond.

"Kaitlyn, this isn't mine," he said reaching his arm in the window and passing Kaitlyn a CD. "I don't like Teena Marie enough to own her greatest hits."

"Oh, that's my sister's," Kaitlyn told him. "Thanks."

"No problem," he said. His hand brushed against Jovia's breast.

"Get your fucking hands off me before I kill you!" she yelled at him. She began breathing so hard that she could see her chest rising and falling.

"My bad!" He scowled at her. "Kaitlyn, you'd better take your friend here and get her some Prozac. She's tripping!"

"Fuck you, bastard," she told him.

"You're one to talk," he laughed and strutted off.

"I hate him," Jovia said as they drove off.

"What was that all about?"

"Nothing."

"I can't—"

"I don't wanna talk about it, DROP IT!" Jovia snapped.

The remainder of the ride to Jovia's house was in complete silence. She finally spoke when Kaitlyn pulled into the driveway. "Thanks again."

Kaitlyn looked at her and Jovia saw the concern in her eyes. "You know you can talk to me about anything, Jovia."

"There's nothing to talk about, Kaitlyn," she said and went inside.

"I'm sooooo proud of you!" Me-Ma ran over and smothered her with kisses as she walked through the door. "Kaitlyn called while you were taking your picture!"

Jovia tried to block her. "Me-Maaaaaa."

"I knew you could do it," she gushed. "Let me see it."

*I'm going to kill Kaitlyn*, she thought, handing the license to Me-Ma. *That wench can't hold water.*

"You look fabulous!" Me-Ma told her. "We've gotta go celebrate!"

"It's no big deal," Jovia said. "You knew I was gonna get it eventually."

The councilman had barely walked in the door when Me-Ma told him the great news. "I'm proud of you, Jovia."

"Thanks, Councilman," she said.

"I told her we have to go out to celebrate," Me-Ma gushed.

"Sounds good to me," he replied, reaching into his pocket. He tossed Jovia a set of keys. "You drive."

Jovia's hand reached out and caught them out of the air. "No way. I'm not driving your car."

"You got that right," he laughed and took her by the hand. He pulled out the front door and she gasped. "You're driving your own car."

Sitting in the driveway was a silver BMW 335i with a bow on top. She was flabbergasted. She hugged the councilman and Me-Ma then ran to check out the car, squealing, "This is amazing. Thank you, thank you, thank you!"

She opened the door and sat behind the wheel, inhaling the scent of leather. The car was fully loaded and better than she could ever imagine. She was so busy checking out the details that she almost didn't see the pink envelope sitting on the seat beside her. She picked it up and then looked over at her parents. Me-Ma nodded and Jovia hesitated then opened it.

Inside was a card with words written in Me-Ma's handwriting:

*To our daughter Jovia,*

*We are so proud of the young woman you are be-coming. Continue to grow, blossom, love, succeed and dream and know that we love you always.*

> *Love,*
> *Me-Ma and the Councilman*
> *(Mom and Dad)*

She looked and saw that there was a check enclosed made out to the community college for the full amount of the summer art program. She was ecstatic and this time the tears she cried were tears of joy.

"You are the best, you know that?" She ran and hugged them again.

"Yeah, we do," the councilman told her. "That car is a privilege, not a right. You go straight to school and back home. No hanging out down there. And you're to wear your seat belt and keep those doors locked at all times. . . ."

"Marcus, she knows all that. Now come on, let's go," Me-Ma told him.

They got in Jovia's car and went to dinner. Jovia realized how blessed she was to have her parents. Even though they didn't see eye to eye on a lot of things, they loved her and she appreciated that.

Having a car now gave Jovia the much-needed freedom she desired and the remainder of the school year quickly went by. Her parents eased up on her somewhat after graduation. She immediately began taking art classes at the community college. The classes exposed her to various entities of art and she learned more than she knew existed. Her afternoons after class were spent shopping and hanging out with Starr and her other childhood friends that she now reconnected with when she attended Deidra's birthday party. Amir was an ever-present part of her life. On the days he didn't work late, they would hang out at his house. Other nights, they would chill at Carey's, who covered for them. Although she was still haunted at night when she was asleep, her wakeful days were pleasant.

"Can I go over to Kaitlyn's for a little while?" she lied one Friday night. Starr had plans and, she decided to go over and spend time with Amir.

"I don't see why not," Me-Ma said, looking over to her husband for final approval.

"Don't be out too late," he said.

"I won't," she promised them. "Thanks, I love you."

"Love you too," Me-Ma told her.

When she arrived at his house, Granny was already asleep and he was watching movies. He greeted her with a sensual kiss and she melted. Amir brought about feelings within that she had never experienced before, sexual ones. They had talked about making love, but he never pressed her about it. Her desire to be with him came natural, but she wasn't ready to sleep with him. She wondered if she would ever be able to sleep with anyone. Jordan's raping her had left her scarred worse than the fire.

"Hey you," he said, smiling.

"Hey yourself," she told him. He led her to the sofa and she lay in his arms, enjoying herself. Her intentions were to stay one or two hours at the most, but soon she had drifted off into a deep sleep in his arms.

Tossing and turning as she slept, she felt the arms holding her tight. Her heart began pounding as she struggled to get out of his grips.

"Let me go! Let me go!" she screamed.

"Jovia, Jovia," Amir's voice called, but instead, she heard Jordan.

"Get off me! Get the hell off me!" She was determined not to let him attack her again. She clawed at his face as if her life depended on it. He grabbed her wrists and she yelled at the top of her lungs, "Not again!"

"JOVIA!"

Her eyes opened and she realized she was dreaming again. She looked at her watch and saw that it was after three in the morning. She jumped up and ran out the door, ignoring Amir's voice. She prayed that her parents were asleep and she could sneak into the house. She rushed out of his building and was about to get into her car when a car pulled into the lot. *I'm about to be jacked*, she thought and turned to run back inside.

"Jovia Grant, you stay right where you are!"

She froze and slowly turned around. She prayed this was all a part of her nightmare, but knew that it was indeed reality when she saw her father standing beside a police officer.

"Jovia," Amir came toward her. He stopped dead in his tracks seeing the councilman. "Shit."

"What the—get in the car, Jovia." The councilman took one look at Jovia's tear-stained face and distraught composure and charged at Amir, grabbing him. A scuffle ensued.

"Councilman!" she screamed.

"Go home, Jovia, NOW!" he yelled as the officer pulled them apart.

She looked back at Amir and mouthed the words, "Sorry."

She jumped into her car and sped home. Me-Ma was waiting at the door when she arrived. "Why, Jovia?"

"Me-Ma, I'm sorry . . . I just—"

"We trusted you, Jovia. I went to bat for you and had your back," she cried.

"I know, Me-Ma. I swear—"

"I don't wanna hear it," she said. "Just go upstairs."

Jovia went to her room, knowing she had just enjoyed her last night of freedom and praying that Amir was okay.

# Chapter 10

"How did they find you?" Kaitlyn asked.

"The GPS system on my car," Jovia told her the next day on the phone. Her parents had yet to say anything to her and she had yet to come out of her room. She tried calling Amir, but didn't get an answer.

"Why didn't you just come and leave your car at my house and take my car?"

"I don't know."

"You've been seeing this guy for two months and using me as your alibi. You could at least let me know what's really going on with you."

"I know, Kaitlyn. I just didn't think to let you know. . . ."

"It's a lot you don't want me to know, I see," Kaitlyn snapped.

"What's that supposed to mean?" Jovia frowned. "What are you talking about?"

"Nothing," Kaitlyn sighed.

"Don't even try it," Jovia responded. "Tell me."

Kaitlyn paused and then said, "Jordan says that the reason you started acting crazy after prom was because you gave it up and then was embarrassed."

Jovia's jaw dropped open. She couldn't believe what Kaitlyn was saying.

"It's okay, Jovia. I don't care," Kaitlyn assured her.

"He's lying, Kaitlyn. That's not what happened at all!"

"I didn't believe him at first, but then when you snapped at his house, I started to wonder."

"He's a lying bastard. You know I didn't even wanna go with him to the prom. You know I can't stand him, Kaitlyn. Why would I do something like that?" She started crying.

"Jovia, please," Kaitlyn's voice was soft. "Don't cry, just forget about it. I'm sorry I even brought it up."

"Forget about it? Forget about it?" Jovia laughed like a madwoman. "Don't you think that's what I've been doing? I've been forgetting about stuff for the past ten years. I forgot about living in Frederick Douglass. . . . I forgot about the fire that killed my mother. . . . I forgot about the fact that I didn't want to even go to the fucking prom and now you want me to forget about the fact that Jordan Capron RAPED ME!"

The phone line became eerily silent and neither girl spoke. Jovia couldn't believe that she had finally told someone. Then it dawned on her . . . she had been seeing Amir for two months . . . the prom was two months ago . . . two months. *GOD NO!!!*

She jumped up, almost dropping the phone and ran over to the calendar hanging over her desk. She flipped back and prayed she was mistaken.

"Jovia," Kaitlyn said.

"No." She began shaking her head.

"Jovia, what?"

Jovia closed her eyes and said into the phone, "It was two months ago, Kaitlyn. Oh God, no!"

"What is it?"

"I had my last period three months ago!"

"What are you gonna do?"

Again, Jovia laughed. She decided if God had a sense of humor, she decided to laugh right along with him. "The same thing I always do, Kaitlyn. Forget about it."

Amir finally called her two days later. She was so depressed that hearing his voice on her phone didn't even cheer her up.

"I miss you," he said.

"I'm leaving here," she told him. "I'm running away. Come and get me."

"Not a good idea, Jovia. Do you know your dad had me arrested for statutory rape and contributing to the delinquency of a minor? I'm in enough shit already."

"I'm sorry for making your life so fucking miserable," she told him.

"The only reason I'm miserable is because I can't see you." His voice softened. "It's only for a little while. We'll figure something out."

"I can't stay here," she told him.

"Why not?"

"I'm pregnant," she confessed. There, she said it again for the second time. It was actually getting easier to say.

"What? How?"

"It doesn't matter. I'm leaving tonight," she sighed.

"Jovia, how can you be pregnant?"

It sounded like the dumbest question anyone had ever asked her and she became frustrated. "Um, I don't know. Immaculate conception."

"Jovia, is your dad—"

"No! He's never touched me. He'd never do anything like that," she quickly said. The councilman may have been a lot of things, but he wasn't a molester.

"You told me you were a virgin."

"I am," she sniffed.

"Then how the hell can you be knocked up," he yelled at her. "I'm in all this trouble and you've been fucking someone else the whole time?"

Jovia hung the phone up without even responding. She couldn't even believe that he would think something like that. She cried as she lay across her bed. She thought about her mother and wondered if this is how Felicia felt when she found out she was carrying her. Her cell phone rang and Amir's name and number flashed on the screen. She ignored it and he called a second and then a third time. Finally, she answered.

"I'm on my way," he told her. "Meet me at Carey's."

Her parents were gone and she was all alone, so it was easy to leave. She waited thirty minutes and then headed to Carey's house. He was waiting on his bike when she got there. She hopped on without saying a word and they drove off. Forty-five minutes later, they were sitting across from each other at Frankie's, sharing a cheesesteak. She told him everything that happened when they left Carey's house on prom night, wiping her tears between taking bites and confessing.

"Damn, Jovia. Why didn't you tell anyone?" He sat back and slowly exhaled.

"I'm telling you now," she said, sniffling.

"I'm sorry."

"Me too."

"No, I'm sorry for being an asshole and saying what I said." He grabbed her hand.

"You were upset." She tried to smile. "So, what's the plan?"

"The plan?" he asked.

"Yeah, I need a plan," she told him.

"Depends on what you wanna do. What about the baby?" He stared into her eyes.

"I don't want it. I wanna get rid of it. I don't want anything to do with it or Jordan. I want it out of me," she said in one breath.

"You're sure?" he asked her.

"Yes, I'm sure." She nodded. She thought about it and knew that's what she wanted to do. When she had a baby, it would be born out of love and commitment. Not out of force and lust. She hated the thought of even carrying it. It wasn't even a baby to her.

"Then we'll take care of it," he said.

Jovia felt relieved and knew that everything would be okay. She leaned over and kissed Amir. "I love you."

His eyes widened with surprise and he smiled. "I love you too."

Once finished eating, he took her back to Carey's house. "You got the plan, right?"

"I got it," she told him. "Thank you, Amir."

"I'll see you later. Love you." He kissed her before driving away. She started walking home, feeling better about her situation.

"Jovia!" She heard her name being called just as she turned the corner. "Wait a sec."

She paused and then saw it was Jordan. Without hesitating, she started running. He was too quick for her and before she knew it, she felt his hand on her, pulling her.

"Let me go, Jordan," she huffed.

"I just wanna talk to you," he panted and loosened his grip on her.

"I don't have shit to say to you." she pulled away from him.

"I got something to say to you, bitch! What the hell are you thinking telling Kaitlyn I raped you," he growled at her.

"Because you did, now leave me alone." She started backing away from him.

"I was drunk and you know it! If anything, you seduced me!" He spat at her, "Besides, you can't prove shit!"

"You've lost your fucking mind," she said and turned to run again.

He grabbed her before she could get away and spun her around. She kneed him in the groin and punched him as hard as she could in his face. His face became contorted and he writhed in pain, bending over. Running as fast as she could, she could hear his footsteps behind her. She willed herself to run faster but he grabbed her by the hair and yanked her back. She fell to the ground in front of him. He was about to punch her when a car pulled beside them.

"Jordan, leave her alone!"

Both of them turned and Kaitlyn was getting out of her car. She ran over and helped Jovia up. She looked back at him and said, "You crazy bastard!"

"Fuck both of you!" he panted.

They hurried into her car and sped away.

"You okay?" Kaitlyn asked her.

"I'm fine," Jovia told her.

"We need to call the police," Kaitlyn said, picking up her cell phone.

"No, don't bother," Jovia said. "Just take me home."

"Are you crazy? He raped you and now he just attacked you again!"

"I can't prove he raped me," she told her.

"But I just witnessed his grabbing you. You can prove that!"

Jovia shook her head and said, "No, I just wanna go home."

"What can I do, Jovia?" Kaitlyn asked as they pulled into her driveway.

Jovia thought of the plan that she and Amir had come up with and told her, "can you pick me up in the morning and take me to the clinic to meet Amir?"

"Just tell me what time," Kaitlyn replied.

\*   \*   \*

The next morning, just as planned, Kaitlyn was ringing the doorbell at eight o'clock.

"Hi Ms. Karen, I told Jovia I would drive her to class today," she heard her friend say when Me-Ma opened the door.

"Good morning, Kaitlyn," Me-Ma said. "You're driving her all the way on the Southside?"

"Yes, ma'am, I have to drop some papers off to my aunt who works in the library. You know her, Sharon Shepperd."

"That's right, I forgot your mother's sister works down there. Tell her I said hello, will you?"

"I sure will. Is Jovia ready?" Kaitlyn asked.

"Jovia, Kaitlyn is here," Me-Ma called. Jovia waited a few minutes and then walked down.

"Hey Kaitlyn," she said.

"Hey, you ready?"

"You girls be careful," Me-Ma said. "Jovia, school then home."

"Yes, Me-Ma." She gave her a kiss then followed Kaitlyn out the door.

"You sure this is what you wanna do?" Kaitlyn asked.

"Yeah, I'm sure," she told her. She reached down and turned the radio up, not wanting to talk. Steve Harvey entertained them on their ride. When they arrived, Amir was waiting.

"Hey, you," he said.

"Hey, you," she said, looking into his beautiful eyes. The butterflies in her stomach settled a little.

"Thanks for coming, Kaitlyn," he said, smiling.

"You know it wasn't a problem," Kaitlyn said. She turned to Jovia and asked, "You want me to come in with you?"

"No, I'll be fine," she told her, taking Amir's hand.

"I'll wait here then." Kaitlyn leaned over and hugged her tight.

\* \* \*

Hours later, she arrived home. Kaitlyn helped her up the steps to her room. She was still groggy, but relieved that it was over. She took the paperwork out of her pocket and tossed it onto her desk.

"You need anything?" Kaitlyn asked.

"No, I'm just really sleepy," Jovia groaned as she got into bed. "Thanks, Kaity. You're my best friend."

"I'll check on you later," Kaitlyn said and closed the door behind her.

# Chapter 11

It was dark when Jovia woke up. She had been asleep since arriving home. She felt the urge to go to the restroom and slowly got out of bed. The anesthesia they had given her was wearing off and she was in a bit more pain.

"Jovia," Me-Ma's voice made her jump.

"Yeah," Jovia answered. She tried to move as fast as she could.

"Where are you?"

"I'm in the bathroom," she answered.

"Okay, I picked up those shoes you wanted from Macy's. I got a size eight and a half, but you may wanna try them on because the rep says they're cut small and you may need a nine."

"Thanks, Me-Ma," Jovia called out. She was feeling dizzy and closed her eyes. "Leave them on the desk and I'll try them."

"Okay," she said. "Dinner's ready."

"I'm not hungry, Me-Ma. I don't want anything."

Jovia walked over to the sink and turned the water on. She looked at herself in the mirror and tried to see if she looked like she just had an abortion. She looked more like death warmed over. Her hair was standing all over her head and her sunken eyes had dark circles under them. She splashed cold water on her face, hoping it would bring her comfort. She was nauseous and her stomach was cramping.

"Are you okay?"

"I'm fine, Me-Ma," she sighed.

"Okay, I'll leave the boots right—" Me-Ma stopped mid-sentence.

Jovia began searching the medicine cabinet. The doctor had given her a prescription for painkillers and antibiotics, but Kaitlyn hadn't returned with them. She found a bottle of Aleve and took two. She opened the door and entered back into her room. Me-Ma was staring at her, looking as if she'd seen a ghost.

"I'm fine, Me-Ma," Jovia said, walking over to her bed and sitting down. "What's wrong?"

"Jovia, what have you done?"

"Nothing, Me-Ma, I have cramps, that's all." Jovia strained to smile. Me-Ma continued staring and Jovia blinked, wondering why she was acting so strange.

"Don't lie to me." Me-Ma held up the crumpled papers that Jovia had taken out of her pocket earlier. Jovia tried to speak, but couldn't. "What the hell did you do?"

"I . . . Me-Ma . . ."

"WHY JOVIA, WHY?" Me-Ma yelled, shuffling through the papers. Jovia knew that there was nothing she could say.

"What the hell is going on?" The councilman rushed into the room. Jovia remained speechless. Tears began streaming down Me-Ma's face and she passed him the papers. He seemed confused at first and then she could see the anger taking over.

"Councilman . . . Me-Ma . . ."

"Stop, just stop, Jovia, please," Me-Ma cried.

"How could you do this to us," the councilman asked. "How could you do this to yourself?"

"I didn't—" Jovia began heaving as she cried. "I tried—"

"You got pregnant and had an abortion! Of all the—" he began to yell.

"I was raped!"

The councilman walked over and stood before Jovia and demanded, "What did you say?"

Jovia looked up at the tall man and repeated, "I was raped."

The councilman stormed out of the room. They heard the front door slam behind him and his car peeling out of the driveway.

"Jovia, why didn't you come to me? You know I'm always here for you," Me-Ma said.

"I didn't want anyone to know," Jovia said, wiping the tears that were flowing.

"He's gonna pay for this, believe me," Me-Ma said.

"I can't prove anything." Jovia shook her head. "He's gonna deny it."

"He's not getting away with this," Me-Ma said, standing up. The doorbell rang.

"That's probably Kaitlyn. I need to take a shower," Jovia said, feeling as if she was going to throw up.

"Go ahead, Jovia. I'll be right back."

Moments later, Kaitlyn walked into Jovia's room carrying a small pharmacy bag. Jovia took the bottle of pills from Kaitlyn after grabbing some fresh clothes and went into the bathroom. She turned the water on and stood under it for what seemed like hours. She wanted to talk to Amir . . . she needed him . . . she wanted him . . . she couldn't do this without him. She got dressed and got back in bed. Kaitlyn was sitting in her chair, watching TV.

"Your mother is frantic. Where did the councilman go?" Kaitlyn asked.

The medication was taking effect and Jovia was drowsy. "He ran out after I told them. . . ." She closed her eyes and fell back into a deep slumber. When she woke again Kaitlyn was still there. She looked over at the clock and saw that it was after eight o'clock.

"Are you hungry? You need to eat something."

"No, I'm okay," she answered. Her cell began to ring. Pain ran through her abdomen as she reached for it and she groaned.

"I'll get it." Kaitlyn told her, "It's Starr."

"Answer it," Jovia said.

"Hello," Kaitlyn said. Jovia watched as her friend's facial expression changed and she became worried.

"Is she there?"

"She's gone," Kaitlyn told her.

"What did she say? Was Amir home?"

"He's in the hospital," Kaitlyn said, looking shocked.

"What? For what? What happened?" Jovia was confused. Everything was happening so fast and she was getting confused.

"Jovia, we need to go," Me-Ma came rushing in.

"Wait, Me-Ma." Jovia snatched the phone from Kaitlyn and dialed Starr's number. Her voice mail picked up. Jovia dialed it again.

"Jovia, now! Your father needs us!" Me-Ma yelled.

Starr finally picked up. Jovia could hear her crying before she said, "Hello."

"Starr, what happened, where's Amir?"

"They just called from the hospital, Jovia. He was beat up. Someone jumped him. It's bad, Jovia, real bad."

"Jovia, get off the phone and let's go!"

"I gotta go. Granny and I are on our way to Lincoln Memorial now," Starr said and hung the phone up.

She looked over at her mother, still confused. "What's going on?"

"Your father took matters into his own hands and went after the man who attacked you. He's at the police station.

They need for you to make a statement." Me-Ma was flustered.

Suddenly, Jovia realized what was happening.

"The councilman attacked Jordan?" Kaitlyn questioned.

"Jordan?" Me-Ma glared at Kaitlyn.

"Jordan Capron, he's the one that raped her."

Jovia's world was crumbling around her. Her boyfriend
was brutalized and now her father was going to jail, and it
was all her fault.

"The councilman was arrested for assaulting Amir Simmons."

# Epilogue

"NOOOOO WHHHHYYYYY?"

"Calm down, Me-Ma, it's not the end of the world," Jovia sighed. She knew her mother would not take her decision very well and was prepared for the reaction.

"Are you sure about this, Jovia?"

"I'm sure, Me-Ma." Jovia nodded.

"But, what about your plans to live in the dorm, joining a sorority . . ."

"Those are your plans Me-Ma, not mine," Jovia told her. They were sitting at the kitchen table. "I know you and the councilman are gonna be disappointed, but I don't want to go. Not right now, anyway. I wanna stay home for a while and finish the art program."

Me-Ma shrugged. "I guess I figured with all that had gone on these past weeks, you'd want to get away for awhile."

It had been six weeks since their world had been turned upside down by the councilman's attack on Amir. For days their family was bombarded by the press who wasted no time plastering the councilman's face on the news and in the newspaper as a madman who had attacked an innocent young man from FDP in a case of mistaken identity. At one point, they were even calling for him to be removed from the city council until Amir and Granny had given a statement during a press conference stating that they supported the councilman and all he had done for the community over the years.

"No, I don't want to go away. I want to stay home."

"I guess your not wanting to go away has a lot to do with Amir?" Me-Ma asked.

"No, not really, Me-Ma," Jovia told her. "I ain't gonna lie, I love him. But I'm settled for now, and I don't wanna leave. Besides, I have to be here to testify against Jordan."

"Did you talk to the district attorney today?"

"Yes, he says I have a strong case because my dress had the DNA evidence and Jordan's parents had a security camera that showed how I looked when I entered the house and when I left," she folded her arms and said.

"That bastard needs to be thrown under the jail," Me-Ma told her. "I can't believe he thought he could get away with it."

"Well, hopefully, he's not," Jovia said. The doorbell rang and she went to answer it. She smiled from ear to ear when she opened the door. She put her arms around Amir and pulled him to her, kissing him passionately.

"Whoa, girl, you know I'm still sore," he said, wincing when she released him. "Wow, is that how you greet all your visitors?"

"Only the ones I'm in love with," she told him.

"Jovia, who is it?" Me-Ma called out.

"It's Amir, Me-Ma," she answered.

"How are you, Mrs. Grant?" Amir said, stepping inside.

"I'm fine, Amir." Me-Ma walked into the foyer and greeted him.

"It's nice to see you're healing well," Me-Ma told him.

"Thank you, ma'am," Amir told her. It was a miracle that he was alive after suffering from a ruptured spleen and several broken ribs.

"We were just about to go have dinner. Would you like to join us?"

Jovia was shocked at her mother's invitation. She looked over at Amir to see his response.

"Uh, no thanks, I was about to go over to my cousin's house and just dropped by for a moment," Amir told her.

"Rain check then?"

"Definitely," he said, smiling.

"Rain check for what?"

They all turned to see the councilman standing in the doorway.

"Uh, Councilman," Jovia's voice was barely above a whisper. "He was just leaving."

"I invited him to dinner," Me-Ma quickly added. "I figured the least thing we could do was buy him a meal since you beat the hell out of him for no reason."

There was a deadly silence, and no one moved. Jovia didn't know how to react. The councilman and Amir stared at each other.

"Well, she does have a point," Amir finally said. "And a brother is starving."

Jovia breathed a sigh of relief and prayed that this was the beginning of the end of her nightmares. She looked over at her father and her boyfriend who were now shaking hands and her emotions swelled. Amir was truly a gift from God and he would always be her Thug Passion.

# All About the Money

*a story by roy glenn*

# Chapter 1

*Jada West*

For me, it was all about the money. I think it's in the blood. I come from a family of hustlers. My moms and my daddy were both hustlers. That's all my mother and father ever talked about. Money, money, money, and how to get it.

They'd known each other all their lives. Moms was born six months and one day before Daddy. They lived next to each other and my grandmothers were best friends. Both my mother and father used to say they don't remember a time when they weren't together. Even though they never got married and we didn't always live together, we were always a family.

My daddy was a gambler; that was his hustle. That's how he put food on our table. He played poker and blackjack, shot craps, played C-low, but his thing was pool. In his day, my daddy could shoot pool with the best of them. He used to always say, that when he truly on his game, "Ain't another man standing can touch me with a stick in my hand." When I was a kid, he would take me with him sometimes when Moms had something goin'. It used to make him madder than hell and he would rant and rave and, "Swear 'for god, this the last time I let her do this to me. She know damn well I got shit to do, 'cuse my French, and if I ever hear you talk like that I'll beat your little ass. But she knows what I gotta do tonight. But if she was to come home and I ain't got no money, what would happen?"

"She would lose her mind," I would always say. 'Cause she would go off over the slightest little thing. It became kind of a runnin' joke, us trippin' on Moms trippin'.

"You damn right she would. I can hear her now. What you mean you ain't got no money. Well, I'll just go on down to the rent office and tell 'hem I ain't got the rent 'cause my *man* couldn't find no babysitter," he went on and on. But the second he got in that poolroom, my daddy was a rock. Makin' shots and takin' money.

My moms used to boost from the mall, identity theft with checks and credit cards, but she would do whatever it took to make money. "Honey, when you got a man's back, I mean truly got his back, a woman gotta step up. Sometimes a woman gotta use what she got to get what she gotta get to take care of her family." The fact that Moms would give it up for money if she felt she needed to used to piss my father off. But when he had a woman on the hook that he was getting money from, Moms wouldn't say shit. For them it was always about the money, 'cause no matter who or where they were gettin' money from, it was always for us. We were always a family.

But money turned out to be their downfall. When I was seventeen, my daddy had a woman who was givin' him money. My father would bring the money home and was givin' it to my moms. That's just how they did it. But one night the woman followed him to our apartment and she waited for Daddy to come out. I was watching from the window and saw her walk up on him, put the gun to his head, and killed him.

"Daddy, no!" I screamed at the top of my lungs and kept screaming as the woman looked up at me and then ran to her car. I wanted to run out there but I couldn't move. My mother came to see what I was screaming about, but I couldn't talk. All I could do was point out the window at my father's body.

"Oh, God, God, no," she said and ran out there. It was like all the life had been drained from my body. He and I were so close and I loved my daddy so much that I couldn't believe what I was seeing. It felt like part me was dying out there.

It still does.

After that, Moms had to go for herself. She went out and got herself a job and worked it for two weeks before she *accidentally* slipped in the ladies' room. She sued them and got a little settlement. But her plan was to do what she called washin' the check. That's when they use some kind of chemicals to erase the amount on the check and then they put in a new amount. She got some fake ID and set up an account to run the checks through and went for it. Good plan, and it worked except for the fact that the insurance company knew who they sent that check number to. So, it was easy for them to match her work ID with the bank's surveillance video. Now Moms doin' fed time in Illinois. If Daddy were alive, he would have never let her make a mistake like that.

I had just celebrated my eighteenth birthday when they took my moms away. With only a court-appointed lawyer at her side, the judge gave her ten years. Now I was alone, and broke. All they left me was a '77 Monte Carlo. That bitch was beat down, but it ran like a champ. I had to get somethin' goin' and quick. Since I had barely graduated from high school, I knew college wasn't in my future. I was determined not to turn out the way my people did, but I had absolutely no clue about how I was gonna do it. I had to learn from what they did and from their mistakes. I remembered what my moms told me about what a woman gotta do, but all the lyin' and fakin' you gotta do just wasn't for me. See, when you gettin' money from men like that, they think they own you. That's the mistake Daddy made. That woman was givin' him her money for that dick and that made him hers. No, no, not a life for me.

For the first couple of months after they took Moms away I wrote to her once a week, you know, keepin' her up on what was goin' on with me. I remember writing her and sayin' how I stayed in our old apartment for three months before they finally put me out. I had moved in with a friend of mine from high school, named Love. She worked at a tattoo parlor. She let me sleep on her floor until I got myself together. I survived those days on whatever money Daddy's old friends gave me. I wrote her that I had to stop getting money from them, because some of them wanted something in return for their money, and I wasn't prepared to do that. I never got an answer to any of my letters, until one day I got a letter from her that simply said that I could stop writing her. She said that reading my letters was too painful for her. She told me that I couldn't even think about comin' to see her, 'cause she didn't want me to see her like that.

With few other options on the horizon, I took a job at a market research company. My job was to call people and ask them survey questions about their buying habits, and direct them to Web sites that they could buy stuff. It didn't pay much, but it allowed me to move off Love's floor and pay the rent for my hole-in-the-wall apartment. Well, at least it paid the rent most of the time, but this month wasn't one of those months and I was late on my rent again. For the last couple of days, I'd been dodging my landlord, a pervert named Chuck.

A few months earlier, I caught Pervert Chuck, the rent collector, building super, and loan shark all rolled into one, sifting through my underwear drawer. At the time, I was 300 dollars short on the rent. I was able to convince him to forget all about the money, in exchange for a pair of my worn Victoria's Secret thongs, but he's been riding my ass ever since.

When the first knock sounded at the door, I jumped, startled by the noise then froze and stood completely still. It wasn't like my super could actually see through the door, but I still tried to stop breathin', and stayed as quiet as humanly possible.

I looked up my reflection in the mirror, which hung above the sofa. "This is really sad," I said under my breath. I swear I could hear him leaning against my door. I knew he wouldn't hear any music or the TV since the power was off. So I stood still and I tried to remain quiet.

"Shit! Missed that bitch again," I heard him grumble. My heart was racing as I stood waiting for sounds of his footsteps walking away. Nothing. I was trembling, praying to God Chuck wouldn't use his key to let himself in and find me standing there pretending not to be home.

When I thought the coast was clear, I tiptoed back into the bedroom. Things were really going downhill for me and I was at my wit's end. I knew that I had to come up with a better plan than the one I was workin'.

Later that afternoon, I was ridin' down Frederick Douglass past the project we used to live in and stopped to pick up a two-piece snack from Fat Larry's. I don't know how he does it, but that was by far the best chicken I've ever tasted. On the way in, I stopped in my tracks to admire what had to be the prettiest drop-top Beamer I had ever seen. It was sweet, royal blue with baby-blue leather and wood panel interior. I mean this car was sparkling in the sunlight and the rims were glistening. A few other people walked by admiring the ride, and I was like damn, will I ever see the day when I can afford shit like that? I sighed and walked up to the entrance. When I pulled the door open, I accidentally bumped into a woman who looked like she belonged in the car.

She was sporting a Baby Phat denim jumpsuit that hugged

her curves. She accessorized with old school Gucci boots and a matching shoulder bag, with a pair of large designer shades that swallowed nearly half her face and a Gucci fedora tilted to the side on her head.

"I'm so sorry," I offered.

"Jada, that you girl?"

I snapped my head toward her hidden face. I didn't catch the voice, but she definitely knew me. When she snatched off the shades and pulled her hat's brim back my mouth dropped. "Diane?"

Diane and I worked together at the marketing company for nearly a year. She rarely showed up to work and hadn't been there at all for a couple of months at that time.

"Yeah girl! What's up? I ain't seen you in a minute!" she said like she was really glad to see me.

I instantly felt self-conscious. There I was dressed in some raggedy jeans and an old sweatshirt that I used to wear to clean the house on weekends.

As Diane spoke, my brain kept trying to understand how one goes from barely coming to work, to being dressed in the finest gear and sporting a look that dripped money. When she pressed the alarm button and that pretty ride beeped I was too through.

"You okay?" she asked.

I looked at the car then back at her, still dumbfounded. "Um, I ah—" I stuttered, but I was taking in everything fabulous about the new Diane. At five feet seven and one hundred and forty pounds, Diane was beautiful. Her once short hair had been replaced by long wavy and flowing tresses. She blinged from her ears to her wrists to her neck. The chick was iced out, and she looked good. "Ah, Diane, what's up, I mean did you hit the number or something?" I needed to know.

She scrunched up her pretty face. "Number? Nah, girl, I ain't hit no number," she chuckled.

I looked at the car again and then back at her. This time her eyes followed mine.

"Oh shit!" she started. "Girl, that ain't nothin'," she testified, motioning toward the car. "You ain't gonna make any real money punchin' no damn clock, I can tell you that much for sure," she said.

"Well, what do you mean?" I asked her.

She pulled me to the side, closer to her car. "Look, why don't you go get you soma' Fat Larry's chicken," she suggested.

I shook my head reluctantly. It was like I didn't want to leave her for fear when I came back she, that car and my chance to make some real money might be gone.

"Gon', I'll wait right here for you," she promised.

I glanced at her and the car one last time before going inside. I walked outside and saw Diane sitting behind the wheel of her car. I gladly climbed into her luxury car and leaned back in the passenger seat like I belonged there.

"Are you ready to make some real paper?" she asked.

"Girl, you just don't know," I said.

Little did I know what she had in mind would change my life in ways I never imagined possible.

# Chapter 2

I thought about the conversation Diane and I that day after we left Fat Larry's.

"Girl, I swear, I was you about a year ago. You remember, I was sneaking in and out of my cousin's dorm room, barely able to eat and shit." Diane shook her head at the awful memories she described. "I just got tired of tryin' to play it straight," she admitted.

"Yeah, but the ride, I mean look at you, girl. You've got to tell me what you doin' to get paid like this."

"It's simple," she said. "I dance at this little club called Ecstasy on Friday and Saturday nights," she said calmly.

I leaned in to her.

"What you mean you dance at a club? What kind of dancin' are we talkin' 'bout here?" I wanted to know.

"I'm a exotic dancer," she said without so much as a whisper to her voice.

"What?" I screamed.

She didn't seem the least bit fazed by my shock. It was as if we were discussing Larry's chicken.

"Say what you want, but I never leave with any less than 500 dollars a night," she said and eased back in her seat.

I could sense she was studying my reaction. I let the figure roll around in my head.

"I know what you're thinking," Diane said.

"No, I don't think you do." Had she said 500 dollars a night? For two nights' worth of work she made 1,000 dollars? That's almost triple what I make for working eighty hours.

She pulled her hair behind her ears and leaned toward me.

"Yeah, I do, Jada. Your ass thinkin' 'bout that paper. And you wonderin' if you can do it."

I didn't say anything 'cause she was right.

I just nodded my head and Diane continued. "Look, I've been to the club with you plenty of times, Jada. I've seen you out there on the floor, shakin' that ass," Diane said and started shakin' in her seat. "You just be shakin' that ass naked."

"Naked in front of a roomful of men," I corrected.

"I don't. I dance for one man," Diane boasted. "Whichever one is standin' in front of me with money in his hand."

"I don't know, Diane. Dancin' at a club is one thing, but naked. I just don't think I could do that in front of a bunch of horny men."

"I'm tellin' you, you could make a grip. You got a bomb-ass body too. Them titties and that ass. I'm tellin' you girl, you sleepin' on your best moneymakers!"

"What, you been sizing me up?"

"Nah, girl, I don't even get down like that. Well I do, but that's only for real serious money," she giggled.

I was used to men commenting about my double-D cups, and I've heard one or two jokes about my bodacious booty, but it was strange sitting there and listening to Diane do the same.

"I'm telling you, all you doin' is dancin'," she persisted.

"Yeah, but you talkin' about dancin' naked," I said, seemingly not able to move past that point. I was just gettin' to the point where I comfortable havin' sex without it being pitch dark in the room, and that was definitely a huge jump from there. "I don't know, Diane," I said and hunched my shoulders.

But there I was, pulling up in front Ecstasy. It was a little building that looked like nothing more than a shack from the outside.

Once the car was in park, I immediately started having second thoughts. *You don't know these people, there could be rapists, murders or whatever hanging out around here.*

I glanced around in both directions hoping no one was paying attention to me as I sat behind the steering wheel of my piece of car, and tried to summon up enough courage to go inside. I wondered if Diane's car was parked on the other end somewhere, or maybe even in the back. I would definitely need her presence to make it through the night.

A couple of guys walked by my car and snapped me back to reality. "Okay, I can do this," I whispered.

I flipped down my visor mirror and looked at the job I had done with my makeup. I had plastered my eyes with so much shadow that I felt like one of the girls in the many porno flicks I'd watched to get myself pumped up. Diane had told me that's what she did to make herself feel sexy. She said after filling her head with X-rated images, that and downing a few shots of Henny, she was usually good to go. I was hoping for the same magic when I felt for a half-pint bottle of Hennessey that I had picked up on the way there. I opened the bottle and took another swallow. *This is nothing more than a new adventure,* the tiny voice in my head encouraged.

I thought back to being cornered by Pervert Chuck and felt up 'cause I didn't have the rent money. I felt disgusted with his hands all over me. If I really wanted to be honest about it, I let him do it. I didn't scream, or fight him off, I did very little in the way of protest. I allowed him to trap me in that corner and touch my body, because that's what it took to cover the rest of the rent.

I knew I'd be meeting the same type of pervert behind

those walls. So I had to ask myself what was the difference? What was the difference between me dancin' naked in front of a bunch of men for money, and being felt up by one because I was short with my rent again? Although neither choice seemed too appealing, the answer was simple. It was all a matter of choice and what I was willing to do. The answer was simple. Money. The truth was there was no difference. It was all about the money.

I fidgeted with my hair and applied more gloss before snapping the mirror shut. I took a deep breath and clutched the door handle. I hesitated and tried to think positive thoughts about what I was going to do, but the truth of the matter was that I was scared to death. So scared that my hands were shaking. "You can do this, Jada," I told myself as I got out of the car. "It's gonna be just like Diane said, I'll be dancin' for one guy," I said as I walked slowly toward the building. "Just one guy."

As I walked, I got a taste of what it was gonna be like, as I could feel the eyes of every guy in the parking lot on me. Undressing me with their eyes and doing worse things in their thoughts. "You can do this, Jada," I repeated. I was used to guys staring at me, but never like this. I felt like an object, a juicy steak on a platter that was about to get served up. Some of the guys were yellin' at me, but I was too deep into what I was about do to comprehend, much less care what they were saying. Truth be told, I was an object now, an object for their entertainment.

At that moment, the club's door swung open and I could hear booming music flooding into the parking lot. When the bouncer stopped me at the entrance, my skin started to crawl as his eyes wandered from my head down to my toes. "I'm lookin' for Bruce," I said to him.

"You new?" he asked in a voice so deep it startled me.

"Um, yeah," I nodded, clutching my thin jacket at the neck.

"I know you ain't shy. This ain't no place for no shy hoes," he insisted.

I started to say something, but no words came out.

He laughed. "Let's see what you working wit'." I jumped when I felt somebody's hand palming my ass.

"What the hell!" I turned to face the culprit.

"Don't touch me!" I screamed at this drunk who could barely hold himself up.

"Aw, baby, you too cute to act all like that," he slurred. "We friendly around here. If you gon' make some money, you gots to be nice," he added.

"Just don't touch me!" I said again.

He stumbled toward me and I took a few steps back.

"Here," he said and shoved a crumbled 5-dollar bill toward me. "Here's something for you, cutie," he continued before stumbling into the club.

I turned my attention back to the bouncer.

"That's just Eddie, he don't mean no harm," he said. "But you definitely got to get used to muthafuckas grabbin' at you. We try to keep that shit down, but it's gonna happen. If you don't want to be touched like that, you gotta figure out how you gonna keep niggas off you without it costin' you money."

"I will."

"Come on, why don't you go in and walk through that first door to your right. That way you can get straight to the dressing room and bypass the crowd," he offered.

Although I was tempted to follow the bouncer's instructions, a part of me was curious about what it was like inside the club. So I stepped past him, bypassed the door and followed the sound of the music.

The room was a pretty good size, but the mirrored walls made the place seem twice as big. The tables and chairs were lined up in sections that surrounded the stage. There were also two dark doorways toward the back of the room. The soft lighting gave off a dark enough hue over the entire room, and the place smelled like a mixture of cigarette smoke, crisp new money, and just a hint of weed. Several men stood huddled in a group surrounding a couple of dancers. They were both naked and dancin' their asses off. There were other men posted up at the bar. A few of them had women dancin' in front of them.

I stopped and looked around the room. A lot of the men that were sitting at the tables had women dancin' for them too. Up until that moment, I was under the mistaken delusion that I would be doin' a couple of sets on stage and that's it. But as I continued to watch, I saw the men givin' the dancers money when the song ended. The dancer would get the money, get dressed in what little outfit they were wearing and move on to the next man.

At that point, I knew that that was how they made their money. If I was gonna clock the kind of paper Diane was talkin' about, I was really gonna have to hustle. I remembered what my moms told me about what a woman gotta do. "You're here to make money, Jada. It's all about the money."

I started to get excited as the music pumped through the massive speakers. It was loud and contagious. Just as I prepared to turn and find the dressing room, I bumped into this completely naked woman. "Hi, you must be Jada," she said, like she was fully clothed. I tried my best not to stare at her naked body, but I couldn't help it.

"Um, how—how'd you know me?"

"Actually, I came out here to find you. I'm Crème. Diane just called me and said she's running late, so she asked me to take care of you 'til she get here," Crème said. She was cute, short hair, olive skin with an hourglass shape, firm breasts, and shapely hips.

I tried not to stare at her nipples, but they seemed to be

pointed right at my eyes. Next to us, two other naked dancers were grindin' their hips and shakin' their breasts all in their customers' faces.

"Oh, okay," I said turning my attention back to Crème.

I kept reminding myself that this was really no big deal. I pulled my gym bag close and followed Crème down a dark hallway.

Before we turned I looked toward the stage; a couple of women were gyrating all over each other. One was wearing a pair of spiked heels and a garter around her beefy thigh. The other dancer, who was laying on the stage, had on white platform boots and a garter filled with bills. Spiked heels dropped it like it was hot and she was bouncing up and down on another dancer's face. On the other stage, I noticed pink flesh when another dancer spread and held her legs up wide in midair. I couldn't hide my shock. But when I saw a group of men throwing bills onto the stage, I finally knew exactly where I was and I was sure that I wanted to be there. "You can do this, Jada. It's all about the money," I repeated silently.

"You comin'?" Crème asked over the music as she walked.

"Yes." I did a slow trot to catch up to Crème.

We weren't in the dressing room for a good thirty minutes before a big burly man burst in through the door. Most of the girls scattered or quickly busied themselves. I never did know what his real name was, but all the girls called him Bruce, Bruce, 'cause he was just as big as the famous comedian and he did kinda favor him.

"Delicious just quit, I need somebody fresh!" he hollered. When he stepped close to me, Crème was standing next to me, but she didn't say anything.

"Oh, Jackie," he said removing the cigar from his lips, where spittle had gathered at the corners of his mouth.

"Um, it's Jada," I corrected.

"Whatever, you're Delicious now. You need to be ready to shake that ass when I call for you."

Before I could protest, he spun around and headed back out the door as abruptly as he had come in.

I glanced up in the mirror to see the other dancers in different stages of closing down for the day, while others were getting ready to go make more money. My head started spinning, and I felt myself get warm.

"God, where's Diane. I can't do this," I said, leaning up against a nearby counter.

"What you mean you can't do it? Much as Diane been braggin' about your ass. You'd better get out there and do somethin'," Crème insisted. But the more she talked the more upset my stomach became. Soon, I felt the bile churning and threatening to erupt. I rushed to the closest trash can and leaned over the top.

The other girls were going about their business like nothing had happened. When I was done, Crème pulled me to the side. "Look, I got a little something for you. It'll help you relax and get into it," she said. She fumbled through her stuff for a second and came out with a small plastic bag. I knew what time it was. She stuck one of her long fingernails into the bag and held it in front of my face.

I had tried cocaine a few times, but I never really got anything out of it. "Naa. That ain't my thing," I said and took a swallow of my Henny.

"Okay," Crème said and took the hit.

By the time it was my turn to dance, Crème had me pumped, a little drunk and feelin' the music. When Bruce, Bruce called for me, I was as ready as I'd ever be. Once I got on stage, I sprang to life, surprising even myself. Every time I went down to the floor, I'd shake my behind and spread my thighs; the men loved it. I'd gyrate my hips to the music, stripping off pieces of clothes as I moved around the stage. When I was down to my last stitch of clothes, which was a thong with fringes, I pulled it to one side and used my fingers to stretch my lips real wide. *That one really surprised me.* These two men stood at the stage feedin' me money like they had an unlimited supply.

Diane never came to the club that night, and I didn't see her at all for a few days, but by the time she came back, I was a pro. After three weeks into my new profession, the money was rolling in and I was ready to change my name. Delicious was okay, but this customer gave me an idea when he came stumbling up to the stage at the end of my performance one night. "I want to see my kitty," he slurred. I was trying to clear my money off the stage before the next dancer came up, but he wouldn't let up. "Miss Kitty!" he shouted. "I want to see her. I live for the part when you stroke that cat for me," he said.

"What?" I yelled over the music.

"Them other bitches just dance. You put on a show for a nigga. Make him want you."

At first, I didn't understand what he was saying, but the more I studied the other girls I realized what he was talking about. They were just dancing. They were merely moving to music. Every so often they may rub a tit, but it was like one, two, stop and turn. Three, four, shake your ass. Five, six, drop and spread. Seven, eight, get back up. That's when I realized just how different I was.

When I was on stage, it was like I was in a trance, dancin' in my very own world. I'd pick a man and stare at him, literally workin' him over with my eyes. When I danced, I moved seductively, and my hands wandered all over my body as if the customer himself was exploring me. I stroked, caressed, and massaged, tryin' to give them an idea of what it might be like if I'd let them touch me.

With his simple request, my new persona was born. I became Miss Kitty. Now, I waltzed out on stage dressed in a short and tight leather miniskirt, with a garter belt and black fishnet stockings. I topped things off with a fishnet shirt and a black leather bra and a long pair of black gloves. My final touch was a small and elegant silk mask. Within two months' time, Miss Kitty had her own small, but generous following. Their money spoke volumes, telling me without a doubt that they appreciated my well-calculated efforts to make them happy and to make me money.

# Chapter 3

I lay in bed one Saturday thinking about how my life had changed. I'm not the same person I was when I walked through those doors. If you had told me when I was fifteen that in five years I'd be the premier dancer at a strip club, I woulda called you a liar and might have slapped your face. But every night, I was the queen at Ecstasy. The truth was I was enjoying this life that I'd been living for the past eight months.

But I had bigger plans for my life. I was gonna be big time. I never really knew what I was gonna be big time at, but I planned to make a lot of money doing it. At least that part of the plan was working. I was making mad money and was a superstar in my own right. Sure, the men came to see the other dancers, but when Miss Kitty sashayed out of the dressing room, it was like the room was mine.

Nothin' could touch the high I felt while on stage. That's the part of all this that has surprised me the most. I'd never been the kind of person that was, you know, stuck on myself. I am by no means ugly, but at the same time I am by no means the prettiest girl in the room. There are women with better bodies and there are a bunch of women that can shake their asses off. What separated me from the rest was my presentation. I just worked harder than every other woman in there, because I wanted it more than they did.

I tried to ease up out of bed, only to lie back down. My head was pounding in the worst way. When the phone rang, I would've paid someone to make it stop. I snatched it up before it could scream again.

"Heeeeey girl, I'm on my way to pick you up now. Nine West is havin' a fierce sale. I know you down, right?" Diane was hollering in my ear.

I slapped my forehead.

"Damn. Why are you callin' here all early with this shit, Dee?"

"Early?" she screeched.

"Shit yeah. I'm a wreck," I tried to reason.

"Bitch, pull yourself together and let's roll," she said sounding far too giddy to me.

I turned to face the wall and caught a glimpse of the digital clock.

"Damn, is it five o'clock for real?"

"Yeah, that's what I been tryin' to tell you, *Miss Kitty*," she threw in somewhat sarcastically. "We hit Nine West, do the rest of the mall, grab some food, then get out to the club and make some cheddar," she said.

I rubbed my face and yawned.

"Okay, how far are you?"

"I'm gettin' off River Drive right now I'll be there by the time you wash your ass and brush your teeth," she said.

Later that night at the club, I tripped off how easy it was for me to drop a grand on shoes during my shopping spree with Diane. I spent a lot more, but I used the grand to cop two pairs of Prada stilettos. Then we went to this boutique that sold La Perla lingerie. Diane's mouth dropped when I easily laid three grand on the counter to pay for a lace bra with matching panty and garter set.

"Are you crazy?" she had asked.

"It's for my show," I said as the salesclerk picked up her pace, hoping Diane wouldn't change my mind.

"At the club?" she asked in bewilderment. "Hmmm, I wish like hell I'd spend that kind of paper to shake my ass for those losers." Diane sucked her teeth.

I didn't respond right away, but in my mind, I pointed to that extra effort as the reason why I was so different from Diane and the rest of the dancers. Considering all I spent on the spree, I knew I'd go to work with a vengeance; no wallet was safe with me on the prowl.

Halfway through my act, to my surprise when I went to the edge of the stage there was a woman calling me with her eyes. She was all but drooling as she stared at me longingly. I slid to her on my knees; steady working my hips like we were the only ones in the room. She was loving every moment of it. Each time I wiggled, she stuffed a crisp new twenty into my thong. "You sexy as fuck," she said when I leaned over to shake my titties in her face. She stroked at me and I scooted beyond her reach. I loved playin' with girls, 'cause it drove the niggas insane and made them drop major paper.

I went to work another section of the stage before return-ing to my faithful fan. This time I turned around and spread my cheeks so she could stuff more twenties into my garter. She didn't disappoint. When she reached up to rub my breasts, I moved out of her way and rubbed them for her, squeezing my nipples for good measure.

I had her hot and wet and I knew it.

After I finished working the room, I made my way to the dressing room to change my outfit. When I came back out, I scanned the room, but my new girl toy was gone. As I walked toward the VIP room to see what was going down in there, this dude grabbed me by the arm.

"Say Miss Kitty, what's up? You looked real good out there," he confirmed.

"I'm glad you enjoyed the show," I said as I tried to move

on. He tugged my arm again, pulling me back closer to his body. Liquor reeked from his pores.

"What's up? You get down like the others?"

"Yeah, for five hundred dollars," I said without blinking. That was my standard answer anytime somebody came at me like that. Once niggas heard that, they usually went on about their business with their heads hangin' low. I was there for the money, not to give up any parts of this pussy.

"Whaat? Five hundred dollars? Bitch, is you crazy? Baby, I can get some ass for a hundred and a half up in this bitch," he yelled.

I sucked my teeth. "One-fifty?" I ran my hand along the length of my body. "What about this body says I'd even consider giving up any of this for a measly hundred and fifty dollar?" I asked with all seriousness.

"Damn, baby, that's a grip though. You want too much."

"Nigga please. Obviously your paper ain't heavy enough, so you need to move on to one of these average bitches around here." Before he could tug me again, I snatched my arm from him and stormed into the VIP room.

When the club was getting ready to close, I walked into the dressing room where everyone was giggling and acting like they'd went in on a winning lottery ticket.

"What's up?" I asked one of the few somber looking dancers in the room.

She turned to look at the group that was celebrating, and then turned to me. "What's up, Jada? They all excited and shit 'cause Bruce, Bruce just came in and picked girls for Sunday night's big private party," she snarled. "I'm really surprised that Bruce, Bruce didn't pick you."

"So am I," I mumbled, taking her response and attitude to mean she wasn't one of the chosen ones. I had heard the talk around the club. The party was being held for The One. He was the hottest rapper in the city and word was when he and his entourage came to the club, it was at least an easy grand for even the average dancer. That told me my goal should be three times that amount. Now, all I had to do was find a way to get invited to the party, but Bruce, Bruce was nowhere to be found.

As I was heading out the back door, a powerful hand clutched my shoulder.

"Miss Kitty. I was lookin' for you. I want you at One's party tomorrow night. Think you can handle it? It's a lot of money to be made," Bruce, Bruce warned.

"I'll be here purrin'," I promised.

# Chapter 4

The next night sheer electricity lingered in the air at the club. This so-called private party wasn't all that private at all. There were fifteen other dancers besides myself and at least thirty members of The One's entourage, and a bunch of the clubs regulars that were friendly with Bruce, Bruce.

When I hit the floor, Bruce, Bruce was sitting at a table in the corner with two guys, but it was the one in the black that caught my eye. I was just about to make my way over there when I was surrounded by three men. "Miss Kitty!" one of them screamed and they all started dropping money at my feet. Without taking my eyes off the man in black, I took off my outfit and went to work.

"Watch this," another one said. "You ain't never seen nuthin' like this before, dog."

I was so into it that a circle formed around me, and before long they were chanting my name. "Miss Kitty! Miss Kitty! Miss Kitty!" There were so many of them that they blocked my view of the guy. When the song ended, I picked up my money and went back to the dressing room.

When I returned to the floor, I looked around the club for the man in the black, but I didn't see him. I was startled when a deep and sexy voice said, "Miss Kitty, right?"

I spun around. It was the guy, and he looked even better up close. He had the most piercing eyes. "That's me."

"I enjoyed watching you dance," he said.

"Thanks. You a friend of Bruce, Bruce?" I asked.

"I guess you could say that."

"I haven't seen you here before," I said and stepped closer. "So I guess you're part of The One's entourage."

He flashed a smile and I got wet. "Not exactly. I own the company that manages The One."

"Oh really," I said, knowing that this was somebody I needed to know.

"You ready to go, Black?" the other guy he was with said.

"Yeah, in a minute, Freeze," he said and turned to me.

"Miss Kitty, it was a pleasure meeting you. Maybe I'll see you again."

"Jada."

"Excuse me."

"Jada, my name is Jada."

"Okay, Jada it is then. Maybe I'll come back to see you. Bruce, Bruce speaks very highly of you. I'd be interested to see why," he said and started to walk away.

Since he'd already seen me dance I assumed that he meant something else. The way he looked; the way that sexy voice rang in my ear, I was ready to forget about this money and go anywhere he wanted. I grabbed his arm. "What's your name?" I had to know.

"Mike Black."

And just like that he was gone.

I kept looking toward the VIP room where the real money was. I knew it was time for Miss Kitty to take the stage. I looked around at the tired-ass dancers who didn't make it into the VIP room and knew I'd have the room chanting my name again soon enough.

When I got on stage, I went into my act. As I was gyrating

my hips, I did a split. When I eased out of it was when I noticed him.

The One himself.

He was walking out of the men's room, flanked by two men. When his eyes caught mine, I took my nipple between my teeth and bounced up and down allowing the tassels on my crotch to touch the floor. He stopped cold in his tracks.

Bills started raining down on me. When I twirled around on my ass and brought my thighs up and did a split in midair, I heard them yelling.

"Goddamn girl!" someone cried.

"Work that shit!" another one said.

I danced like there might not be a tomorrow, and at every turn, his eyes were on me. Before it was over, he was at the edge of the stage, his bodyguards right at his side.

When I crawled to him, he plucked five crisp 100-dollar bills from his wad and held them out for me. He leaned over and whispered in my ear. "You come to VIP with me and my boy Bullet here," he demanded.

I allowed him to put the bills into my thong then shook my head. "Nah, baby, I've got work to do," I said, shaking my hips and wiggling away from him. When I finished my set, he was still standing there staring at my every move. The One went back in the VIP room, while I was picking up my money and cursing myself for not jumpin' at his offer. I was doin' all right controlling the floor, but I knew that The One was in there with a select group, and that's where I belonged. With the real money!

Later that night, I walked out of the dressing room and bumped right into The One's bodyguard. He was massive, a six-feet-four-inch tower, who looked down at me and said, "The One wants you in the VIP."

"And what are you, his mouthpiece?" I asked.

"He told me to bring you," he confirmed.

Since that's where I wanted to be anyway, I followed Bullet to the VIP room, without another word passing between us. When I walked through the door, Crème and the other dancers that were in there rolled their eyes at me and continued what they doin'. They knew what my presence in the room meant. And when Bullet walked me over to The One and he pulled me onto his lap, you woulda thought I'd slapped their mothers.

"You a bad muthafucka, you know that?"

"Thank you," I purred modestly.

"I was watchin' you move on the stage."

"I know, and thank you, for the tips," I said and ran my hand across his chest. "Do you want me to dance for you?"

"I wanna fuck you," he demanded more than asked.

I was shocked, but at the same time, not at all surprised at his directness. "It'll cost you," I said.

"You ain't said shit to me, mommy," he said sucking his grill. "Why don't I double what you usually charge? I always gets what I want."

I looked at him, studying him.

The One was fine as hell, but since I wasn't plannin' on fuckin' him, or anybody else in there, I decided to get ridiculous. "Two grand," I said quickly, thinking that his reaction would be the same as everybody else. I thought that he would say I was crazy, and have Bullet drag me outta there.

"Why don't we make it three," he said with ease.

My eyes lit up. *He can't be serious*, I thought. He just couldn't be. When he started ripping bills from the most massive wad of cash I'd ever seen, I knew The One was no joke. At that moment, I had to make a choice. *Three grand just to fuck him.* I thought about all the shit I talked to the other dancers about doin' exactly what I was thinking about doing. I'd taken pride in the fact that I wasn't that kind of woman. They were lettin' those drunk-ass niggas have them cheap. I wasn't goin' out like that. I was a dancer, an entertainer, not a ho.

"So, what's it gonna be, mommy?"

*Three grand.* I nodded my head slowly, and began eating my words.

"Get your shit then, we outta here," The One said and nodded at Bullet. He stood up and escorted me to the dressing room and waited outside like a sentry, while I got dressed. Thinking that I could still change my mind and tell Bullet to tell The One, *thanks, but no thanks. Miss Kitty don't roll like that.* I took a swallow of Henny and knew that wasn't gonna happen.

As I got ready to walk out, Crème burst through the door. "Where you goin'?" But before I could answer she said, "You ain't slick, bitch, I saw Bullet's big ass standing outside the door." She leaned close to me and whispered, "You gonna fuck The One."

"For three grand," I whispered back.

Crème didn't say a word. She just held up her hand for a high five, and I was on my way.

We took his Hummer limo to his hotel, where he took me up to a plush suite. I swear I felt just like Julia Roberts in *Pretty Woman.*

He ushered me into the room while he stood in the hallway talkin' with Bullet and some of the other members of his entourage. I eased into the bedroom and prepared myself for his arrival.

Knowing how guys like to talk and brag about their conquests, I knew I'd have some time. I had never done anything like this before and I never thought that I would find myself in a situation like this. To this point, all of my sexual experiences have been with only three guys. Two of them, Dwayne and Thomas were boyfriends, and this guy named Roy. I met him a couple of years ago and we'd been fuckin' ever since. We don't have a relationship, I mean we don't go anywhere or do anything, he just comes by when I call him and he takes care of my needs. The whole idea of doing it for money was completely foreign to me, not to mention something that I had promised myself that I would never do. But when he said he would pay me three thousand dollars just to have sex with him, I couldn't refuse.

I was determined to make sure he knew that I'd definitely be worth his cash. I selected a little black and lacy number and positioned myself on the bed, but I knew that I wouldn't be there for long. The moment he walked through the bedroom door I was all over The One.

"Damn girl, you vicious, huh?"

"You just don't even understand just how vicious I am. But you will, I promise you that." I had his clothes off in no time and was ready to rock his world.

The One laid out on the bed. "Come here," he demanded and I quickly complied.

He was very well-endowed, but I didn't hesitate to climb on for the ride. I put my hands on his chest, grabbed hold of his dick, and slid down on him.

"You like Miss Kitty?"

He was so deep inside me I swear he was poking my womb. The One was that and then some—massive, thick, and long.

"Shit! Take this dick, bitch. You want it, take it," he encouraged.

And I was definitely trying to take it all. I leaned forward, placing my weight on my arms and pounded him. "That's right, bitch! Throw the fat, juicy pussy, bitch!"

I wasn't real happy about him callin' me a bitch, but he was paying well for the privilege, so he could call me whatever he wanted to. I rotated my hips, grinding my pelvic area onto him until I was certain he couldn't go any deeper.

"Damn, bitch!" he yelled. "Get that dick!"

I leaned forward allowing my nipples to graze his face. He tried to shove both of them in his mouth. "Yeah, you know what I want. Do that shit."

I pumped harder.

I could see the look come over his face. "Oh shit!" he cried out.

I pumped harder.

"Damn, I'm about to bust."

It had been a long time since I had any dick, and even longer since I had one this big and I wanted to make it last. But when I tried to move he grabbed my hips, pulled me closer and started pumpin' that big dick like there was no tomorrow. I felt him expand and explode inside me. I wasn't even close to cummin'. He had been beating up my walls, but he hadn't quite hit my spot. But for three grand, I felt like we could go several more rounds at least.

The One, the only name I got from him, released a gut-wrenching grunt and suddenly shoved me off his body. "Watch out, I gotta piss," he said. I wanted to protest, remind him that I hadn't gotten my fill, but the thought of the three grand made me think better of it.

When he didn't come back to bed right away, I thought about checking on him, and then decided against that too. Finally, he stumbled out of the bathroom, wearing a pair of boxers and a massive platinum iced-out chain.

"Yo, look, you was tight and shit, but I'ma have Bullet take you down to the lobby."

That caught me completely off guard. "Um?" I said, once again stunned by his directness. But I wasn't about to say anything.

"Um, sure, I can see myself out."

"Whatever. He's gonna take care of you. Cool?"

"That's cool."

The One went back in the bathroom and closed the door behind him.

*Whatever.* I shrugged my shoulders and got out of the bed. While I got dressed, I wondered if maybe he was a little embarrassed because I'd made him cum so quick.

Bullet was standing by in the hall. He counted off three thousand dollars and handed it to me. I quickly shoved it in my bag and gave him a half-ass salute letting him know I could handle it.

"Later," he said, then turned and stumbled down the hall.

As I made my way to the elevator, I felt used, probably because I had been used. I don't know what I was expecting to happen in there, but it wasn't to get humped, dumped, and asked to leave. I stepped onto the elevator, smiling inside at the grip I'd made in less than five minutes and I wondered who really used who. I began to think about how easy that actually was, as opposed to what I was doing dancing at the club. If I busted my ass and hustled all night, I mean really went cutthroat, I could make a grand, maybe more on a good night. But I made three times that amount and barely broke a sweat.

When the elevator stopped on the twenty-sixth floor, I wondered who the hell was going somewhere at six-thirty in the morning.

The doors opened and a curvy white woman stepped into the elevator. Her hair looked a little rustled and her makeup was smeared a bit, but she still looked classy.

"How are you?" she asked, like she was simply being polite and didn't really care that it was two minutes before dawn.

"Oh, I'm good," I yawned, "and you?"

"You sound a bit tired like me." She flashed a fabulous smile and yawned herself. "Those are very contagious, you know," she yawned again.

"My name is Sasha," she extended her hand. "Sasha De-verox."

I reached for hers. "Jada West."

She tossed me a knowing look then snickered. "Are you here doin' what I think you're doing?"

"It depends," I said, really curious about what she meant.

She looked around as if we weren't alone on the elevator. Then she leaned in toward me. "I mean who do you work for? Which service?" Sasha wanted to know.

I was really confused, but I needed to know just what Sasha was talking about. She was iced from her ears to her chest and her fingers. I noticed a thick diamond tennis bracelet dangling from her arm when we shook hands.

"Why? Do I look like someone you know?" I asked stalling, but hoping for more information.

"Yeah, as a matter of fact, you do. But I know she got out of the business a long while back. A shame too, 'cause she used to make serious money. She's the one who encouraged me to go out on my own," Sasha confirmed.

My interest was very piqued at this point. She didn't look like a dancer, she had this air of elegance about her that told me she was clocking some serious dough, and if she was shaking her ass to earn it, she was doing some type of private shit.

"Well, how's it been on your own?" I asked, still fishing.

"It was rough at first, but once I built up my clientele, it's been paradise ever since," she said, smiling again.

"Your clientele, huh?"

"Best part is I don't have to worry about splitting my fees. Of course, I don't tell the client I'm an independent contractor. It seems like they just feel better thinking you're part of a service; you know, a real escort service," Sasha said easily.

My mouth dropped, but in my mind, I knew Sasha was somebody I needed to get to know better. I looked at Sasha,

*Roy Glenn*

the way she was dressed, the way she carried herself, and I knew this was a much better hustle than stripping. I would make it my business to find out all I could about the escort business. Sasha didn't know it, but she was about to take me to the next level and hopefully to riches beyond my wildest dream. And my dreams were pretty wild.

# Chapter 5

Two weeks after we met in the elevator in those wee morning hours, I sat across from Sasha at the trendy and upscale Feleani's Chateau on south Broadway.

"I could tell when I first saw you that you weren't in the business," she said.

I let out a little giggle. "Was I that obvious?"

"Yes," Sasha reluctantly admitted. "But I knew that you needed to be."

"It was my first time," I reluctantly admitted.

"What do you do?" Sasha smiled. "I mean before your first time."

"I dance at a club called Ecstasy."

"Everybody got to start somewhere." Once we ordered our meal, Sasha got down to business. "So, like I told you over the phone, what I do can be very lucrative. It's just a matter of knowing how to handle yourself in every situation."

Sasha offered to let me work under her until I felt comfortable going out on my own. Sasha was very big on independence, and I liked that about her. She had convinced me it was best that way. Under Sasha's tutelage I leaned how to walk and talk like a lady. There were days when I felt like I was Eliza Doolittle and Sasha was Henry Higgins in *My Fair Lady.*

Sasha and I had spent weeks "fixing" my wardrobe. "I don't mean to criticize, but what you wear is too—too ghetto for what we do, honey," Sasha criticized as she went through my closet. "This stuff may be all right for the club, but the look you're going for is elegant and classy." I already had compiled a stash of sexy lingerie, so that wasn't going to be an issue. But I swear, it was like the woman had a line of credit at all of the most exclusive boutiques. For a while after I hooked up with Sasha, I still danced at the club so I had money to reinvent myself.

Once Sasha felt that I was ready to be seen in public with her, she encouraged me to quit dancing so she could introduce me to the world. We went to executive networking events, exclusive VIP mixers, and just about every high roller's private party there was. It amazed me to see just how many people she knew.

Sasha had discreet and elegant business cards. I noticed when Sasha attended these events she was often friendly, but never a chatterbox. She'd carefully scrutinize all of the men who were present, especially those with dates. By the end of the night, she would have distributed a small and select number of her cards. I really liked the way she operated. If the men were loud and flashy, drunk or obnoxious, she avoided them. Sasha had a good nose for money, and oftentimes it was the quiet and laid-back ones who were her ideal targets, and they usually paid off.

We'd spotted a couple of celebrities and I remembered feeling like I wanted so desperately to be a part of Sasha's world. We'd talked for hours about the ins and outs of the "biz," as she called it.

It would take about a month before I felt completely comfortable with the idea of sleeping with men for money. Even though I had already done it, the idea was still somewhat foreign to me. I gave some thought to how I'd been livin' for the past year. None of this was part of my great plan. Well, almost none of it. I had always planned on makin' this kind of paper, just not like this.

One Friday afternoon, I had just finished a mud bath at a spa Sasha recommended when I got her call. She informed me that Douglas, no last name provided, was in a pinch and needed a date for an exclusive event.

Once I agreed, she informed me that I should check into the Peninsula Hotel on Fifth. Douglas would be picking me up at the hotel room. I chose a carmel-colored Chanel skirt suit with soft, camel leather sling backs, and a matching Chanel evening bag. Sasha had warned me to dress tastefully when I checked into the room.

When I walked into the grand lobby of the Peninsula Hotel, it was like stepping into Wonderland. A cascading staircase that forked into two directions took center stage in the massive lobby. I stepped to the right and went to the front desk. "Good evening, madam," the clerk greeted.

"Ms. Green," I said like Sasha instructed. "I have a reservation."

He checked his screen, then looked up at me and smiled. "Of course, here's your key card. Will you be needing help with luggage?"

"I've got it, thanks," I said as I took the card and headed toward the bank of elevators. I stepped off the elevator and into the deluxe suite. It was a one-bedroom corner suite with a glorious view. I opened one set of French doors that led to a terrace. I looked over the rail and felt my stomach nearly give way when I looked down.

The room was luxuriously furnished in earth tones and neutral colors. There was a decorative fireplace and even walk-in closets. I marveled at the separate dressing area with its own vanity, and a separate guest bathroom. The room had a stereo system with a CD player, and the master bathroom had double sinks with a television mounted over the bathtub.

Maybe thirty minutes after I was relaxing in the California king-sized bed, there was a knock at the door.

"Shit!" I bolted upright in the bed. I looked at the clock wondering if I could've misunderstood about Douglas's pickup time.

"Ah, who is it?"

"Room service," the cheerful voice called back.

I jumped up, a bit confused. "Room service?"

"Yes, ma'am. Compliments of Ms. Deverox," he answered.

I rushed to the door and pulled it open. When I did, the bell-man wheeled in a silver cart, like they do in the movies.

"Fresh strawberries with melted chocolate, and a bottle of Moët," he announced in a grand way.

"Oh, wow," I said as I searched the room for my purse.

I slipped him a ten-dollar bill and giggled as he closed the door behind himself.

"Shit, I could really get used to living lovely like this!" I plucked one of the juiciest looking strawberries and dipped it into the bowl of melted chocolate. I bit into it and savored the flavor.

An hour later, I stumbled over to the bed. I had indulged in too much champagne, and I knew I needed to pull myself together before Douglas arrived. I was glad Sasha suggested the earlier check-in.

By the time Douglas knocked on the door, I was still hanging on to a nice little buzz. I leaned against the open door wearing a simple but elegant Donna Karan silk slip dress. The fine fabric felt so good against my skin.

Douglas was a big man, with great taste in clothes. He was wearing a tailored tuxedo that looked like it may have been made specifically for his body. "You must be Stacy," he said.

I thought about correcting him, but I wasn't sure what

Sasha had told him, so I figured I'd be Stacy tonight. "And you must be Douglas. Please, come in," I said and I moved to the side so he could come into the room. He looked around and I could tell he was impressed.

"Ah, this is nice," he said, as his eyes rolled over my body. "Real nice," he added.

"So where are we going tonight?" I asked.

"Excuse me?" he asked looking a little confused.

"I was asking where we were going tonight?" I repeated. "I was under the impression that we were going out for the evening."

"Oh, that stuffy affair," Douglas said and took a seat in a chair by the window. "I showed my face and snuck out to see you," he said. His pudgy cheeks broke into deep-set dimples when he smiled.

"Oh?" I wasn't sure what to say or do.

He used thick fingers to tug at his bow tie. In my mind I had prepared myself for polite conversation over a nice meal at his stuffy affair, maybe even some dancing. I thought I'd have enough time to think through what I had to do and get myself motivated over drinks. But Douglas made it clear the only thing he had on his mind was getting me out of the dress as quickly as possible.

I looked at Douglas again. Although his clothes fit him well, Douglas was shaped like a pear. He wasn't exactly the type of man that I found particularly attractive. But that was something I would have to get used to if I wanted to get paid in this business. I thought back to my experience with The One. Being with him was easy because he was fine as hell. This was going to be a bit harder.

I started thinking about the kind of man I wished Douglas was, and that's when I noticed I was getting wet. Visions of being loved by my faceless man flashed through my head, and I zoned Douglas completely out.

"So, what'd you think about that?"

I snapped out of my wishful thinking and shook my head. "I'm sorry, what did you say?"

"I said, you should come over and sit on my face so I can suck you dry," he repeated without as much as a flinch or stutter.

I hesitated.

"Oh." He held up one of his fat fingers. Douglas peeled his jacket off, quickly unbuttoned his shirt, and stepped out of his wingtipped shoes. He then dug into his pocket and pulled out a wad of cash I hadn't seen since my nights at the club.

He quickly peeled off several bills and held them out toward me. "I guess once we get this out of the way, we can get down to business."

I looked at the cash then up at him.

"I know this isn't a freebie, so let's cut the theatrics and get to it," he said in a cold no-nonsense fashion.

I took the bills from his hand, careful not to snatch them and placed them on a nearby table. I fought the urge to count as I turned and tried to lead him into the bedroom.

"Where are you going?" he asked.

"I thought you wanted me in the room," I offered.

He held out his hand, "Nah," he shook his head and extended his arms to me. "Why don't you come over here?"

The instant I walked over to Douglas, he snatched up my dress, ripped off my panties, bent me over the edge of the couch and was about to ram himself into me when I said, "condom."

"Oh, yeah," he said and did what amounted to a giggle.

By the time I got the condom out of its package, Douglas's dick was hard and his pants were down around his ankles. Once I got the condom on him there was no caressing, no gentle touching, or foreplay. Douglas spun me around, bent me over the edge of the couch again, and rammed himself into me. He banged me like he had something on his mind and the work he put in with me might help make things better.

When Douglas grabbed the back of my hair and slammed himself into me deeper, I wanted to howl out in pain, but I bit my lip and dug into the sofa's upholstery.

"Emmm, you are gorgeous!" he squealed. He grabbed my waist, holding me in place before slamming into me again. After the sofa, Douglas took me on the coffee table, a nearby sofa table with my leg hitched up on one side and then again on the floor.

When we were done, I thought he might want to relax on the bed and catch his breath, but he didn't. I watched as he picked up his discarded clothes and went in search of the restroom. Ten minutes later, a fully dressed Douglas was standing in front of me. "I like you. Tell Sasha, we need to see each other again," he said.

Before I could think of what else to say, he was gone. I picked up the money he had given me and counted it. My fee was 1500 dollars. I counted it again and realized there was an extra 300 dollars there. I saw that as a bonus Sasha didn't need to know about. She and I had worked out a deal. My fee for use of her connections was 25 percent, until she thought I was ready to do my own thing.

Sasha had two hotels we used for our business. And it was simple really. I'd go to the Peninsula about twice a month, and that was always my favorite. In the past six months, I had seen Douglas twice since our last encounter. During that time I was starting to get the hang of things. I knew what to expect in most, if not all, situations and was very comfortable with myself and what I was doing.

I was at home one afternoon when my BlackBerry rang. I reached for it and answered without checking caller ID. It was Diane. I hadn't seen or talked to her since I stopped working at the club. She and I tried to keep in touch with one another, but we had been playing phone tag for months.

"Well it's about damn time you actually answered the fuckin' phone. A bitch been tryin' to call your ass for mo-than-a-minute," Diane's voice rang out in my ear.

"I swear I was just gonna call you," I quickly defended.

"Yeah, yeah, whatever, bitch. What's been up wit' you?"

"Nothing much."

"Cut the bullshit, Jada. Crème told me she saw you pushin' a new big-body Benz. Bitch, I need to know what you been doin'! And let's not even talk 'bout how your ass just bounced and been MIA for months now!" she hollered.

"I know, I know," I said.

"You know my nosy ass, I gots to know what the fuck is up wit all that. I wanna know what you been up to. I mean, you hit the numbers or something?" she asked bringing back memories of a similar conversation I had had with her.

My other cell rang and I checked to see Sasha's number flashing across the screen. "Dee, I need to grab that, but I swear we'll get together soon. I promise," I said wanting her to hurry and hang up, because Sasha was calling with information for my appointment for the evening.

"If you don't call me back, I swear-fo'-god, bitch, I'ma hunt your ass down like a runaway slave," she testified.

"Dee, I'm gonna call you back, I swear!"

My heart was racing at the thought of missing Sasha's call, but luckily, Diane let me go. "Hey, Sasha," I said.

"Randolph is meeting you at the Peninsula at nine," she said.

"Are we going out?"

"No, he wants a romantic evening in. He mentioned something about pay-per-view movies in the room and all. Oh, he wants you in a teddy and high-heeled slippers," she informed me.

"Okay, cool."

"Remember, ease up on the slang. Remember, classy and

elegant, not ghetto and fabulous," she warned before hanging up. I had already learned a lot from her.

Six months after that, I felt I had a nice little list of my own clientele. Sasha and I had agreed when the time came for me to venture out on my own; we'd talk about it so there wouldn't be any kind of hard feelings. That talk was to take place at the Pen-Top Bar & Terrace inside the Peninsula Hotel.

When Sasha arrived, we ordered drinks and some food. I had marinated shrimp cocktail with Marie Rose sauce, while Sasha ordered sushi and sashimi with wasabi, pickled ginger and soy sauce. "How'd it go last night?" she asked, sipping a the Blue Crystal, a drink made with Beefeater gin, triple sec, and a splash of blue Curaçao. I had a white chocolate martini, made with Absolut vanilla, Godiva white chocolate liqueur, and cream.

"Everything went fine," I said and discreetly handed Sasha her cut of my money for the last time.

Sasha took the money and put it in her purse before taking a sip of her drink. "You know I just absolutely love the view from up here," she said.

"I know what you mean. It makes me feel like I'm on top of the world," I said.

Sasha folded her hand in a very ladylike way in front of her and looked at me. "So, Jada, tell me what you wanted to talk to me about."

"Well—Sasha—I umm—"

"Don't tell, let me guess. You think you're ready to fly solo. Is that what you think you wanna tell me?"

Her attitude caught me a little off guard. I had known Sasha for almost a year and in all that time, she had never copped the kind of attitude that she was throwing off now. But I never had to tell her that the envelope I'd just handed her would be her last. I had become a good earner for her. Most weeks I'd give her no less than 2500 dollars, and all she had to do for it was pick up the phone. On top of that, my company was requested quite frequently and by some of her better clients. Some of which I planned on taking with me.

"I think I'm ready. No, I know I'm ready."

Sasha laughed at me and I wanted to kick her ass over it, but I did business regularly at this hotel, so I kept my cool.

"Look at you, Jada. All dressed up tryin' to be a lady." Sasha took a sip of her drink. "Do you remember who you were when I met you?"

"Yeah, I remember." Now it was me that had the attitude.

"You couldn't talk, you could barely walk without falling on your face, and you definitely had the most ghetto taste in clothes."

This bitch was one insult away from getting this white chocolate martini thrown in her face.

"I made you," Sasha leaned forward and said sternly. "It was me who taught you how to walk without falling. How to talk without having to end every sentence with a curse. And it was me who taught you how to dress like a lady. I taught you all those things. If it wasn't for me, you'd still be shakin' your ass at that dive. I made you, Jada," she said again, but this time she stuck her finger in my face. "Never forget that."

"No, Sasha," I said to her. "I won't forget any of that."

I was on fire, my eyes were squinted, my teeth were grinding together and my fists were balled. I seriously wanted to punch Sasha in the mouth. Although I hated to admit it, Sasha was absolutely right about me. When I met her, I was just a ghetto shake dancer. It was just the nasty way she said it that was pissin' me off.

Then Sasha smiled. "Stop looking like that." Her smile turned into laughter. "I was just playing with you."

"You sure?" I asked, but I was still hot.

"Yes, silly." Sasha laughed and ate some of her sushi. "Had you going for a second there, didn't I?"

"I was about to start acting very unlady like." I laughed and tried to relax.

"Listen honey, I am so proud of you and the way you handle yourself now. Jada, you have come so far. You've been ready to fly solo for a long time."

"Really?" I questioned with childlike wonder.

"Of course you have. But I figured that if you wanted to keep giving me your money that it would be rude of me not to accept."

"And you know a lady is never rude," we both said almost in unison.

I was glad to go with Sasha's blessings. Working with and studying Sasha taught me one thing. She was on top, in charge, the boss and I worked for her. I walked the way that she did, talked the way she told me to talk and I dressed and conducted myself the way she said a lady should.

Sasha was my madam, even though I hate the word, she was my pimp. That's where the money was, not laying on my back with my legs in the air. I was ready to leave Sasha all right, but I wasn't going solo. I was giving Sasha two, sometimes three grand a week. If I were to get a couple of girls working for me, I could pull in five, six grand a week and whatever I made would be gravy. In the New World, I would be on top, 'cause that's where the money was.

And you know, I was all about the money.

# Chapter 6

I looked around my new spacious two-bedroom apartment and marveled at how far I had come. I had a nice new luxury car, a large apartment, the finest clothes and tons of money in the bank, maybe not tons, but more than I've ever had in my life. I was finally living the good life.

I strolled over to my dining room table and glanced at the pictures I had laid out. Each one was personally selected to get started. And while I figured that one other person and myself would be good, I liked each one of them, and I couldn't choose, so I decided to keep them all. Diane was the only one I was iffy about, because she was straight ghetto. I was sure that Diane wasn't ready to work with the kind of exclusive clientele I was working with. "Come on, Jada," Diane pleaded when she arrived at my apartment. "I could be a good fuckin' ho for you," she said and laughed.

"That's just it, Diane, I'm not looking for hoes. I'm targeting a more upscale clientele," I told her.

"Come on, Jada. I'm tired of dancin' every fuckin' night. And I'm so fuckin' tired of them scandalous-ass bitches. Shit, if could make three times that layin' on my back, come on, Jada, you gots to count a bitch in."

"And that another thing, Dee."

"What?"

"You curse too much," I said.

"What about it?"

"It's not very ladylike," I said.

Diane looked at the expression on my face. Then she looked me up and down. "Look Jada. Don't think I ain't been checkin' you out. You changed."

"I have changed, Diane. But that's how—" I started but Diane stopped me.

"Like I said, the way you talk and shit. You even walk different, don't be lookin' like you 'bout to fall all the damn time." Diane smiled and I did too. "You know, I been seein', you know, how you dressin' these days and how you carry it and shit, and I'm like yeah, Jada, you doin' it. So, if that's what it take then you got to teach me to be like you."

"We'll give it a shot and see how it goes," I said quietly.

Diane gave me a hug. "You watch, Jada, I'll be the best ho—I mean escort you ever seen."

The ringing phone broke up our moment. It was the doorman.

"You have visitors. A Miss Bella and Miss Simone," he announced.

The minute I first laid eyes on Bella and Simone, I began thinking about all the money I could make by investing in these two beauties. "Yes, Alfred. Please send them both right up." I quickly gathered the pictures and placed them in the folder I had nearby.

When I opened the door, Bella strolled in. She was a caramel-skinned beauty with long curly hair, wicked curves, full breasts, and a smile that lit up the room. We met one morning when I was coming in from an appointment. "Excuse me," Bella had said that morning.

I turned to verify she was talking to me. "I think you dropped this," she said holding up a tube of M·A·C's lip gloss.

"Damn!" I squealed. "Thanks, honey. I lose these things like they're free," I said.

When she smiled, I was like, whoa! "You live around here?" I asked.

She shrugged. "I wish. I was actually trying to meet a friend, but I got lost," she said.

We grabbed coffee at a nearby Starbucks where she poured out her life story. Bella told me how miserable her life was. She was on the outs with her very repressive parents and had been going from one bad job to no job at all and desperately in need of money. But what I saw in her was spirit. I found her to be a quiet and easygoing young woman with an almost childlike enthusiasm for life. Bella was the kind of person who sought variety in what she did. Bella also told me she had tried to be a dancer, but didn't go back after she slipped and fell from the stage. "I figured that was a sign that I needed to find a new way to make some extra cash," she had giggled.

My other selection was Simone. She too had a sad tale to tell about how she desperately needed money. Simone was tall and thin. She was flat-chested, but looked like she was gliding instead of walking. Simone had a short Halle Berry–type haircut, light eyes, and smooth skin. Simone was a stunner who had raw sex appeal and determination. I met her working in one of the boutiques I had frequented with Sasha. She was frustrated after a rude customer had ripped her a new one over not being able to return a gown that had been visibly worn. When the customer stormed out of the shop, I heard her sigh. "I don't know how much longer I can take this shit," she had hissed.

I walked over and looked around to make sure her manager was nowhere in sight.

"You could probably make a substantial amount of money if you just used some of your other assets," I said.

Her eyebrow crept upward, but she didn't dismiss me right away.

"You a headhunter or something?" she wanted to know.

"I'm not. I'm what you can call an entrepreneur. You're not afraid to make a little cash and have some fun while you're at it, are you?"

"I don't sell or do drugs," she said.

"I understand." I slipped her my business card then slid the stack of crisp 100-dollar bills toward her.

She looked at the money then up at me.

"When can we get together?" she asked.

Once everybody had a drink and made themselves comfortable, I explained what we were going to do and how we were going to do it. "The most important thing that I'm going to teach you is how to conduct yourselves in a ladylike manner in every situation. Elegant and classy, ladies, that is who you are at all times." I stood up and moved to the middle of the living room. "I'm going to teach you how to walk, how to talk." I looked at Diane and she rolled her eyes. "And how to dress and how to conduct yourself at any occasion. Knowing what to say and what not to say, will make your company more desirable and therefore requested on a regular basis.

"Now I've been thinking a lot about this and I realized that Sasha will be working all the CEOs, CFOs, and other suits. Wealthy people that are discreet with their money. They don't have anything to prove to anybody."

"That's old money," Simone said.

"Old money is good money," Diane added.

"True. Old money is good money, but," I said and paused to emphasize my point, "those people are used to having it and know what to do with it."

"So, what you talkin' 'bout us doin'?" Diane asked.

I wanted to make Diane repeat that sentence in proper English, but we'd have plenty of time for that. "Our plan doesn't involve targeting her rich crowd. We're going to leave those clients to Sasha. She has both a knack and a nose for them." I also knew I'd be creating bad blood by going after Sasha's established clientele. Especially if I didn't have to. "Our target group is going to be the new rich. The ones who just stumbled into money. The ones who don't quite know how to act now that they have it."

"Ballers," Diane said.

"I'm talking about music industry insiders, rappers, producers, actors, and movie and television producers and of course, ballers. Now, unfortunately, people like that don't attend the kind of mixer and events that Sasha's crowd go to. But they do have their own functions and that's where we'll target them."

"Sounds like a plan to me," Bella chimed in quickly.

I fronted them five grand each to let them know I was serious about business. It was like a signing bonus. The ladies and I had spent the next month or so getting to know each other. Bella, Simone, and Diane had spent many nights at my place during our late-night bonding session that lasted well into the early morning hours.

Sasha and I still met once every couple of weeks, to catch up, but for the most part I was either shopping, which the ladies all excelled at, or hanging out with one or all of the ladies. In my mind these little outings were all training sessions.

After one of many shopping trips, I walked in the bedroom while Bella was on the phone. "Well, if that's how you feel about me now, I guess I have no choice but to make it on my own," I heard her say into the phone before sniffling. Before I could tell what was going on, Simone came rushing out of the bathroom with a wad of tissue.

That's when I realized Bella had been crying. She turned and I noticed her bloodshot eyes.

"What's wrong with her?" I whispered to Simone.

She walked over to me, leaned in then whispered, "She's been fighting with her family for nearly an hour now, something about them not wanting her back home."

"But I—" Bella managed before breaking down and sobbing again.

I looked over at Bella who was crumbling on the phone. I walked over and slowly removed the receiver from her shaking hand. I placed it back into its cradle and took her into my arms.

"My mother called me a streetwalker," she sobbed onto my chest. "She said she never wants to see me again," she added.

I rubbed her back. "We're your family now, don't worry about it," I told her.

"Her parents are devoted Jehovah's Witnesses, you know, like they go door to door, and all," Simone said.

"I just didn't want to follow the faith," Bella said.

I stroked her back. "Don't worry about it. Like I said, we're your family now." By the time I looked up, Diane had walked into the room. I didn't know how much she had heard, but I could tell by the look on her face that she agreed with my statement.

"If your parents don't want you because you don't want to go door to door, you ain't ever gotta worry about them again," Diane said walking over to us.

Bella finally pulled back and looked up at me.

"I'm so sorry," she sobbed.

I looked at her, moved hair from her face then said, "That's what I'm trying to tell you. You have nothing to be sorry about." I looked around the room. "I know everyone here agrees, we don't ever have to worry about feeling left out, or like we don't belong; by the time we're done, we'll rule this town." For the first time since I walked into the room I realized that we were at a turning point in our relationship. If things went the way I planned, our little close-knit family would be unstoppable.

"Thank you, Jada," Bella said sniffling. She turned away from my embrace, "Thank you all," she added. We enveloped her in a group hug and laughed at ourselves for being so emotional.

# Chapter 7

Two months into my self-employment gig and business was very slow. As a matter of fact, business was a bit too slow. We were for the most part, living on my back. I still had my regular clients. When I had an appointment, or when the client would allow it, I would send Bella or Simone. Diane was still a little too ghetto for prime time, but she was working hard. I had thought about doing some work for Sasha, until she informed me since I was now the competition that her fee had increased to 51 percent. "It's just business, sweetie," she said, then sipped her mimosa.

I couldn't fault her, but talking with her gave me an idea. Working with Sasha business was steady, because of her clientele and connections. But now that I was on my own, maybe I needed a different approach.

"So what's up, Jada?" Bella asked.

"Yeah, when do we get to see some real money?" Simone had asked.

"I've got an idea," I said, shedding thoughts of Sasha from my mind. "

I think we need to go out and see if we can drum up some business."

Bella had a worried look across her face, but it was Simone who fired questions at me.

"Drum up business? Why? I thought you had that all under control, you mean we gotta go out and get the johns?" She sucked her teeth.

"Okay, first off, these are not johns, these are very important clients who are a bit lonely and are willing to pay for the company of an attractive lady," I corrected.

"Whatever," Simone snapped.

"I think what she means is, we thought things were a bit more organized and set up already," Bella informed me. "I didn't think we'd actually go out there and have to get our own clients."

Simone jumped up. "I don't know about this," she said.

"I thought you guys were ready to make some paper. I guess I was mistaken," I said, shrugging.

"Yeah, but I ain't about to go on the stroll," Simone said, and smacked her lips.

"Nobody's asking you to go on the stroll. All I'm saying is, right now my client list isn't enough to sustain us all, and I don't think it would hurt to do some networking at some exclusive events."

"So how do we get ourselves invited to these exclusive events?" Simone asked.

"I know exactly where we'll start."

"Where?

"Sensations."

Sensations was a nightclub frequented by our target clientele. My plan was a simple one.

Advertise.

If you have a product, and you wanted to get maximum product recognition with your target group, you have to advertise. Get that product out in front of your target group. Once a week, we would go to Sensations.

"Are you guys gonna trust me or what?" I needed to know. "I'm telling you, we're doing the right thing."

Simone was a bit reluctant, but after some convincing, quite a bit, actually, she agreed. Once I had Simone, Bella fell right in line. By the time Diane arrived, it was agreed we'd go to Sensations the very next Friday night.

That night I realized that my new family had found their voice. Simone was by far the strongest personality of the three. Bella was soft as butter, and Diane was just glad to be down, so she went along with whatever everybody else was doing.

But not Simone, her favorite line was, "I don't understand this at all," she would say, laced with attitude. Which to me always meant that she wasn't with what I was sayin', and before we moved on, I needed to make it clear what we were talking about and more importantly, how it would benefit everybody. I knew that once I had Simone on my side it was over.

We spent the day shopping for that evening's attire. Simone chose a Nicole Miller stretch, satin-ruched slip dress with spaghetti straps. I couldn't really appreciate the straight neckline, but I did like the ruching at center bust and at the front and back bodice. When she first walked out of the fitting room, I wasn't sure I liked the dress.

"Work it, girl," Diane encouraged.

And when Simone worked it, it was like she gave the dress a life of its own.

"I think that's the one," I told her.

"You like it?" she asked Bella.

"It's nice, and obviously you know how to work it," she said excitedly.

With Simone out of the way, we turned our attention to finding just the right outfit for Bella. I was flipping through a nearby rack of dresses when my head snapped toward a squeal coming from Diane.

"Well, I'll be damned!"

I turned to see Bella strolling out in a bodysuit. But this wasn't just any bodysuit; it was a sleek one-piece that hugged her curves.

She strutted and ran her hands along the length of her body.

"I feel so sexy," she giggled. She spun, then struck a pose.

"Girl, you are too fierce in that getup," I said.

"You think I should get it, Jada? I mean, you don't think it's . . . I don't know . . ." she shrugged, "too much?"

"Too much?" I stepped a bit closer to her. "Girl, you look hot!"

"For real, with that outfit on, I just pray we'll be able to get some play up in the club standing next to you," Diane cosigned.

"Okay, if you guys like it, then I'll get it," she said before turning and rushing into the fitting room.

Once we piled into the car, Diane turned to me and said, "How come you didn't get anything?"

"Yeah," Bella added.

"Please, all the stuff I have in that closet, some of that shit still have tags dangling from them."

When Snoop's new cut came on, we all started rocking to the beat. All the while I thought about the black Just Cavalli satin bustier dress laced with leopard-print tie, it was just the right mixture of elegance and class, the perfect outfit for the queen bee. When I thought about it, I knew for sure that the night would belong to us.

Everyone agreed to meet at my place by seven. After I went over the plan again, we got dressed and were sipping champagne while we waited for the bewitching hour. Our game plan didn't involve going to the club to party, we were strictly there for business. I had put in a standing reservation for a limo to pick us up every Friday night at eleven o'clock sharp. We would arrive at the club and make our grand entrance at exactly midnight.

Knowing that the club would be crowded by the time we got there, I made arrangements with Sherman, the club's manager, to have one of the circular couches close to the VIP room to be reserved for us. "Money isn't an issue," I said when I talked to him over the phone.

"I think you and your party would be more comfortable in the VIP room," Sherman said.

"No, Sherman, but thank you. I'm sure we'll be just fine outside the VIP room."

When I got off the phone, naturally, Simone questioned my logic. "Why don't we wanna be in the VIP room?"

"Because all of our target market won't be in VIP room. We need to position ourselves where we would get the maximum exposure. The driver will be here soon," I said, as the clock got close to eleven. "Is everybody ready for this?"

"Shit, I been ready," Diane said quickly. "Let's do the damn thing. Oh, I mean, yes, Jada, I am ready to proceed to the club," she laughed at herself, as did everybody else.

"We're gonna take Sensations by storm, ladies. They're not ready for this," Bella added, standing up to do a model's runway turn.

"The world is ours!" Simone began shouting, and Diane and Bella joined in. I was so proud of them, especially Diane because she had worked so hard and came so far from where she was. The chant of *the world is ours* continued until the phone rang. "Quiet down, ladies," I said and answered the phone. "Yes, Alfred."

"Your driver is here," Alfred the doorman called to say.

"We'll be down in fifteen minutes."

While the ladies talked amongst themselves, I hung up the phone and slipped into the bathroom and took one final look. Once I was done, I joined my family. I stood in front of Diane until everyone was quiet. "What?" she asked.

"Let's do the damn thing."

When our stretch Chrysler 300 limo pulled up at the club's entrance, I noticed the stares from people in line. Some were blatantly staring, while others tried to act like the vehicle's sleek appearance was no big deal. We sat parked for at least ten minutes before the driver stepped out to get our door.

He opened the door and extended his hand to me. I accepted his hand, stepped out of the limo and struck a pose. I could hear the buzz of small talk from those who were in line. The driver held out his hand for Diane and she stood next to me. By the time Bella was out of the limo and standing next to Diane, I knew we had everyone's attention. When Simone got out and stood next to Bella, the only sound to be heard was coming from cars passing by.

I started walking toward the entrance, as planned. Diane walked next to me while Bella and Simone followed single file behind her. "Where they think they goin'?" I heard one woman say as we passed.

"I don't know, but they need to get their wannabe cute asses in the back of this line like everybody else," the woman in line with her said. That was exactly the response I was hoping for. I wanted to set the tone from the start. I wanted everybody to know that these ladies were special.

We walked right up to the door, where security removed the velvet rope and allowed us in without any questions. I could hear the mumbles as the door closed behind us.

"Can I help you, ladies?"

"Yes, I'm sure you can. My name is Jada West. I believe we have an area reserved for us?"

"Yes, Ms. West. We've been expecting you, and welcome to Sensations. A bottle of Moët is waiting at your table, compliments of the management," the hostess informed us.

"You ladies look so good tonight. It would be my honor to escort you through the crowd to your table," one of the club's security staff said with his eye on Simone.

"Thank you," I said.

"Why don't you ladies follow me?" he said and along with another member of security, escorted us to our table. The security escort wasn't planned, but I was gonna work it to our advantage.

Sensations was a very big club, with a huge dance floor, a big stage, and five bars. The VIP room was in the back of the club directly across from the stage, with a small staircase that led to the entrance. It was elevated so guests in the VIP could watch the show without having their view obstructed by the crowd.

As I expected, the club was packed. I was glad for the security escort, because had it not been for them clearing a path with flashlights, we would've never made it to our area. Not to mention, our entrance wouldn't have had the same impact. As we made our way through the crowd, I could see that we were getting a lot of attention from the men and quite a few women.

When we arrived at our couch, we found it had been roped off for us. I reached in my clutch, pulled out two 100-dollar bills. "Thank you for getting us here," I said and handed a bill to each of our escorts.

"You didn't have to do that," one said, but Bella had his attention.

"But thank you," the other said and practically snatched the bill out of my hand. He quickly rushed off and grabbed a waitress. "You take good care of my friends here."

Once they were gone, she popped the cork and poured each of us a glass. I raised my glass. "Well, ladies," I said over the music, "here's to us. The world is truly ours and tonight is just the beginning."

"Damn this is the bomb," Diane commented.

"I told you guys to have faith in me. I know what I'm doing," I said, relieved that it worked out that way.

A man walked up to the table and asked Simone if she wanted to dance. He was nicely dressed and kind of cute, but I could tell that he only had enough money in his wallet to buy somebody a few drinks. Maybe he could spring for breakfast after the club closed, but that would be a stretch. He wasn't even on my radar. In the short time we had been there, I had already scoped out a few targets.

Before she could answer, I spoke up. "No. She doesn't want to dance with you," I said with a smile.

He looked at me like I was crazy. "I wasn't talkin' to you."

"Yes you were."

"What about you?" he asked, thinking he'd get a different result from Bella.

"She doesn't want to dance with you either."

He looked at Diane, she held up her hand. "Don't even waste your time," Diane told him and he went away.

"Why does it seem like all the cuties are broke?" Bella asked.

"I know what you mean. It wasn't too long ago that I would've jumped up and been on the floor right now," Simone said with a smile as she watched him walk away. "I might have even given him some."

Diane laughed. "Jada's right. He's the type of guy that will try to keep you on the dance floor so he ain't gotta buy you no drink."

Finally, members of our prospective clientele started approaching us, and one at a time I allowed the ladies to dance, but we had a strict one-song limit. I put that rule in place for two reasons. First off, dancing was not what we were there for. Dancing makes you sweat. Sweat ruins your hair and suddenly your outfit doesn't look perfect anymore. I wanted them to look perfect. Perfect objects for the pleasure of man. Two, you give a wolf a taste, and then say "Thank you," and walk away with that "you know you want me" look in their eyes.

We weren't in the club for a good hour before I had spoken with several men who I knew from their conversation, would become my clients. There was Alex, the accountant. He couldn't get enough of Bella. Then there was a guy who introduced himself to me as T-Love. His ballin' ass was drippin' money. I knew that with her experience in dealing with guys like him, that Diane would be the one he wanted.

While the ladies were on the floor, I was giving bedroom eyes to some eye candy sitting across the room. I didn't know what he did, but I knew he was rich. He was iced out from the large diamond nuggets that hung from his ears, to the large diamond-studded bracelets on his wrist and the Presidente Rolex. He was drippin' money too, literally wearing his riches for us all to see.

Simone and Diane had just returned to the table when the waitress came over and leaned down toward me. "Compliments of the gentleman over there." She placed the standing ice bucket with a bottle of Cristal on ice near our table. Once the waitress had filled my glass, I glanced in his direction and raised it in acknowledgment of his gesture, but he was on his way over to me.

"So, whassup?" he asked.

"You," I said.

He looked at Simone then back at me. "You ladies mind if I join you?"

They both shook their heads.

"I was just about to use the ladies' room," Diane said as she stood, Simone followed.

"I like your style," he said. "You know, the way you carry it."

"Is that right?"

"So what's up with you? I ain't seen you here before," he said.

"Are you a regular or something? Keeping tabs on who comes and goes?" I inquired.

"Nah, I just recognize a dime piece when I see one," he countered.

"I understand," I said, but I wasn't getting a good vibe from this one. The way he was talking just didn't fit what he was wearing.

"Would you like to dance?"

"No. I don't dance," I replied coldly, as Bella came back and slid in next to me. He started to say something, but I cut him off. "I don't mean to be rude, but, I need to speak with my friend. I really appreciate the Cristal, but if you'd excuse us."

"I really did wanna talk to you."

"Do you have a card?"

He stood up and reached in his pocket, pulled out a solid gold card holder and handed me one. "I'll look forward to hearing from you," he said and walked away.

Once he was gone, Bella looked at me. "He was cute. What does he do?"

I looked at his card. "Investment banker," I told Bella. "But there's something about him that doesn't quite feel right. But I'll check him out."

By the time we left the club, I had a collection of business cards and phone numbers that I was confident would turn into money.

# Chapter 8

Since we began going to the club, business had picked up, and not a moment too soon as far as I was concerned. The club had become a mandatory event, unless you had an appointment, and had been every Friday night for the last three months, but it was starting to get old. Fact of the matter was, I was getting enough referral business from our clientele that we really didn't need to go there. But the ladies love it. It was the one night of the week they looked forward to. At first, I thought it was because it gave them a chance to be stars. "That's not it, Jada," Bella corrected. "It's because it's the only time that we all get together and hang out."

"Yeah," Diane added, "just hangin' together, you know, like we used to, shoppin' or whatever. But we were always together."

"Like a family, Jada. Ain't that what you used to call us? Well, that's what we are."

The limo picked us up at my apartment, we made our usual entrance, and we were escorted to what had become our spot at Sensations. That night the club was packed, more packed then usual. But as packed as it was that night, our usual targets didn't seem to be in the house. So I allowed

everybody to cut loose a bit, which meant doing more dancing and drinking than usual.

We had been there an hour and a half when I decided that
nothing was up for the night and Simone advanced the idea
that we go to another club. "You know, see what else is out
there."

"Yeah, I'm for that," Diane added. "Have some fun. I ain't
got drunk and wild in a minute."

Bella laughed. "Now you know any time you start drinkin',
you start lookin' for a woman to seduce."

We all laughed, but it was true. When she used to dance at
Ecstasy she'd get with a woman, but only if the price was
right. That was her policy until she ran up on this one client
that turned her out. After that, any time I ran up on a female
client, she belonged to Diane. "Keep talkin', Bella," Diane
threatened. "And I'll be suckin' on one of those fat, juicy nipples you got," she said and playfully reached for Bella.

"Back up off me. You know I'm in it strictly for the Ben-
jamins."

"I am too. So for you, I'll only charge you half price to suck
on those titties."

Just then, a commotion started not too far from us. The
next thing I knew there were shots fired and everybody
started running for the exit. Not wanting to get caught up in
the stampede, I ushered the ladies into the VIP room.

When things quieted down, I found out from one of the security staff that a man had been shot. It seemed that his
woman showed up at the club and caught him with another
woman. He told me that the police were in the club, and that
they wanted to ask everybody who was in or around the VIP
room some questions. "Questions? What kind of questions?"

"Don't worry, Ms. West. They wanna talk to everyone who
was in the VIP room at the time. Since you were sitting right
where it happened, they just want to know what you saw. No
big deal," he assured me. But I wasn't feelin' that at all. There

was no way I wanted to talk to the cops about a murder, or anything else for that matter. I looked at the ladies. Diane was borderline drunk, and Bella was just a little too easy to rattle. I knew I didn't want them talking to the cops either.

"You need to get us outta here," I said digging in my purse for some money to give him.

He looked around. "Okay, okay. Let me think for a minute."

"Well think fast," Simone told him and touched his face. She knew that he liked her and would do anything for her.

"I'll make like I'm takin' y'all to the bathroom and let you out the back door. But it would be better if you all didn't go at once." He grabbed Simone by the hand. "Come on, let's go."

"No," I said quickly. "Bella, Diane, y'all go with him. You stay with me, Simone."

"Why?"

"Not now, Simone."

"Okay, whatever. Whoever's goin', let's go," he said and Diane and Bella followed him out.

Once they were gone, Simone looked at me with angry eyes. "Why you do that?"

" 'Cause you are stronger than they are, Simone. If somebody gotta talk to the cops, I'd much rather it be you."

She looked at me and then her look softened. "You're right. Diane is drunk and Bella is just Bella. The cops start sweatin' them, there's no tellin' what they might say."

"I'm glad you understand. I need you to be a rock for me, Simone."

"I am," she protested.

"I know, but you gotta have faith in me and not question everything I say. Especially at times like this."

"My bad," Simone said to me as the cops bum-rushed the VIP room.

"When are we gonna be able to leave?" a woman asked in a whiny voice.

I didn't say a word; the last thing I wanted to do was give the cops a reason to toss attention my way.

"We ain't see shit, we been posted up in here all night," this rapper I had met but couldn't name, offered up. They asked us a few questions, took our names, told us that they would be in touch if they needed us and let us go.

I felt relieved that that's all it was, but the next day I got a call from the cops. They wanted to ask me some more questions and wanted me to come down to the station. My first thought was to ignore their request, but I knew that wasn't the answer. They would probably think I was trying to hide something and start looking at me. Not that I was worried about the murder, I didn't see shit, but I knew how cops were. My next thought was to show up with my lawyer, but I talked to Sasha and she didn't think that would be a good idea either. "No, Jada. You walk in with a lawyer, it would be the same as saying look at me, coppers, I got something to hide."

So, I dressed down, no makeup and definitely no ice, and went down there. I thought that it was a little strange that Simone hadn't gotten a similar call to come in, but I just figured that they would get to her in due time.

After a short wait, I was taken to what they called an interview room and was introduced to detective Albert Gineconna. "Thank you for coming in, Ms. West. I won't take up a lot of time. I just need to ask you a few questions about what happened the night before at Sensations," he said and placed a tape recorder on the table in between us. "I'll be recording our conversation, if that's all right with you."

"Not a problem."

"So, tell me what you saw."

"I really didn't see anything. I was there with a friend of mine," I started, but the detective stopped me.

"What's your friend's name?"

"Simone Frazier."

"And it was just the two of you?"

"Yes," I said slowly.

"Go on."

"We were just sitting there, when all of a sudden we saw a commotion in front of us. When we heard the shots and saw the people running, we ran in the VIP room."

"You say you heard shots."

"Yes."

"Was it a single shot or more than one?"

"Well, the music was playing so it's hard to be sure, but I think I heard more than one shot."

"What happened after that?"

"Nothing. We were told that we couldn't leave until the police talked to us. After that I went home."

Then his questions got personal. Where I lived, what I did for a living and how often I went to the club. I told him that I came to the club pretty regular and gave him my correct address, 'cause he could check those things if he wanted to know. I told him that I sold insurance, glad that Sasha got one of her clients to get me a license without having to take the test. After that, he thanked me for coming in and told me that I was free to go.

As I left the interview room was when I saw him. The eye candy I had the bad feeling about the first night we came to the club. He wasn't iced out or as well dressed as he was the last time I saw him, but it was definitely him. I knew right then that he was a cop.

As quickly as I could, I put on my sunglasses and dropped my head. I walked out of there considering the possibility that he could just be there like I was, to give a statement about what happened the night before at the club. I didn't know and didn't care which one it was, I just got out of there and hoped he didn't see me. Once I got to my car and was on my way out of the parking lot and thought about it. They only made the people that were in the VIP room stay and he wasn't one of them. No. He was a cop, I was sure of it. And since that was the case, I had to consider the possibility that this wasn't a coincidence. Maybe they brought me in for him to ID me. I made the decision right then and there; we needed to stay out of the clubs for a while.

# Chapter 9

After that incident, we laid off Sensations for a couple of months. During that time, business had been very good. I no longer felt the need to make elaborate public displays in order to market the ladies. I had reached the point where I wanted to be in this business. Now that I had stronger contacts, I was always one of the invited guest at social gatherings. I was running my program exactly the way Sasha ran hers. Now it was me carefully scrutinizing all of the men, making note of those who were there with dates. And before I left, I'd have leads on new clients. With all the new business, I was thinking about adding some new talent.

I was sitting around the apartment relaxing with Diane one afternoon and we were talking about our increase in business. I had just offered her choice of the last three appointments that came in. "What times are they?"

I ran my finger down the appointment schedule on my laptop. "Uh, seven, ten, and a late night will call."

"Jackson?"

"Of course."

"I'll take them all," Diane said.

"What?"

"You were just sayin' that business was so strong that you had to handle some new clients."

"And?"

"I'm trying to keep you from havin' to go out like that." One thing I had to say about Diane, she was true to her word. She was a good ho. "If business is so good why don't you recruit somebody?"

"I've been thinking about it, Diane, I really have. And I've been looking at some women, sizing them up. I just haven't found what I'm looking for."

"What about Crème? She's been all over me to talk to you."

"Oh hell no. Crème likes to powder her nose too much."

"True that," Diane agreed as Bella came in the apartment.

"Hey, Bella," we both said.

"That is not the type of person we want to invite into our family," I continued.

"What type of person?" Bella asked.

"You remember my friend Crème?"

"The one that used to work with y'all at the club?" Bella questioned.

"That's her," Diane said.

"What about her?"

"Jada thinks she would be a bad influence on us because she sniffs."

"I don't know about her being a bad influence, we're all grown and capable of making our own decisions, but I agree with Jada."

"Why, Bella?" Diane asked.

"I don't know. I just never liked being around people that do that," Bella said.

"People that do what?" Simone asked as she came dragging out of the bedroom.

"Well good afternoon, sleepyhead," I said. "Glad you're still with us."

"Yeah, well, y'all are making so much noise out here I couldn't sleep. So what y'all talking about?"

"Diane wants us to start hanging out with her crackhead friend from Ecstasy," Bella said.

"She is not a crackhead," Diane insisted. "And I only brought it up because Jada was talking about recruiting somebody new."

"Why?" Simone asked quickly. "I think we're doing just fine. We don't need anybody else," she added.

"Jada thinks we do," Diane said like a pouting child.

"I just said that business has picked up and I was thinking about it. But let's talk about it."

"I say no," Simone told us firmly. "It's true we all have been working a lot and I am a little tired, but what I'm not, is ready to give up any of this money."

"I agree with Simone," Bella said.

"Well, when you put it that way," Diane said and winked at me. "There's just enough money for us."

"I guess that settles it," I said. "But from what I'm hearing, we all could use a break."

"Maybe we could take a trip," Bella suggested. "Go to one of those resorts in the islands and have West Indian men wait on us hand and foot."

"That's sound like a great idea," I said. "But I was thinking of something a little more immediate. It's been a while since we went to the club." I didn't have to say another word. The ladies were all for the idea and we quickly agreed that we were ready to go back to Sensations.

The moment the limo pulled up in front of the club, flashes of the last time we were there flooded my mind. "You thinking about the last time we were here, huh?" Bella asked reading my mind.

"Yeah, that shit was foul," Diane added.

When our driver got out and opened the door for us, there was a small round of applause from the few members of security that were standing outside. "Welcome back, Ms. West. The place hasn't been the same without you ladies." He walked up to Bella. "I really missed you, cutie."

"Thank you," Bella said to him and kissed him on the cheek.

Just as they always had, security escorted us to our spot. It did feel good to be back. Sherman, the club's manager, sent over a complimentary bottle of bubbly and it seemed like old times.

It didn't take long for the ballers to pour into Sensations that night. I noticed this chick walking around like she owned the place. I wasn't mad at her though, she was working the hell out of this bad-ass white Gucci pants suit. She gave me a knowing look as she passed, hot on the tail of this up-and-coming actor.

Later in the ladies' room, I noticed the chick in the white suit as I stood next to her at the sink. "This place is always such a mess," she commented.

"I know. You would think that they would keep somebody in here to keep the place clean," I told her.

"If these men only knew how nasty some of these women are, I don't think they'd be in such a hurry to jump in bed with them." Then she paused and thought about it. "What am I sayin'. They wouldn't give a shit as long as they get what they want."

"You ain't told no lie there," I said and looked around for something to dry my hands with.

She reached in her purse and handed me a few bar napkins. "I'm Chante," she said extending her hand.

I dried my hands and then shook hers. "I'm Jada."

Her eyebrows wrinkled. "Like the actress?" she asked.

I nodded my head.

"I've seen you here before," she said as we walked out together.

"Yeah, I've been here a few times."

"You and your friends always look so nice every time you're here."

"Thank you, Chante. I was telling my friend earlier that you're wearin' the hell out that Gucci."

"Thank you."

As we made our way through the crowded club, a guy grabbed my arm with so much force, that I bumped onto Chante. "What the hell?" I screamed. I could tell he was drunk, but that didn't stop him from trying to manhandle me. I struggled to pull free from him. Before I knew what was happening, Chante did a quick move and sent a blow to his neck.

"Goddamn! You see that shit?" I heard someone say as the drunk cowered over grabbing at his neck.

Chante turned to me. "Are you okay?"

I stood stunned to silence. I slowly nodded my head, but I was still in shock over the way she put him down.

She pulled me by the arm. "Come on, let's get out of here before he gets up."

"Why don't you come back to my table and I'll buy you a drink," I offered.

She smiled. "I'd like that."

Chante was cute, brown-skinned, shoulder-length hair that she wore bone straight with a part down the middle. I couldn't pinpoint her age, but I immediately started wondering if she'd be interested in our line of work. Of course that's not the kind of question you go asking complete strangers. When we got back to the table I introduced Chante to the ladies. After a round of drinks I asked, "So, tell me, Chante, what do you do?"

"Oh, nothing really," she said. "What I mean is, I used to be an executive assistant until my uncle died and left me a nice little stash. So I chunked the nine to five three years ago and just been havin' a good time. But you know what they say about all good things, soon or later, they come to an end.

Lately my money is starting to look real funny." She shrugged. "Guess I could've done some better planning, should've kept the job. But I'm hoping to find a generous donor," she giggled.

"Well, when you find him, please let me know if he has a brother, uncle or even a father. I've been looking for a member of that family for quite a while," Simone said, sending us all into a laughing fit.

# Chapter 10

Over the next few weeks, Chante had hung out at the club with us a few times. I took her along a couple of times when I was going to private parties or CD release joints. She was cool to be around and the ladies liked her. I liked Chante because she was easy to talk to and she always kept it real. No pretense at all from Chante. She was straight up, no chaser, that's what I liked about her. Whether she would make a good addition to our family was another matter. After my experience with the police over that shooting and seeing Mr. Investment Banker at the precinct had left me a little leery about new faces. But I still gotta eat, so I decided to invite Chante to meet me at my favorite restaurant. Besides, it would give me a chance to observe her in another atmosphere.

As I strolled into Jill's for dinner, the place was packed and buzzing. I loved walking into a place and realizing heads were turning in my direction. I glanced around the bustling restaurant and still hadn't seen Chante, so I figured I'd arrived early. I squeezed by two men who had been eyeing me up since I stepped onto the scene. "You looking for me?" one of them asked. I smirked at his tired-ass line and kept moving.

By the time I looked toward the back of the restaurant, I

noticed none other than Chante, curled up with some sexy roughneck. "Ahem," I cleared my throat.

Chante stuck her pretty little head around her friend's and smiled up at me.

"Jada! I was just looking for you," she said, looking like I had caught her with her hand in the cookie jar.

"Emp-hmm, looking for me all up in his face, huh?" I teased.

"Girl!" She winked. The guy finally turned at the sound of my voice.

"This is, ah, what's your name again, sweetie?" she cooed.

"Richard," he offered in a deep voice.

"Yeah, this is my new friend Richard," Chante said. "See, I told you I was waiting on someone," she said to him.

Richard's beady little eyes ran up every inch of my body then back down before he pulled away and glanced back to Chante.

"Well, my girl's here, so I'd better spend some time with her," she told Richard who hadn't taken his eyes off me. "You know how it is, gotta spread the love around."

He looked at her then back at me. "What's up? She don't like to party?" he asked.

Chante and I looked at each other then started cracking up. "Come on, Richard, my girl and I need to catch up. We'll get together later, I promise. But right now, we've got some private business to discuss," she said like she was talking to a three-year-old.

Richard took her hand to his lips and planted a kiss there. I rolled my eyes, but waited while he worked his jelly. "I'll be at the bar waiting on you," he promised. You'd think the two knew each other for years.

We admired the view as he walked away then started looking over the menu.

"It is so packed in here,'" I said.

"That's why I grabbed this table. I figured if I had waited

any longer, we might be eating outside on the sidewalk," she said.

Dinner went pretty well. We talked about clothes, music, and the latest black celebrity gossip. I marveled at how easy-going Chante was, and how we interacted like old friends. By the time we had wrapped up dinner, Richard had passed by our table at least three times. Each time he did, he and Chante exchanged *fuck me* looks. I thought it was funny. I thought about telling girlfriend she shouldn't be giving up the goods for free, but that would have led us down a conversational path I wasn't ready to go down, so I kept it to myself. "Well, so what's up for tonight?" I asked as I rose from the table with my doggie bag in hand.

"I'm gonna see what Richard is talking about, then I'm gonna hook up with you guys. Where are y'all partying tonight?'" she asked.

"We'll be at Sensations tonight. Or at least I will. Simone has an appoint—I mean a date tonight and I'm not sure about Diane."

"Even if it's just you, me, and Bella, I'm sure we'll have a good time," Chante said.

"Why don't you meet us at my place and ride with us?"

"Sounds good."

"You sure lover boy is gonna cut you loose?" I asked.

"Please," she said as she stood up. "After I work him over for a few hours, he'll be begging me to get out." I gave her a hug and turned to leave.

Hours later, when we walked up into the place the way we did, Chante fit right in. We watched from our table as other half-naked women jockeyed for attention. Some tables were stacked with drinks. To the left of our table, a few ladies were having a divorce party, with the guest of honor wobbling in and out of her seat. A couple of her friends were doing a se-ductive lap dance in their chairs as her friends cheered on, while another one held a camcorder.

"You having a nice time?" Chante asked.

I nodded, and then took a sip from my drink. I was having a blast. The dance floor was packed and the music was thumping. I sipped my drink again and enjoyed the atmosphere. Waiters walked around like busy mice, quickly running through the maze of a club from table to table.

It was about one-thirty in the morning when Simone and Diane walked into the place. "Hey, ladies. How'd it go tonight?" I asked as we each exchanged hugs.

"Great, Jada," Diane said quickly. "It don't even take me long to do what I gotta do."

"Must not have been all that. Who comes to the club after a great date?" Chante asked.

Bella quickly looked away like she didn't know us. Simone and Diane looked at her and then to me with that *handle your girl* look on their faces.

"What?" Chante smiled and hunched her shoulders. "Did I say something wrong?"

"No, Chante. You didn't say anything wrong," I said, searching for something to tell her. "A great date doesn't mean you got to give up the goods." Then I flipped it back on her. "I see you here after your date with Richard."

"That's 'cause I checked out his package early in the evening," Chante came back quickly.

"What you talkin' 'bout, Chante?" Diane asked.

"When we were leaving Jill's I bumped into him and felt for his dick. I couldn't find it." Chante grabbed her head. "I started getting a headache right then."

The bass in the music was thumping and some blinged-out baller grabbed Diane's hand. She looked at me, I looked him over and motioned with my eyes that it was cool. Watching Diane on the floor, feeling the music, had me feeling like I needed to go find me something to rub up against, you know, let Miss Kitty out of the bag. I quickly decided against it. I hadn't danced with anybody since we started going there and I wasn't about to start now. I was there for business. But a few minutes later I was rocking to the music in my seat. I wondered if Chante noticed that I collect business cards any time we're out, and if she did, did she wonder why.

This well-dressed guy came and stood over Simone. They didn't look like they were strangers, and she didn't bother to introduce him to us. Without a word he extended his hand to her and she accepted. Eyebrows raised and a few smirks popped up when Simone and her mystery man walked away from our table. "I guess she was bored with our company," Chante joked.

I shook my head and got up from the table. "I'll be back," I said and headed toward the ladies' room. A waitress arrived just as I walked away, and I told her to bring me another drink. I glanced over my shoulder and considered whether it was wise to leave Bella alone with Chante. I figured it couldn't hurt, so I was on my way.

On my way back, I couldn't hear what they were talking about, but the look on Bella's face told me she wasn't feeling the conversation.

"Hey. Everything okay?" I asked as I took my seat.

"Yeah, it's cool," Chante answered, a little too quickly for my taste.

"You guys seen Diane?" I asked.

"Not since she left the table with that baller," Bella answered.

Before I could take another sip of my drink, I looked up to see Diane walking toward us. "Jada, lemme holla at you for a sec," she said.

I got up again and walked a few feet away.

"I've got a live one here, so I'm about to bounce," Diane

said and motioned toward a delicious-looking thug who was waiting for her near the bar.

I usually didn't allow that type of thing, but I recognized him. He was already a client, so I made sure he saw me.

"How much longer y'all gonna be here?" Diane asked.

"Not much longer, maybe another hour. I don't see many new prospects."

"Well, I'll catch up with y'all later then," Diane said then sashayed over to her client. Again, when I came back to the table, I felt like I was interrupting something between Chante and Bella. But I wasn't about to start trippin; I made a mental note to get the 411 from Bella later.

Just then, Simone came back to our table. I could tell by looking at her that she'd been crying. I jumped up from my chair and rushed to her. "Simone! What's the matter?"

"That guy was my ex-boyfriend," she said, fighting back the tears. "He heard what—" she started and then cut her eyes at Chante.

I quickly grabbed her hand, "Come on, Simone. Let's go someplace quiet. Excuse us, ladies," I said to Chante and Bella, and led her to the VIP room. Once we were inside I said, "Now, tell me what's going on?"

"That guy who I left with, he's my ex-boyfriend. He heard from some of the boys what I've been doin'," she said and began to cry again.

"How would any of his boys know about what you're doing?"

"He told me that his boy is a client."

"Oh." What else could I say?

"He came to make me stop."

"What did you say?"

"At first I said that I didn't know what he was talking about, but he just kept pushin' it. Callin' me a ho and a slut and this and that, tellin' me I was better than this and that he was taking me away from this life of sin, 'cause I was a ho and needed to find God or whatever." Suddenly the tears stopped and I saw the fire return to her eyes. "Then I just lost it, Jada, and started goin' off on him. Then he grabbed me by the arm and tried to drag me out the club. Well you know security wasn't haven't that. They grabbed him and dragged him out of the club. When they got him outside they started kickin' his ass. I tried to stop them and tell them that it wasn't that serious, and he just needed to go and not come back. But once they let him go, this fool spit in big Kevin's face."

"Wrong move," I said, having seen how security here deals with problems.

"Kevin hit him in the face so hard that blood was everywhere and then the police came and took him to jail, but he was trying to fight them too. He kept callin' my name, callin' me a ho and that this was my fault. I swear, Jada, I didn't want him to get hurt and I damn sure didn't want him to go to jail."

"It's not your fault, Simone. He shouldn't have tried to manhandle you like that." I reached in my purse and gave her the card of a bail bondsman. "But if you're feeling that badly about him going to jail, here is the number for a bail bondsman. Let me know how much his bail is." That was the very least I could do for her.

The next afternoon I made it a point to talk to Bella about the conversation she and Chante had the night before at the club. It must have been on her mind as well, because as soon as I sat down, Bella came to me with her concerns. "Chante doesn't know what we do?" she asked one afternoon.

"No, what's up?"

"Just curious, 'cause last night, she just seemed to be all up in my grill. I mean she was fishing for information. I didn't say nothing, though," Bella had reported proudly.

"What exactly was she questioning you about?"

"Well, she wanted to know how we made money, what we did for a living, how we were able to buy such nice clothes and things like that."

"And what'd you say when she asked?" I had to handle Bella gently; I didn't want her to think she'd done anything wrong.

She shrugged. "I just told her she needed to talk to you."

"What'd she say after that?"

Bella thought for a moment, smirked then said, "You know, I don't think she really said anything about it. But she wasn't like salty or nothing like that. I just remember saying it to her, then I think you walked back up on us, so we dropped it."

"I see," I had said.

"Did I do good, Jada?" Bella asked, waiting for my approval.

"Yeah, Bella, you did just fine. You tell Chante or anybody else with questions about our family to come to me, and I'll handle them from there."

Bella actually breathed a sigh of relief. The fact that she went at Bella was a bit troubling. I mean, Chante and I had spent a lot of time together and she had plenty of chances to ask whatever she wanted to ask. In fact, I'd been waiting for her to come at me with questions. I knew for sure I needed to check Chante out a little closer.

# Chapter 11

*Chante*

I woke up early that morning and got ready to go. When I started up my car, I sat there for what seemed like an eternity, thinking about what I was doing. "It's just another job," I told myself. "No different from any other. Then why am I making it so complicated?" I knew the answer and I was afraid of what I'd discovered about myself.

I know what they're doing. They're high-priced hookers. Even though they are all so discreet about it. They were breaking the law and I had violated the rules and gotten personally involved.

The truth was I liked Jada, she was mad cool. Over the last few weeks I'd really gotten to like her and the ladies, as Jada called them. We were friends.

Jada rarely goes anywhere without calling me and inviting me to hang out with them. We have lunch and dinner together all the time in some of finest spots in town. We've gone to clubs, release parties, and we shop. Damn, Jada West is one shopping—don't give a fuck what it cost—I just know it fits and I want it—woman.

Jada has a style about her that I liked, even envied. She always wore the finest clothes; she's chauffeured around like a celebrity just about everywhere she goes. And I loved being a part of that lifestyle.

I put the car in drive and pulled off. While I drove, I thought about how I got into this in the first place. "Come on in and have a seat, Rachael," Gineconna said the day he gave me this assignment.

First off, my name is not Chante. My name is Rachael Dawkins and I'm a cop. "Thank you, lieutenant," I said and took a seat in front of his desk.

"How's it feel to be back?"

"I was happy to be able to sleep in my own bed after seven months." I had been on loan to the DEA, infiltrating a drug ring that was operating heavily on the East Coast.

"You'll be glad to know that thanks to the work you did, three dozen arrests were made, as well as a substantial amount of drugs and money confiscated. Damn fine piece of work."

"Thanks, Lieu."

"So, are you ready to be a cop again?" he asked, knowing that I had no say in the matter.

"No. I was hoping for a little time off. You know, an all-expense-paid trip to the Bahamas. At the DEA's expense of course," I replied, since I knew it wasn't happening anyway.

"Wouldn't we all, Rachael. Wouldn't we all."

"So what you got for me?"

"You ever hear of a club called Sensations?"

"Big club, upscale clientele, I've been there once or twice. Why?"

"Well, Sam's been working there, trying to get a handle on what we believe is one of the largest drug operations in the city. He reported that there's also a prostitution ring that's been operating out of there. It's run by a woman named Jada West."

"A woman?"

"Yes, a woman. What's the matter, Rachael, I know you aren't going to tell me that you're discriminating against women being pimps?"

"Not at all. A crook is a crook is a crook, all day long. I'm just a little surprised."

"So far, Sam hasn't been able to get close to them."

"Say it ain't so." Sam used to be my partner. I can't stand him. "What's the matter, Super Sam can't crack a girlie pimp?"

"He's working the drug angle and doesn't want to tip his hand. A couple of other male officers have tried to get close to her, but she won't bite."

"Sounds like she's got good instincts. She can smell a cop."

"I agree. That's why we're trying a different approach with you. Anyway, there was a murder there, totally unrelated to the drugs or the prostitution ring, but since then they've stopped coming. I want you start hanging out there, see if you can find out where they disappeared to. If they show back up, you get close to them and let's see if we can shut them down."

"So, you want me to be a prostitute?"

"No. But if it comes to that, we'll work something out so you won't have to take it there."

That's how it began. During the time that they were absent from the club, I went to work. The address and phone number she gave when they brought her in for questioning were dead. She had moved out of that apartment and changed her cell number. Knowing Jada like I know her now, she probably sniffed Sam out as a cop. Bringing her in for questioning on that murder was what made her go underground, not the murder. So I was at the fuckin' club every night, because I had a feeling they'd be back. Every night I'd talk to men. It wasn't easy, but I finally found one of her clients and bought him a drink. I told him that I was a lesbian, which kept him from being all over me, but also served another purpose as well. Once I got him drunk and talkin', I told him that I'd seen one of her girls and, "She was a goddess. I would pay anything to get with her, but they stopped coming here."

"I know which one you're talking about," my drinking buddy said and began describing Diane. "Here," he said and reached in his pocket for a pen. "Here's her number."

Jackpot.

By the time they came back to the club, I knew everything about Jada West. Father dead, mother doin' fed time. I knew about her and Diane at Ecstasy. I knew all about Simone and Bella. The lieutenant was happy to hear that I had made contact with them rather easily on their first night back in the club.

Since then, I've had nothing to report and he's growing impatient. At our last meeting he reminded me that I was better than this. "I understand from talking to her that Jada West is smart. But shit! It shouldn't take this long for you to crack her. Either way, Rachael, I need to see some results soon or I'll have to pull you off this thing."

I parked my car behind the building and went inside. I saw my old partner Sam coming toward me. "How's it going, Rachael?" Sam is the most disgusting man I've ever met. Always talkin' 'bout his big dick and what he could do to me with it. You can't turn you're back on him or his hands will be all over you. Fuckin' pig.

"Great, Sam. How about you?" I replied like I was happy to see him.

"Same old same, day in and day out. We should get together, you know, to catch up."

"I'd like that," I lied. "I'll stop by when I'm done," I lied again. *I'm not giving you any pussy and nothing you have to say is of any interest to me,* I thought as I made my way to an appointment that I was already very late for.

"Good morning, Rachael," Gineconna's admin said to me.

"Is he in?"

"Yes, but he's on a call and wants you to wait for him."

I nodded my head and took a seat. Suddenly, Gineconna's door swung open. "Come on in and have a seat, Rachael," I heard him yell.

I came in his office and made my report, which was basically the same as the one I made last week. "Nothing new to report."

"So you mean to tell me nothing has happened yet?"

"No, sir. I mean we go out clubbing a lot. Sometimes we go to these parties, mostly for up-and-coming rappers. We've been to a few celebrity birthday parties and that kind of stuff. And we shop, a lot," I said, only half lying.

"No mention of where the money comes from?"

"Not a word. When I asked, all I got was giggles, and I'm told to ask Jada. These things take time. You know that."

"And you've never witnessed any exchange of money for sex or sexual favors?"

"None that I've witnessed personally, no. As far as I know and can prove, they're just four girlfriends that hang out together. Jada never speaks to me about what they do. And the ladies, as she calls them, basically only speak when Jada says," I said.

"Okay, so when you're at these parties what's goes on? What does she say she does for a living?"

"She says she sells insurance."

"And?" Gineconna asked.

"She has a license, a Web site and she speaks knowledgeably when she has to. When we're at these events she collects business cards, just like everybody else. My guy says that he met her at a record company party and he gave her his card. A couple of weeks later, she calls and sets up a date for lunch. She broke it to him over salad."

Gineconna let out a frustrated sigh and I took the opening. "What it comes down to is how bad you want them?"

"Will your guy testify?"

"Not likely."

"What about the girls? Can you turn one of them?"

"I'll stay on it and see what I can do, but I'll be honest, those ladies are loyal to Jada. She walks on water in their eyes. Turning one of them will take time and I'll run the risk of blowing my cover."

"Right now we don't have enough evidence to make a case that will stick," Gineconna said. "You think you can turn up another client of hers?"

"Sure, but it will take time, how bad you want her?"

"Bad, but I can't continue to justify the use of resources and the overtime on the four little girls sellin' pussy with no results in sight. I need you back in the rotation catching cases."

I tried my best to look disappointed. "Damn. I just need a little more time." But that was exactly what I wanted. "I tell you what, Lieu, you do what you gotta do, I'll continue to work it on my own time. I'll stay close to Ms. Jada West; try to flip either one of her clients or one of the girls."

Gineconna smiled. "That's what I wanted to hear, Rachael. I knew I could count on you. As flamboyant as West is, and the way these girls seem to love the spotlight, I'm sure they'll make a mistake."

I left Gineconna's office feeling great. I got exactly what I wanted. I was officially off the case, but still had an official reason to remain in contact with them. After a while Jada would be off of Gineconna's radar. I'd already told them I was going to have to get a job, so I've got a reason to be unavailable at times, but I could go on being Chante.

I loved being Chante and I was starting to wonder if Chante was who I really was. I didn't believe it. But I do. I love being Chante.

The last time we were together, Jada asked if I could take a weekend trip with them. "All expenses paid of course,"

Jada explained. "It's just going to be us and the ladies hanging out in the Bahamas."

I told her I'd think about it, but I knew deep down inside I wanted to go. And since how I did my job was pretty much my business, I figured I'd be able to go with no worries.

But Gineconna was right about one thing, I know Jada could live without it, but the ladies do love the spotlight. Sooner or later hangin' out at that club will be their downfall. My job now was to keep Jada out of the clubs or this could all come crashing down on me. I've had nightmares about blowing my cover and fearing Jada's disappointment once she realized the truth. My challenge was to find a way to prevent that from happening at all cost.

# Chapter 12

*Jada*

It was a little before midnight on a Wednesday night and the ladies and I had been sitting around talking and drinking. Everybody, myself included, had an appointment earlier that night and had come back to my place. "So, I say we polish these off, and go find some real trouble to get into," I said looking around the room.

"One more of these and I ain't gonna have to try too hard to find trouble," Diane said hoisting up her glass.

"Okay, we're all feeling real nice, and nobody's got an appointment." I winked. "So we should just call an end to this bonding—then go kick up some dust." I glanced at the ladies, "Who's down?" I asked.

"Count me in!" Diane said, hyped and drunk at the same time.

"You ain't said nothing but a word," Simone tossed in, as she turned up her glass.

Just then the phone rang.

"Does this mean I can give it away for free tonight?" Bella giggled.

Diane got up and removed the drink from Bella's hands. "I

think you've had enough," she said in a dramatic fashion. We all started cracking up as I picked up the phone.

"House of Beauty, this is cutie," I sang into the receiver.

"Hey cutie, sounds like there's a party going on over there, how come I didn't get an invite?" Chante said into my ear.

"Oh, hey Chante. We're just sitting around trying to decide what to get into," I answered. I had planned on talking to Chante about her conversation with Bella, but it was a conversation I wanted to have in person.

"Hmmm, seems to me like that's where I need to be," Chante said.

"Well, come on through then," I challenged.

As I hung up, Simone turned to me and asked, "Who was that? Chante?"

"That was her," I confirmed.

"So, what's up? Is Chante gonna be down or what?" Simone asked.

"I don't think so. I mean she's cool and all, but ours isn't the kind of business you can just welcome someone into," I said to Simone even though that was exactly how I got her. I placed the phone back in its cradle and swallowed the last of my drink. I had a nice buzz going and this wasn't really a conversation I felt like having with Simone. But I knew she wasn't about to give up.

"So we just continue to have her hanging around? I mean, pretty soon she'll figure it out, don't you think? Nobody can be that fuckin' dumb," Simone snickered.

"Well, she hasn't said anything to make me think she's even curious," I lied just to shut Simone up. She had a way of questioning everything. I hadn't forgotten about the questions Chante had asked Bella, but a part of me was a little suspicious about why Chante never approached me. "Why don't we think about getting our groove on," I offered, trying to keep things light.

"Yeah, I feel you on that. So what's up with the bachelorette party Diane mentioned?" Simone asked.

"Bachelorette party?" Bella questioned. "Diane, you are getting too gay for me."

"Look, it's like I told her. I don't think we need to even start doing shit like that. I mean, we make good money now; we start going out like that, I'm just afraid it could turn into something we don't want."

Simone didn't look like she agreed too much with my response, but I meant what I said. "I didn't start this business only to go right back to where I'd started. I see no real money in the stripping thing, especially since we make three or four times what a stripper earns on a good night. This is easy money for a few hours on your back." I knew for sure that old saying, *been there and done that*, applied in this case. It made no sense to start stripping at parties and honestly, I was a bit pissed at Diane for even bringing it up in the first place. I went and sat down next to Diane. "Did you ever imagine things would turn out this way?" I asked.

"I always knew you were destined for the big time. I watched how you came to Ecstasy and took over. Yeah, there were prettier girls working there. Better dancers too. I was a better dancer than you," Diane said, laughing. "But you knew how to give those men what they wanted and you made the money. So when you said you were gonna do this, I knew this was where the money was gonna be. Why do you think I begged you to be down?" Diane smirked.

"Smart girl." I leaned closer to her. "So why do you want to take a step backwards and go back to shaking your ass? I know it can't be the money."

"Honestly," Diane said softly. "Crème asked me if I would do the party with her. I already told her what you said, but she wants to get with us bad and she's trying anything."

"I knew there had to be something else to it. I tell you what,

why don't you and me go by Ecstasy and I'll tell Crème myself. That should get her off you."

"Thanks, Jada. Once she hears no from you maybe she'll
stop bugging me about it."

Diane and I stood up and started getting ready to leave.
"We're gonna make a quick run, ladies," I said to Bella and
Simone. "Chante is on her way. Give me a call and let me
know where y'all end up and we'll meet you there."

"Where y'all going?" Simone asked.

"Ecstasy," Diane replied.

"The place where you guys used to dance?" Bella asked.

"That's right," Diane said.

"What are y'all going there for?" Simone asked. "You're
not still thinking about asking that crackhead to join our family, are you?"

"Of course not," I assured Simone.

"She getting on my nerves, so Jada's going to shut her
down."

"I wanna go," Bella said quickly. She stood up and started
shaking her ass. "I might even dance while I'm there."

"Why, so you can fall off the stage again?" Simone asked
and started to get ready to leave.

"Why you gotta go there, Simone, with your no-dancing
ass," Bella came back.

"Aren't we getting a little loose with the language, ladies?"
I asked.

"Sorry, Jada," they both said and Diane stuck out her
tongue. It was usually her that I had to chastise about her language, but lately it hadn't been an issue.

"Where are you two going?" I asked.

"With you," Simone said.

"No. You guys have got to wait here for Chante."

"She has a cell phone, am I correct?" Simone said in as
proper a manner as she could.

"Simone, you are absolutely correct. Chante does have a cell phone," I said and took out my cell phone.

Bella walked up to me. "Can we talk for a second?" she asked quietly.

"Sure."

"Jada. I don't feel comfortable around Chante after the other night," Bella told me.

"I understand. But that's why I want you to wait here for her. I'm going to talk to her tonight, but I wanna know if she comes at you again."

"What about Simone?"

"Have you told her anything?"

"No."

"You let me worry about Simone," I said and headed for the door. When I opened the door, there was Chante.


## Chante

"Oh, hey, Chante," Jada said, obviously startled to see me standing there.

I almost went for my gun when the door flew open. "I was just about to ring the bell."

"Good, now we don't have to wait for her," I heard Bella say in the background.

"Y'all weren't trying to leave me, were you?"

"Me and Diane were gonna make a run," Jada said and looked at Diane. "But we can do that anytime," she said and kept walking out of her apartment.

"Hey, Chante," Diane said, hugging and kissing me on the cheek. After she squeezed my ass she followed Jada to the parking lot. I can tell by the way she looks at me that's she interested; and I'm curious.

Bella was standing in the hallway, but when I looked at her

she looked away. I'd wondered if I had come on a little too strong when I tried to get Bella to talk the other night. "How you doin', Bella?" I asked and followed Diane. Bella didn't answer. I looked over my shoulder and saw she and Simone coming behind me. "What's up, Chante?" Simone said.

"Hey, Chante," Bella finally said. She was smiling the way she always does so I couldn't be sure.

"Where we going?" I said as we got to Jada's 500 Benz.

"Sensations," Simone said.

"Again?" I said quickly.

"What, you don't like Sensations?" Simone asked.

"I like it, but we were just there the other night," I said and Bella looked at me. "Why don't we go someplace else?"

"It doesn't matter to me," Jada said and got in the car. Diane got in the front seat, I sat in the back between Simone and Bella. Once we were all in, Jada asked, "Where you wanna go, Chante?"

"What about the Twenty-Grand Club?" I suggested, but anywhere other than Sensations was fine with me. The only reason they were even on Lieutenant Gineconna's radar was because they were operating so high profile in the middle of his drug investigation. I was sure that if I kept them out of Sensations and out of Sam's reports that Gineconna would forget all about these ladies.

"Haven't seen you in a couple of days, Chante. What's been up?" Jada asked. I could see her piercing eyes in the rearview mirror.

"You remember I said my paper was getting a little short? Well, I've actually been thinking about looking for a job." I wanted to start laying some foundation for when my job started preventing me from doing lunch. Diane and Jada exchanged glances. Diane smiled and Jada looked in the mirror. "I just been gettin' my résumé together and what not, but it's a start, right?" I couldn't tell if she was looking for a reaction from Bella. I glanced at Bella. She was staring out the window as if nothing I said amounted to a hill of beans. I was way too paranoid and it was starting to get on my nerves.

"Tough break," Diane said. "Having to get a job and all. Maybe you'll get lucky and find a job doing something that you like."

"Yeah, maybe I will," I said and shrank into my seat.

It was a completely different event when we went to other clubs. No limousine, no major entrance, no reserved table. We parked the car three blocks from the club and had to walk. We stood in line for twenty minutes and there was nowhere to sit once we got inside. Low profile. That's how I intended to keep them. I think they prefer it this way, except Simone. She more than Bella and Diane reveled in the attention they got at Sensations. Out of the spotlight, Jada, Diane, and Bella don't leave the dance floor, but not Simone. Not being much of a dancer, you'll always find her posted up at the bar, surrounded by men and holding court. The dance floor belongs to the three former shake dancers. Men come and dance with them, but eventually they fade away. Usually when they realized that each lady was trying to out dance the others and were paying them no mind.

Of the three, Diane was by far the better dancer, while Jada was more seductive, and even though she may stumble every now and then, Bella is a saltshaker that had men mesmerized. Me, I flow somewhere in between. I can hold my own on the dance floor, but I'm nowhere near the level the ladies are on. So I drifted to the bar, where Simone was in rare form. One of her suitors asked her to dance. "I won't dance with you, but maybe Chante will," she said and dismissed him with a hand. He was fine, so I danced with him.

When I came off the dance floor, Jada did too. She followed me back to the bar where Simone was. It wasn't long before some good-looking man was handing me a drink. "Here you go, sweetie," he said and began talking to me like

I had known him all his life. Suddenly, I became aware that Jada was standing nest to me.

"Chante," Jada said and touched my arm. "Do you have any plans after you leave here?"

"No. What's up?"

"Nothing. I just wanted to ask you something."

"What?" I asked, knowing she wanted to talk about me sweatin' Bella.

"It's really nothing," Jada started. "But I was just wondering what you thought of me, Chante."

Of all the shit that could've come out of her mouth, she asks me what I think of her. I wasn't at all ready for that. "I don't know." I giggled and thought about an answer. "I like you, we're friends, I guess." And giggled again.

"I like you too, Chante. So that's why when Bella said that you were—" Jada started.

"Hello, Ms. West," a voice came from behind Jada.

When she turned to see who the voice belonged to, I got ready to give the speech I had ready.

"Ricky Stanton," Jada said.

*Oh shit!* I thought as he stepped between us and kissed Jada on the cheek.

"How are you doing?" Ricky asked. He took a step back and looked at me. I could tell I looked familiar to him.

"I'm doing fine, Ricky." Jada turned to me. "This is my friend—"

"Chante. We met a couple of months ago at Sensations. How's the music business?" I asked him quickly, before he remembered that he gave me Jada's number after I got him drunk.

"Busy. Always something going on," he said and turned to Jada. "Look, I gotta run, but I wanted to tell you, we're having a little party tomorrow night at my house. The One finished his next album, so if you're not doing anything stop by."

"I'll do that," Jada said.

Ricky turned back to me. "Now, Chante, is it?"

"It is," I flirted.

"You say we meet before. Did we get along?" Ricky asked me and Jada rolled her eyes.

I looped my arm in his and winked at Jada. "We got along very well." I leaned toward Jada. "We'll talk later, girl," I said quietly to Jada. *Anything to get away from that conversation,* I thought and left the club with Ricky.

After we left the club, Ricky Stanton took me to breakfast, after a while, he took me to my apartment in his limo.

Damn, I loved being Chante.

She was living a life that I only dreamed of and knew would never happen for me.

# Chapter 13

## *Jada*

It was good seeing Ricky Stanton the night before. He was The One's producer and one of my first clients. I've seen The One a couple of times since that night. As much as that night represented a turning point in my life, it was apparently just another night at the tittie bar for The One. He doesn't remember it at all, not that I've gone out of my way to remind him. Each time he sees me it's like the first time we're meeting and I always have to remind him that we've met.

I decided early in the day that I was going to the party, so some maintenance was in order. I called the spa and made an appointment. I was able to drag Bella and Diane along, but Simone rolled over and pulled the blanket over her head when we tried to recruit her.

"Go awaaay," she shrieked. I had no idea when she had made her way in, because she was nowhere to be found when we left the club. Diane had come in just before sun-up, but still she was down for the spa. I called Chante to see if she wanted to go, but she didn't answer. She slipped out the club with Ricky Stanton before we had a chance to talk, but I was sure I'd see Chante at The One's party.

Chante don't like to miss anything.

After the day at the spa, we prepared for the evening. Bella and Simone had early appointments for the evening; however, both planned to come to the party if it was at all possible.

As for me and Diane, we had a stop of our own to make before we headed for the party. Once we left the apartment, it wasn't too long after that me and Diane were seated at a table at Ecstasy.

We were definitely overdressed for the occasion. Diane dressed in her Carmen Marc Valvo satin cocktail dress, with the plunging V-neck in the front and back. And me in my new Betsey Johnson Battenburg-lace dress. "A lot of new faces in here," Diane said.

"You know how it is, they come and go," I replied as one of those new faces approached the table. She was a caramel-skinned beauty with big pretty eyes, curvy hips, and large breasts. "Y'all wanna dance?"

"Yes," Diane said quickly.

I looked at Diane as the dancer began peeling off what little outfit she had on. "I think Bella is right about you."

"What?"

"I mean it's cool, you know, if you're into woman."

"I am definitely bisexual and leaning that way. It's like, you know, dick is just a job for me now. I don't know," Diane said and turned her attention back to the dancer.

While Diane got her eyes full, I flagged down a waitress and ordered two Absolut and cranberry juice on the rocks. "If you see Crème tell her that she has guests in the house," I said and gave her a fifty.

Before the waitress came back with our drinks, I saw what looked like Crème coming toward the table. If it was Crème, she had lost a lot of weight. I leaned close to Diane. "When was the last time you saw Crème?"

"I don't know, it's been a while. Why?" Diane answered without taking her eyes off the dancer.

"Diane!" I yelled to get her attention and pointed at Crème.

"Damn" was all that Diane could get out before Crème was at the table.

Crème was still cute, but her face was drawn and her olive skin had blotches. She had let her hair grow long and now it looked unkept. Her hourglass shape was gone, and her once firm breasts were sagging. Remembering what she looked like then, it was hard looking at her now.

"Look at you two," Crème said and pulled up a chair. "Diane and Miss Kitty herself."

"Crème, what happened to you?" Diane asked.

"I had been sick. Had the flu and shit, lost a little weight. But I'm feeling better now, startin' to get my weight back up."

"How's it going here? I was just saying to Diane that there are a lot of new faces."

"It's a'ight, but I'm 'bout burnt out on this. I need to do something different. That's why I been hollerin' at Diane about gettin' wit' you." Crème looked at Diane. Diane looked away.

I held up my hand to stop her. "Crème, don't bullshit me. You know as well as I do that the flu didn't make you lose all that weight. How much are you smoking?"

"You right, Jada, you right. I was on it pretty hard for awhile, but I got it under control now," Crème assured me, but I didn't believe her. It looked like she had taken a hit before she came on the floor.

"You are in no condition to work for me."

"Come on, Jada. I got that shit for real." Crème looked around the room. "I just need to get outta this place."

I looked around the room and thought back to my first days at Ecstasy. Diane was missing in action, so it was Crème who looked out for me, taught me the ropes. I looked at her now and I saw the desperation in her eyes. "You are in no condition to work for me," I said, but feeling like I had to do something. "But I tell you what I will do for you." I reached in my purse and handed her my card. "When you ready to get off the rock, call me and I'll help you." I stood up and looked at Diane. "Let's go."

It was after midnight when Diane and I arrived at the party. Bella and Simone were there when we got there, and so was Chante, of course. The living and dining rooms at Ricky's house were fully packed with invited guests. They had gathered two hours after the exclusive event began to toast the host. Quite a few of our clients were there, but there were a lot of others who weren't. The room was filled with upcoming rappers, and a bunch of video vixens, one or two that I considered recruiting.

I looked around the room, nicely decorated with people mingling and having a good time. Not only was there a DJ who was spinning the hits, but there was a microphone in case any of the rappers felt like going freestyle.

"To a successful and profitable year," Simone said, hoisting up her crystal champagne flute.

"Hear, hear!" I agreed.

I also noticed a couple of athletes were in attendance. Simone, the closest thing I had to a right-hand man, had already talked about luring the elusive men onto our clientele list. Simone leaned over as we watched Chante seductively dancing with a football player who was one of the targets. "Is she on board?"

"Nah, I don't trust her like that."

Simone brought the glass to her lips then looked at me,

her eyebrow raised. "You don't trust her? I can't tell, I mean the way she hangs with you. I mean it's like she's already on the team," she said.

"Well she's not."

I glanced over at Chante and the ballplayer again. The two looked like they'd soon be headed for a room. When Simone cleared her throat, I looked to see what or who was holding her attention. She was watching Bella and the guy she was with.

"Who the hell is he?" she asked.

I looked at the roughneck who Bella was with. "Oh that's Bullet. He's The One's bodyguard."

I motioned for Bella to join us. She excused herself from Bullet and came over to where Simone and I were standing. I asked her what was up with that, because from where we were standing they looked like they were in love.

"Yeah, he's been on me real hard since I got here," Bella admitted.

"Well is he a potential customer or a freebie?" I asked.

Bella looked at me and sucked her teeth. "Girl, please, who you talking to? You of all people should know, aren't you the queen of not giving up the goods for free?"

I shrugged my shoulders. "Yeah, you got that right. But I was just checking," I said.

When Chante walked up, Bella slipped away and a few minutes later, I saw Bullet walking over to her. "What happened to dude you were all up under?" I asked.

"Jada, I'm telling you, he's a trip. All over me, but wanna talk about we need to go back to my place because his fiancée is at his house!" Chante said with tons of attitude.

"Hmm, interesting," I said, storing the information for later use. "I'm kind of tired. I'm thinking about getting out of here soon."

"Yeah, you mind if I ride with you?" Chante asked.

I shook my head, "Not at all." It was obvious that she had too much to drink. "Let me go check on the ladies." After wandering around the house for a while, I found Diane. She told me that Simone was out by the pool talking with a couple of football players. "You seen Bella?"

"Simone said she left with Bullet."

"We're getting ready to leave. I'm tired and Chante is drunk."

"I'm not drunk, Jada."

"Whatever, Chante."

"I'm gonna go too. Nothing here I'm interested in. I'll let Simone know we're going," Diane said.

On the way back to my place, Chante went to sleep in the backseat. She was able to make it as far as the couch before she was out cold again. It was funny, I couldn't wait to leave the party because I was so tired. But once I got home, a burst of energy popped up. So while Chante slept, me and Diane talked about Crème. How sad it was to see her looking like that.

I remember her offering me a bump before I went on stage that first night. "I was so nervous that night, Diane, and I was so tempted to hit it."

"You see where you'd be if you did," Diane reminded me.

It was maybe an hour after that when Simone came in. Once Simone started talking, Chante woke up and joined the conversation. I looked up and realized we'd been sitting around chitchatting for nearly two hours. It was almost seven in the morning.

Just as I was about to break things up and retire to the bed, the door opened, and Bella stumbled in.

"What the fuck!" Simone screamed. Her horror was well justified. Bella's clothes were torn and stained with blood. One of her eyes was bruised, and blood was trickling down her lip and chin.

"What the hell happened to you?" I jumped from the couch. By the time I got to her, she nearly collapsed right into my arms.

"Somebody call nine-one-one!" Diane screamed. She rushed to my side and helped me move Bella's body to the couch.

"Forget nine-one-one," Chante said. "We need to get her to a hospital now. We can get her there a lot faster."

What she said made sense. We piled into my car as Chante nursed Bella in the backseat. When we arrived at the hospital, I didn't even take time to park the car. I pulled up at the emergency room entrance and I ran inside screaming for help.

"Please, my friend, she needs help, she's in the car," I yelled. Two ER workers ran out to the car. I was so glad to have Chante there. She talked to the police and told them everything we knew, because the rest of us were useless. By the time Chante came walking into the waiting area where the rest of us were, everyone was silent with our own thoughts.

When the doctor came out, he told us that the beating Bella had taken had caused some internal bleeding. "Internal bleeding?" Diane questioned.

"Internal bleeding is the leaking of blood from blood vessels into spaces in the body. Deeper bleeding that involve arteries and veins can result in severe blood loss that can result in shock."

"What causes that?"

"It can be caused by a violent blunt force, such as being thrown against an object or the beating she apparently took."

"But she seemed all right on the way here," Simone said.

"Signs and symptoms of internal bleeding are less obvious

than that of external bleeding. In fact, an injured person may appear normal at first."

The doctor promised he would do all he could to help Bella, but when he came back an hour later, he didn't even have to say a word for us to know the diagnosis.

"I am so sorry, ladies. There was nothing more we could do," the doctor offered up.

"The beating she took caused a lot of internal bleeding. It was just too severe," he said somberly.

My head was spinning and pounding at the same time. I was fuming! I still couldn't believe Bella was gone. Before the doctor could even finish, two detectives walked into the room.

"We need to know who was the last person to see her alive," one officer said.

Bullet.

Unfortunately, I didn't know his government name, but I knew where to find him and once I did, he'd be sorry he ever laid hands on Bella.

We sat through the intense questioning with the detectives. When it was over, Chante drove us all home, and the ride was the longest I'd ever endured.

I couldn't be sure just when Chante went home, but I know none of us ever got any sleep. We stayed up talking about Bella, still unable to come to grips with the fact that she was dead.

"I'm about to go find this nigga," I screamed.

"What? And do what when you find him?" Diane wanted to know.

I stormed across the room and dug into a nearby closet. After pulling out several boxes, I found what I was looking for.

"When I find this muthafucka, I've got a bullet with his name on it."

"Okay, you need to chill out," Diane said. "You know the cops will find him."

I looked at her, sucked my teeth, and tossed the gun into my bag.

"I'm going to the studio. I'll be back," I said, leaving the rest of the ladies in the room in awe.

# Chapter 14

*Chante*

I could tell something was wrong the moment I knocked on the door and no one answered. I knew for sure they were home. It was as if they were just sitting there, listening to the doorbell. I reached for the knob, and without much effort pushed the unlocked door opened. "Hhhello?" I started to reach for my piece, thinking something just wasn't right. "Is everything okay?" I walked down the short hall slowly, not sure if I should have my weapon drawn already. When I rounded the corner, I was confused by what I saw.

Somber faces stared back at me. I looked around trying to figure out where Jada was. "Hey, guys, what's going on?" I asked no one in particular.

Diane buried her face into the palms of her hands and started sobbing.

"What's wrong?" I looked around at Diane and Simone. They sat there stone-faced, not even acknowledging my presence.

"Where's Jada?"

That's when Diane looked up at me. Her eyes were swollen and red from crying. "She went after him," she cried. "She went after him and I'm afraid of what's gonna happen when she finds him."

I stepped closer to Simone. "Who'd she go after? What are you saying?"

Simone sucked her teeth and rolled her eyes. "She went after Bullet. And I hope she finds his ass. Bella never hurt a soul. That muthafucka deserves exactly what he gets. I should've gone with her."

I immediately started blocking Simone out. "How did she find him?" I asked Diane.

"She-um—she said—" Diane hunched her shoulders. "I don't know, she just said she was going to the studio."

"What studio?" I demanded to know.

"Triple Platinum," Diane mumbled over her tears.

I turned to leave, but Simone grabbed my arm. "Where you goin'?"

"I'm going to find Jada."

"I'm coming with you," Simone said.

"No. You stay here and take care of Diane. Maybe Jada will change her mind and come back here. If she does, call me," I told her and dashed out of there. I couldn't allow Jada to go out like that.

## Jada

I was crying my eyes out when I got to the studio. I just hoped that he would be there. There were a lot of cars parked outside, so I didn't want to walk in there waving my gun and yelling where's Bullet. Even though that's what I wanted to do.

Then I got lucky. Bullet came out and walked to his car. I started mine and was about to follow him when he shut the door and went back inside. At least I knew he was there. So I turned off my car and waited.

A few minutes later, a group of guys, including the One

came out and within minutes, Bullet's car was the only one left. I got out of my car and walked toward the door. As I passed his car I looked in the backseat. It was full of suitcases. He wasn't getting away after what he'd done. I took out my gun and went inside.

It didn't seem like there was anybody left in the building. Maybe Bullet had left with everybody else and I just missed him. That wasn't likely; if that big-ass muthafucka had come out, there was no way I'd miss him. And besides, if everyone was gone, why would they leave the door unlocked?

I wandered around the building looking in every room without success. "Where is he?"

As I continued my search, I began to hear the sounds of music playing and followed the sound. The closer I got, the louder the music became, the madder I got. I was so mad I couldn't think straight. How could Bullet have done that to her? Bella was the sweetest, most kind and considerate person I knew.

When I reached the door where the music was coming from, I smelled smoke. Not weed, it smelled more like something was on fire. I opened the door slowly and walked in. There he was. Standing over a metal garbage can with a fire extinguisher in his hand. The muthafucka was probably trying to burn the clothes he had on when he beat Bella to death. "Bastard."

The music was so loud that he didn't hear me come in. With his back turned and his attention on the fire I was able to walk up on him.

"Put the fire extinguisher down and move away from the fire," I said with my gun aimed at his head.

Bullet hit the extinguisher button a few times to put the fire out and turned around smiling.

"I said put it down!" I yelled over the music.

Bullet laughed a little and put the extinguisher down. He tipped his head to one side and looked at me. When he started to move toward me, I took a step closer to him and screamed, "Don't move!"

"Okay, okay," Bullet said and began looking around the room before turning back to me. "You know the whole night I been tryin' to remember where I knew those pretty-ass titties from. Now I remember you, Miss Kitty."

"Shut up!" I yelled and my hands started shaking a little. This may not have been the time to think it, but I had never shot, much less killed anybody before. But there I was, ready to put a bullet in Bullet's head for what he had done. Bella was like a sister to me. I couldn't let him get away with it.

"You might as well put that little-ass gun down, Miss Kitty. You know you ain't gonna shoot."

"That's where you're wrong. You're gonna die." I knew that he could see my hands shaking. I was so mad that it felt like my whole body was shaking. I gripped the gun tighter.

"No I'm not. Look at you, can't even hold the gun you're shakin' so fuckin' bad."

"Why'd you kill her?" I yelled.

"I didn't kill that ho."

"Yes you did! She died this morning in the hospital from the beating you give her."

"She was alive when she left me. I can't be responsible for what happens to a ho when you're finished with her. That bitch probably went out and found her another john and he killed he ass."

"No, it was you. If you didn't kill her, what you trying to get rid of? Why is all your shit in the car?"

"You can't prove that, dead hoes tell no tales."

All of a sudden, Bullet kicked the garbage can in my direction and I jumped back. When I moved he dove behind a desk. When he came up he had a gun pointed at me. *Shit!*

"Now I know you ain't gonna shoot me, but I will kill you just like I killed your ho. Now put the gun down."

"Fuck you!"

Bullet took another step closer. The door flew open.

"Freeze!"

Both Bullet and I looked toward the door, and to my surprise, it was Chante. *What the fuck is she doin' here?* Whatever the reason, I was glad she was here with that big-ass gun.


## *Chante*

"Freeze!" I yelled as I came through the door with my gun drawn. Jada and Bullet had their guns pointed at the other.

"Who is this? Another one of your hoes come to have a little threesome?" He laughed.

"No, muthafucka, she here so both of us can kill your ugly-bitch ass," Jada said.

"I'm not here to help you kill him, Jada. I'm here to stop you," I said without taking my eyes off him. I knew neither one of them was going to shoot the other or it would be over. They were both looking for a way out. All I had to do is stall.

"Stop me? What the fuck are you talkin' about? This is the muthafucka that killed Bella."

"I know that. The police are on their way. Let them handle this."

"NO!" Jada shouted at me. "He killed Bella, and he's gonna die for it!"

"No, Jada," I said slowly and quietly. The tears were flowing from her eyes.

"Fuck that!" Jada screamed and took a step closer to him. Whether he meant to kill her or not, Bella didn't deserve the beating she got from him. I had to defuse this situation fast or she just might do it. I couldn't blame her, 'cause in reality I wanted him dead too.

"Jada, please put the gun down."

"NO!"

"He isn't worth it."

"I'm gonna kill him," Jada said almost in a whisper.

"Please, Jada, don't do this. Don't throw your life away on this worthless piece of shit. The police will be here any minute. Just put the down, Jada. I got him, he's not going anywhere."

Jada slowly began to lower her gun. "Thank you, Jada," I said and glanced at her. When I did, Bullet fired at me. I felt the shell rip through my left shoulder. The impact knocked me off balance. He tried to run.

I was about to return fire when Jada screamed, "NO!"

I saw Jada raise her gun, close her eyes and empty her clip. The recoil put her on her ass. While she was down, Bullet turned and fired at Jada, but he missed her. I took careful aim and fired. I hit two with two shots to the chest.

He went down and I moved in on him. I held my gun on Bullet and kicked the gun out of his hand.

I looked down at Jada. "You okay?"

"I'm okay—I'm all right."

Just then the doors burst open. "Freeze!" one uniform yelled.

"Put your weapon down," the other yelled.

I immediately put the gun down, raised my hands, knowing how trigger-happy some of my brothers in blue could be, I yelled, "I'm a cop!"

"What?" I heard Jada say.

I could see the look of hurt and disappointment in her eyes. "Yes, Jada. I'm a cop."

# Chapter 15

*Jada*

Ain't this a bitch? Chante's a cop. I can hardly believe it, but here I am sitting in the backseat of a police car, somewhere I thought I'd never be, because I was just too smart, too careful. I knew that I wasn't under arrest because nobody had read me my rights and I wasn't wearing handcuffs. Bullet was dead though; Chante killed him. The bastard got what he deserved for what he did to Bella. Now she could rest in peace.

I heard Chante tell the other cops that I didn't hit a thing, so I wasn't all that worried. But the fact that Chante was a cop and she was all up in my world couldn't be a good thing. A million things were going through my mind as we drove to the precinct. Along the way, I tried to think of everything I said to her. I tried to remember who she'd seen us with. I had a lot of high-profile clients and now their reputations, and maybe their careers, were on my back.

I should have known better; should have seen this coming. Chante's a cop. Ain't that a bitch?

We arrived at the precinct and I was taken to the same room that I had been the last time I was questioned about a murder. I had been in there for about an hour and a half before anybody came in the room.

It was the same cop that questioned me the last time, and one I had never seen before. "Ms. West, my name is Detective Sergeant Banner, I'm with the homicide division, and I believe you already met vice Lieutenant Gineconna."

Now I was scared. If this asshole was vice, then they'd been on me for a long time. It was all starting to make sense to me now and the more it made sense to be me, the more scared I got. I was the target and Gineconna questioning me about that murder at Sensations was just the beginning of it. I should have stayed out of that club after that night; never gone back. But then I thought about it. If I was the target, club or no club, they would have come at me anyway.

"I'm sorry to keep you waiting so long," Banner said. "I only need to take your statement and then you're free to go."

I started to say something dumb like, "You mean your not going to arrest me for running a prostitution ring?" but I simply said, "I understand."

Banner placed a tape recorder on the table and asked me to tell them what happened. While I told my story Gineconna stood behind Banner and never took his eyes off me. Once I was done, Banner turned off the tape recorder, thanked me for my time and got up to leave. Naturally, I stood up too. I followed the two cops to the door, but when I got to the door, Gineconna turned and blocked my path.

"I hope you learned something from all this, Ms. West," Gineconna said to me. Then he stepped aside and let me pass.

As I walked out of the precinct, I thought about his question. *Had I learned anything? And if so, what was it?* I was glad he didn't want an answer, because I didn't have one. Maybe in a day or two I would, but not now. Right now I was too shaken to think. Bella was dead; murdered by Bullet. Chante was a cop assigned to get close to me. There was definitely a lesson to be learned from all this, but all I wanted to do was go home.

When I came outside the building, the first thing I saw was Chante. She was leaning against my car. "How'd my car get here?" I asked her.

"I had it towed here instead of the impound."

"Thanks," I said and walked past her.

"Jada, wait," she said and grabbed my arm.

I jerked my arm away. "What do you want, Chante? Is that even your name?"

"It's Rachael, Rachael Dawkins. Chante is my middle name."

"And you're a cop."

"Yes, Jada, I'm a cop."

"How could you, Chante? I mean, Rachael or whatever your name is. I trusted you."

"I was just doing my job, Jada."

"Yeah well, if your *job* is to betray your people who considered you a friend then your job sucks."

Chante looked away from me. I could see the pain in her eyes. "You're right. It does suck."

I leaned against my car next to Chante. "So, what's next?"

"Nothing."

"What do you mean, nothing?"

"I mean that's it. Gineconna told you that you were free to go, right?"

"Yeah."

"Well, there you go. If there was going to be any charges, you'd be under arrest now. I never told Gineconna anything."

"I understand that, Chante. What I don't understand is why, Chante? Wasn't that your *job*?"

"You're right, it was, but something happened to change all that. I wasn't completely honest with myself, Jada. 'Cause if I were, I woulda had to admit to myself that I really loved being Chante. The truth was that I found your lifestyle exciting. I mean look at yourself, Jada, you always wear the finest clothes; you get chauffeured around, and you're making mad money. But it was more than that, Jada. I came to like you. We became friends." That one made me smile on the inside because that's how I saw her, as a friend.

"That's deep, Chante. The cop and the madam, friends."

"Ain't it?" Chante laughed.

"What you gonna do now, Chante?" I asked her.

"I don't know."

"Wanna go get a drink?"

"I could definitely use one."

"Come on then," I said and got in the car. Chante got in the passenger seat and broke out her sunglasses. As I drove off, I thought about the fact that it wasn't all about the money at all. In the end, money didn't matter at all. It was about friendship.